SHATTERED · SNOW

RACHEL HUFFMIRE

Appropriate for Teens, Intriguing to Adults

Immortal Works LLC
1505 Glenrose Drive Salt Lake City, Utah 84104 Tel: (385) 202-0116

© 2019 Rachel Huffmire
www.rachelhuffmire.com

Cover Art by Ashley Literski
strangedevotion.wixsite.com/strangedesigns

Interior Illustrations by Kaelin Twede
kaelintwedeart.wixsite.com/kaelintwede

Formatted by FireDrake Designs
www.firedrakedesigns.com

ISBN 978-1-7324674-5-3 (paperback)
AISN: B07K5MJ7CT (Kindle edition)

To David.
For always cheering me on.

"Man's first experiment with time travel destroyed the twenty-first century. Small changes in the past created wars and famines in the present day that erased millions of people. The International Time Travel Agency spent fifteen years reconstructing history to match the original timeline. Today, time travel is strictly limited to observational research. Any other use is illegal."

-Sample taken from A History of ITTA

CHAPTER
ONE

K eltson tapped on his earbud, drowning out the sounds of the busy street corner with the steady beat of a bass drum. A guitar began accented strumming patterns – his signal to start walking. Cars kicked up wakes of mist from the recently rain-covered street as they drove past. Keltson ignored the spray on his face and measured his steps with the even rhythm of the song while gripping two black duffel bag handles. He passed a filling station and glanced toward a low-tech security camera attached to an awning above the fuel pumps. It recorded his steps, creating the perfect alibi.

Keltson always made sure he could be seen when he stole something.

Continuing his steady pace, he reached into his jacket's pocket and gripped the pen-sized ignition button hidden inside. He counted along with the beats, waiting for the musical drop he used as a signal to jump. One...two...three...drop. Keltson pressed the ignition linked to his vest, and space shifted around him. The cars speeding down the street stopped, frozen in time, then faded into the ground. Walls rose around him, forming the workshop of the Palais Garnier in Paris.

Keltson stumbled to a stop and tensed his shoulders. A chilled stillness rushed across his skin, the frozen air bit into his lungs, and the light formed shadowy rays that darkened after he passed through them. Nothing about the Pause felt comfortable.

Rows of clothing racks towered around Keltson, filled with carefully crafted costumes that had been prepared for an upcoming performance. Around the workshop, designers stood like mannequins caught in the motions of measuring, cutting, and sewing. They would never know about the man who stole between the quantum Plancks.

Keltson studied the costumes on velvet hangers, looking for an ideal dress. He pulled out his photovoltaic transmitter and isolated a fifteenth-century noblewoman's gown. Pressing a button, he slid the clothes into the Pause with him. He folded the fabric into one of the oversized duffel bags. Next, he selected a men's peasant outfit and put it into the smaller duffel.

"Sorry for the inconvenience," Keltson muttered as he zipped up the bags. He glanced around at the designers. The frozen people quivered under his gaze and he quickly looked away. "My clients will put this to better use."

Turning back down the corridor of costumes, he started the song over, waiting as the music built to his cue. He began his measured steps and at the drop, pressed the return ignition.

The Carntyne street corner rose around him and his skin tingled with the sensation of being pulled back into the flow of time. Cars rushed by again as Keltson continued his stride. To the world, he hadn't missed a beat, though his duffel bags looked more stuffed than before. No one knew that he'd jumped from Scotland to Paris and back again in no time at all.

He turned past shops and picket fenced houses on his way toward the molting grey box he called home. Symmetrical bay windows stood on either side of his front door and a stone chimney stuck straight out the center of the roof, just like every other house on this street. He strode confidently up the dilapidated stairs and pulled out his key. The worn teeth jammed in the knob, refusing to let him turn or pull it back out.

"Blasted lock," Keltson muttered as he balanced the duffel bags on the splintered stair rail and tugged. The peeling door swung open on its own, revealing a muscular man who had a butch haircut and scruff on his chin.

"Baigh?" Keltson asked as his older brother smiled and pulled him into a crushing hug. Worry flushed through Keltson. He released himself from Baigh's grip and closed the door behind him. "What are you doing here? I thought you weren't supposed to leave Kilmarnock. You want to get lifted by the Polis again?"

Baigh took a step back, lifted his pant leg, and revealed a bare ankle. "No more parole for this reprobate," he said, a wide smile lighting his face. He shook his pant leg back down. "Though I still don't get my license back."

"That's a reasonable penance for getting caught in a stolen car," Keltson said, dropping the duffle bags on the floor.

Baigh shrugged his shoulders. "I didn't know my boss lifted that junker. The cell phones I transported, sure. But not a whole car."

Keltson stepped into his front room, ignoring the peeling yellow wallpaper covered in dark spots where the previous owner had once hung pictures.

Baigh leaned over the armrest of the sunken couch and pulled a case of Vibe energy drinks from the floor. Keltson hung his keys on a nail near the door and turned just in time to catch the aluminum can that Baigh tossed at him.

"Today deserves a little revelry," Baigh said, opening his own can.

"Ah, Baigh, I wish I'd known you were coming. I have work in fifteen minutes." Keltson rolled the can around in his hands, offering his brother a truly apologetic smile.

"Work? Is that what's in those bags?" Baigh asked with a look of mischievous curiosity. Keltson's stomach dropped. It was that same curiosity that always seemed to get Baigh sucked into trouble. Finding out the contents of those duffel bags would be no exception.

"Is'na anything," Keltson popped the tab on his Vibe and hid his face behind the can as he took a swig of the bitter drink. If Baigh recognized his nervousness, he'd dig even deeper.

Baigh wrinkled his nose. "I know that look. You've something rich in there."

Keltson hesitated before he lowered the can and shrugged. "Someone had to keep the streets running after you left."

"Aw! Has my baby brother finally come around to being a scoundrel?" Baigh laughed.

"I wouldn't call myself a complete scoundrel. There's a whole lot of grey between those black and white lines, Baigh." Keltson folded his arms.

"Took you long enough to realize that," Baigh said, straight-faced. "I certainly got my fair share of moral lectures from you growin' up." A smile cracked through Baigh's somber expression and he winked. "Don't worry. If it's paraphernalia for the Carntyne gangs, I'm leaving it alone. I can't afford to go back to court again." Baigh dropped onto the couch, slouching into the cushions. "Might I offer a bit of advice though? Stay off Edinburgh. My old crew is'na what it was. In fact," Baigh eyed the bags, "perhaps you could make those scarce and we could jam for a while?" Baigh pulled Keltson's guitar onto his lap.

Keltson took the guitar and placed it back on its hook. "I told you, Baigh. I have work."

Baigh groaned and slapped the cushions as he pushed himself up from the sofa. "Daylight's no time for crime, Kelts."

"I did'na quit my day job yet," Keltson said.

Baigh clicked his tongue then sighed in disappointment. "Fine, you keep the Vibe then. I'll be back for it tomorrow." Baigh did a sloppy jig on his way to the door, celebrating his freed ankle. Before stepping outside, he paused.

"Kelts, I know we don't know much else besides backstreet deals, but be careful with—" He nodded toward the duffel bags.

"Thanks." Keltson sighed in relief as Baigh closed the door behind him.

He couldn't be late.

Keltson shut the blinds, picked up his bags, and headed toward the hall cupboard. Inside sat a rusted 20-gallon water heater. He reached around the corner and yanked on a hidden pulley system, lifting the tank from its base. A trap door opened into the cellar below. Keltson dropped the bags into the darkness, then remembered the Vibe. It might come in useful. He likely had a long shift ahead.

Tucking the case beneath his arm, Keltson made his way down a thin ladder into the cellar. His trap door and water heater slid back into place as his feet touched the ground. The blue fluorescent lights attached to the underbelly of the house lit up, illuminating his headquarters.

The cement walls radiated cool humidity across his various workstations. He crossed to the line of monitors and flipped them on for the day. After returning his photovoltaic transmitter to its hook in his workshop, he hefted the case of Vibe into a mini-fridge next to his sound station—a corner filled with speakers, soundboards, and guitars. Music didn't have anything to do with time travel, but it helped him process problems when he hit a wall. Besides, now that he had some Vibe, it would get him amped up for the job.

It wasn't glamorous down here, but the room gratified Keltson. It combined his childhood surrounded by crime with his strict moral compass. This was a place where he made a difference.

He selected a song by the Coroners and pressed play. He closed his eyes and listened as the gentle guitar solo eased into a heavy bass line. The energy drink seemed to rush beneath his skin as the volume built.

Time was set in stone
now it's fluid, bottled sand.
You could shape fate if you want
but instead, you stay your hand.

Hindsight loses meaning
on a king whose heart runs dry.
You study others' pains
watching as they die.

Saving what you see
in the veins of history
to defend ancient remains
shows your morals wax and wane.

You say that if we pull
on the slightest living thread,
the tapestry of time
would be torn to tissued shreds.

Preserving what you see
on the skeins of history
to preserve ancient remains
leaves a million lives in chains.

This song became Keltson's mantra six years ago when he was still a teenager. Baigh had just been arrested for the first time and in order to fend for himself, Keltson took an apprenticeship with one of the best renegades in the hacking and tech-refurbishment business. The man commiserated with a group of time travel activists and though some of his ideas were a bit radical, Keltson found himself agreeing with a lot of what the man had to say.

When the first time travel broadcast aired worldwide, people sanctioned it as the greatest frontier to be explored since the moon. However, within moments of sending back the first agent, the International Time Travel Agency released a special broadcast. They claimed that attempts to improve history had caused catastrophic wars and famines that nobody seemed to remember. ITTA also claimed their agents took fifteen years to restore the timeline to its original form, even though to the world, no time had passed at all. It was further proclaimed that time travel was too dangerous to tamper with. From here on out, it was for observation only.

Countries rioted, insisting ITTA fabricated the videos to suppress the greater good. But the laws remained firm. Time travel became a mere reality TV mechanism and photon acceleration technology became one of the best-kept international secrets.

Until Keltson cracked their system.

After quietly breaking through ITTA's secure database, Keltson had the world of time travel tech at his fingertips. He could have sold his findings on the black market, but he knew what happened when bigger, stronger, stupider people got hold of tools they weren't prepared to use. So, he kept them to himself, developing a mission to change history for the better without ITTA noticing.

Keltson took on clients who became vigilantes in the past. He didn't break the law because he wanted to screw up history. He wanted to fix it. Even if politicians said his efforts were "illegal". Their rules were for people who wanted anarchy. Keltson's strict vetting process ensured he didn't give power to any extremists. Crazies deserved the rules. Not him.

The music faded and Keltson moved toward his desk, straightening a short pile of notes before grabbing a beanie, thin gloves, and a disposable cell phone. He usually wore plenty of layers when he jumped into the Pause. The trip to the Palais Garnier had been an exception since he wanted to be visible and the present weather didn't justify gloves and a beanie.

Keltson expected his newest client to call in a matter of minutes. He plugged an extension cord into one of the four full-length mirrors next to his desk. His shoulders tensed. Taking new clients often required long stretches of problem solving and physical labor. He already felt exhausted just thinking about it. He shook out his hands, then started the timer on his wristwatch to keep track of his hours.

The phone rang. On time. Keltson took a deep breath and answered the call.

"Once, some time ago, I sat in my bantam tower flat with a view of my neighbor's cinderblock wall and recognized the depth of my entrapment. My career is filled with ladders I cannot climb and glass ceilings that hold me down like a casket. So, to answer your question, no. Leaving my lifetime behind is not an issue."

-The application of Lilia Vaschenko

CHAPTER
TWO·

L ilia stepped out of her oil-stained coveralls, resenting how the smell of petrol followed after her like a stray dog. A career spent scrounging through old engines in the Zapasnoy Junkyard was degrading enough without taking the scent home every day. Throwing her uniform into a plastic sack, she yanked the ties into a knot, wishing it would never come undone.

Above her, Andrei whistled and clanged his slugger wrench against the catwalk rail. "I forget how skinny you are under that circus tent, Lilia."

"If you worked harder you might lose a few pounds yourself," Lilia said, not bothering to look up at him. She punched the junkyard's time-clock, ignoring Andrei's continued taunts. Her muscles ached from salvaging in the upper lot and she didn't have the energy to respond.

The smell of grease faded behind her as she stepped through the chain-link gate. She folded her arms tightly against her ribs now that she no longer had the shroud of the junkyard to mask her scent. On the Metro, the other passengers gave her a wide berth. She didn't blame them. The best she could do was to crouch next to the ventilation duct and hope it pumped her putrid essence outside.

She hopped off at the Ulitsa Chapayeva station and darted down a narrow alleyway toward the cinder block high-rise she lived in. She took the metal fire escape to the tenth story. It was the only way up. Lilia opened the door to a minuscule room and stepped inside.

"Not evicted yet, Misha?" Lilia asked a bear-shaped mildew stain on the ceiling. She dropped her uniform into a cooler by the door then picked up a half-formed device off a crowded shelf. "Now, where were we?" she asked the gadget. It had once been a flashlight, but she was repurposing the circuitry to also be an infrared heat detector. Her best customers were usually the ones who lived in the darkest alleyways. It would earn her a few extra rubles once she finished. She sat down at her rickety table and reached for the soldering gun.

She stopped.

A white legal envelope rested on the edge of the table. Its stark cleanliness stood out against the bundles of wires and tools that cluttered the surface.

Lilia looked around, checking for signs of a break-in, but everything sat in its usual place.

Her heart fluttered as she lifted the envelope. Could this be…?

She left greasy black fingerprints on the paper as she ripped the seal open. Inside, she found only three sentences on a single page.

Application Accepted. Call 1754-9522-9357 @ 9 PM. Prepare for immediate departure.

She closed her eyes and pressed the note to her chest with shaking hands. The Mirror had accepted her application.

Lilia checked the envelope again, but it contained no further instructions. No packing list, no directives. Just a phone number.

Immediate departure. Was she ready? Of course she was. She'd spent the last three years preparing for this moment. She'd learned old German, watched footage from the ITTA studies, and recorded herself practicing sixteenth-century etiquette. Adrenaline rushed through her veins.

She was going back in time.

As a child, Lilia constantly daydreamed about going back in time. She could find her father and beg him not to leave. Or, she could warn her mother about the tainted water that would kill her. But after a few years of growing up in the slums, she realized that even with her parents, life wouldn't have been much different. She would still live in the same dirty neighborhood. What she needed was a new life entirely.

And today, she no longer had to dream.

Lilia ran to her shower and tried to scrub the grease from the creases in her hands and beneath her fingernails. Years of grit and grime crowded every crease of her calloused skin. Though the floor pooled with grey suds, her hands still held telltale signs of her work. As the lukewarm water ran over her, she closed her eyes.

Perhaps fate had never meant for Lilia to stay here. Her job certainly wasn't glamorous, but it had kept her alive. Her ability to understand electrical currents and mechanics gave her food to eat and a community among the cheap-rate junkyard engineers. There, she had first heard the rumblings of a tech-hacker who had successfully replicated ITTA's technology; a rogue time traveler the others called "The Mirror". But when Lilia had questioned them further, no one could prove the rumors.

"If I were him, I'd be rolling in lotteries and stocks," Andrei had said, smoking a vapor pipe with his feet propped through a broken car window.

"ITTA would never allow someone like him to exist," her boss had argued, slamming the empty cash register closed. But while her coworkers dreamed of money, Lilia's interest focused on the man with the power to change her fate.

Turning off the shower, she dressed in her most professional clothing- a pair of baggy slacks and a faded blue linen work shirt. The wrists had been worn thin by its previous owner who must have nervously picked at the threads. She hated that their habits looked like her own. As she brushed her long brown hair, it dampened the back of her shirt.

Pacing, she fingered a bit of scalar wire wound around her finger. The wire that changed her life. Three years ago, she'd received an order to pull six centimeters of scalar wire from the junkyard. Oddly, there was no name or address attached. But as soon as the order was set on the back counter, it disappeared, replaced by a currency code.

No one else seemed to think much of it, but a voice deep inside Lilia whispered that whoever placed this order didn't want to be known. She received shady orders all the time, but this one felt different. And the rumors felt so real. So, the next time it happened, she placed a note in the delivery box:

Mirror,
You're leaving a trail I can hide. If you're sending people back, I want in.
-Lilia Vaschenko

A few weeks later she had received an envelope under her door with a digital application inside.

The Mirror was real and he changed history for the better. But to be a part of it, Lilia had to find someone to save.

She crossed to her bed and lifted the sheets, revealing a slit cut into the side of her mattress. Inside rested a portfolio wrapped in a plastic bag. She opened the packet and flipped through the pages. The Mirror's questions required months of traversing through historical documents to find the perfect vigilante mission. Her target had to be someone inconspicuous in history. The slightest risk of ITTA flagging her endeavors in the past would get her denied. At first, she'd felt frustrated that she couldn't fix her own life, but quickly realized *anything* would be a welcome lifestyle change.

She turned through the pages of the portfolio to a character summary and an oil painting of a young girl in a beautiful white dress.

Name: Margaretha von Waldeck - a 16th century German countess
with only a handful of legal documents and a wives' tale recorded of her.
Injustice: The king of Spain poisoned her for falling in love with his son.

When Lilia first found Margaretha's story, she felt a connection with the girl. Her childhood misfortunes *almost* matched Lilia's own sorry life.

Every day for the next two years, Lilia came home from the junkyard covered in grease and imagined herself instead draped in soft folds of fabric and soaked in sweet-smelling rosewater. She fell in love with the idea of living near a castle instead of working under catwalks and chain-link fences.

The easiest question of the application had been:

Are you willing to go back in time and never return?

Lilia knew the peril of breaking international law. But even if she was caught, a cell in an international prison would probably be a step up from her flat.

9:00 pm.

Her hand shook as she picked up her cell and dialed the number. The phone clicked as someone answered.

"Hello?" She felt like a little girl again, begging for scraps.

"I don't ever take clients like you," a man said in a grave and distorted tone.

Lilia grimaced. Deep in her heart, she had hoped The Mirror was a woman. She didn't care for men. Men always proved to be *bespredel* in the end.

"Don't disappoint me," he said.

She straightened. She wasn't a helpless orphan anymore. She would show him just how strong she could be.

"I don't plan to."

"The Master Document contains the original history of the world and is locked in an unalterable vault. Each half-hour, ITTA computers compare contemporary history to the Master Document, ensuring that no notable events stray from their original course."

-First Amendment to ITTA laws and regulations

CHAPTER THREE

K eltson spoke to Lilia in German, the only common language they shared. A kindly German grandmother had taken him and Baigh off the street for a few months when they were teenagers and taught them to speak the language. He wasn't an expert by any means, but Lilia's thick Russian accent made him grimace. Whatever. He could make anything work.

"Do you have the payment?" Keltson asked, picking up the duffel bag with her dress. Lilia shuffled through papers on the other end of the line. She didn't have money. Instead, she offered clearance codes for supply orders. With her codes, Keltson could order enough scalar wire to last a lifetime without anyone tracing him. As agreed, Lilia would release the codes after he successfully assisted her through her directives.

He set down the cell phone and programmed the coordinates on his vest.

Location: Yekaterinburg, Russia (56.825422 N, 60.581876 E)
Time: 9:02:25 PM (Pause)

Keltson pressed the ignition and slipped into the Pause. Despite the chilled surroundings, Keltson always felt safest there. It was his best-kept secret. ITTA knew how to travel through history from point A to point B, but Keltson could hover between the two without being noticed.

Lilia sat frozen at her table, surrounded by scrappy knick-knacks on every side. Though he had already been here to deliver her acceptance letter, her living arrangements still shocked him. He hadn't seen such squalor since seventh grade when he ran away with Baigh for the first time. The room felt even more suffocating now with Lilia, the oversized duffel bag, and the portable mirror taking up space.

"Not afraid to leave this all behind?" Keltson asked. Her frozen expression remained hard and her hands stopped in midair, ready to cram his clearance codes inside a metal lockbox. He made the mistake of staring too long and her body shattered like a piece of glass. The shards flew across the room, then gathered into new, fully formed reflections. One woman was far more plump and motherly, a second more sallow and pale. Keltson clenched his teeth and shook his head to clear the images, not wanting to see what Lilia *could* have been. He hated how the Pause messed with his mind. All organic matter shattered whenever he focused on it—one more reason he didn't like to stay too long.

Keltson set the duffel bag on the edge of Lilia's bed. As he let go, the fabric dissolved into the flow of time. To her, the duffel bag would appear out of thin air. Next, he crossed to the portable mirror.

"This should be the best angle for you," Keltson said, shifting the mirror toward Lilia. He pulled a keypad from behind the frame. His mirror's controls could only be accessed from the Pause. Once time resumed, the mirror sealed, preventing his clients from messing with it. He programmed the dials.

Location: Weilburg Forest, Germany (50°29′N 8°15′E)
Date: 5 April 1539 - 4:02:25 PM

Once she stepped into the mirror, the entire device would travel with her, vanishing from this point and appearing in the location he had just programmed.

"That should do it," he said as he unplugged the mirror from the extension cord and watched it melt into the dim light.

He shivered, pressed a return button on his vest, and braced himself for re-entry into the cellar. Materializing back into time made his skin feel carbonated. He returned to his desk, shaking the cold from his fingers, and hung up on Lilia before activating the mirror. Lilia appeared on his monitor, being recorded by the mirror's surveillance feed.

The mirror and the duffel bag appeared and the crackling noise they made startled Lilia. She stood up, assuming a defensive stance that knocked her cell phone and the box of codes off the table. It wasn't unusual for his clients to be jumpy these first few seconds.

Lilia crept forward, her shoulders relaxing as she recognized her own reflection in the mirror. He pressed a button, activating the video feed and the glass flickered and faded into black. The corner of Keltson's monitor showed the broadcast Lilia saw.

A hazy glow formed in the center of the mirror and the clear image of a porcelain mask appeared, suspended in the darkness. The glossy reflection of his avatar illuminated her room in milky light.

The mask didn't look like him at all. Keltson's square jawline clashed with the heart-shaped mask and Grecian nose. Even the white finish contrasted his dark hair and permanent five o'clock shadow. He couldn't afford to have his clients recognize him, so he also dampened the mask's facial expressions to hide his mannerisms. The avatar made him look older and melancholy. He preferred his clients take him seriously.

"This is all fairly theatrical, don't you think?" Lilia said, raising an eyebrow. Keltson smiled, but the mask didn't flinch.

"So, what is this?" She ran her fingers along the mirror's sleek, modern frame.

"The mirror is for communication. Cell phones are too traceable..."

"It's a little big for a cell," she said.

"...it also serves as a door."

Lilia raised an eyebrow and looked behind the frame. Keltson rolled his eyes. All of his clients insisted on doing this.

She straightened and stared into the mirror. "Is this a joke?" She tested the glass. It held firm.

"You let me worry about the mechanics of time travel. You just open that bag." Keltson nodded his head toward her bed and Lilia turned. Hesitating, she stared at the duffel that had mysteriously appeared on her pillow. She unzipped the top and found petticoats, bodices, undergarments, and a blue silk noblewoman's dress.

"The junkyard rumors certainly don't give you sufficient credit," Lilia said, looking over her shoulder at him.

Keltson smiled again. He allowed the avatar to fade into blackness, giving Lilia the cue to go get dressed.

She stepped into the small bathroom, struggling to pull the clothes through the narrow door with her. Authentic clothing from the sixteenth-century would have required a dressing assistant, but theaters had quick costume changes in mind. Stealing from them suited his clients just fine. When Lilia emerged, she looked decent enough and held herself with surprising grace in the foreign clothing.

"Spin," he commanded, twirling his finger despite her not being able to see it. He pursed his mouth to the side as she turned. "Your rouge is too thick and your hands are in terrible condition. No one will believe you're a Russian noble. You'll have to wear gloves full-time until they soften. And remove that piece of wire around your finger."

Lilia looked down at her finger and bit her bottom lip. He worried that she might fight him over it, but she turned and slipped it off her finger, quickly sliding the gloves over her hands.

"You have your first directives memorized?" Keltson asked.

She nodded again but didn't speak.

"Then proceed with preparing your cover story," he said.

Lilia shook her head. "No one is going to come looking for me. Let's get on with it."

"Someone always comes looking," he said. "Especially when you stop paying rent. Go unlock the front door. I'll hire a crew of looters to come through and mess the place up."

"They'll be disappointed," Lilia said, unbolting the lock. Keltson sniffed.

"When you're ready, the mirror is activated. You may step through at your leisure. You'll receive a full briefing on the other side."

His avatar's mask faded away and a beautiful summertime forest appeared in the display. As Lilia stared into the soft sunlight falling through the leaves, she rolled her shoulders back and tilted her chin up as if to welcome the warmth.

Keltson's clients usually tensed at the prospect of stepping through the mirror, but Lilia looked more comfortable now than she had been the entire conversation. She reached forward, resting her hand against the frame, and stepped into the glass.

The mirror disappeared from the crowded studio apartment and reappeared in a clump of tall boulders and shimmering trees atop a hillock near the Waldeck family castle. As Lilia stepped out with her back to the glass, he activated the transmission on the mirror and cleared his throat. She turned at the sound of his voice.

"Welcome to the Weilburg forest. A road lies at the bottom of this hill. Herr Waldeck will ride past in twenty minutes."

"Twenty minutes? That's..." Lilia trailed off, smoothing down the front of her dress while her eyes flitted around to the trees surrounding her. Keltson nearly chuckled at the awestruck expression on Lilia's face. He remembered the first time he had stepped into the past. Jumping from one reality into another felt indescribably disorienting.

"Do you remember your first directive?" Keltson leaned forward trying to study her for the tell-tale signs of cracking.

She straightened, her eyes darting back to his mask in the mirror. Her glazed-over eyes focused and she again appeared determined.

"I am to establish myself as a strong and respectable woman. I will make a favorable impression on Herr Waldeck, then suggest his daughters need a mentor."

"Excellent. Don't forget to explain that you are a Russian noble headed to Munich to explore German culture and society. Your carriage driver stole your goods and abandoned you in this forest."

Lilia fiddled with her gloves, rubbing the spot where her wire ring had been. "Won't he be suspicious of a Russian all the way out here, unaccompanied? Won't he..."

"I know this is all a lot to take in at once, Lilia. Take a deep breath," Keltson said.

Lilia clamped her hands at her sides. "I can prove I'm the role model he needs for his daughters." Her voice sounded stiff and overly rehearsed.

Keltson arranged his notes on the desk in front of him. "Remember, if anything goes wrong, come right back. I expect you to make mistakes. That's why you need me."

Lilia cocked her head to the side as if she didn't understand. It was always hard for his clients to grasp the idea that he could go back and change their mistakes before they even made them. He leaned forward.

"I hold a reset button. If you succeed, come back here and we'll move to step two. If not, tell me what went wrong and we'll do this over again. I'll be watching for you."

Lilia nodded, brushing a wisp of hair from her face. Then she turned and descended the hill to the road below.

Keltson sat back and pressed against his chin till his neck popped. Getting his clients into the past was always easy. Now came the hard part. His clients rarely executed their first directive gracefully. Hopefully, Lilia could pull it off. Though she looked nervous, her composure surprised him. He'd seen individuals with far more training break under such pressure. Perhaps it was because Lilia had more to lose than his other clients if she failed. He couldn't blame her for wanting to leave the life she had. Everyone else had poured buckets of money at Keltson, but Lilia had no funds to offer. Her payment, however, might prove to be his favorite payday yet. He smiled, thinking about her clearance codes. No more exhausting orders for wire by the inch. No more hopping into the Pause to secretly pick them up.

But Lilia still held the code keys. Keltson still needed her to succeed.

"Margaretha's stepmother despised her and sent her away to live with relatives. While attending the Spanish court, the Prince of Spain fell in love with her kindness and beauty. Once the King recognized the depth of his son's attachment to Margaretha, he poisoned her."

-History taken from the application of Lilia Vaschenko

CHAPTER
FOUR

Margaretha stood on her tiptoes next to the new cradle and peeked her nose over the rail. The baby inside smelled like fresh linen and sweet milk. But all the comforts of the nursery didn't keep the baby from squalling. Someone needed to care for her. Margaretha looked over her shoulder at her nurse who whispered to the housemaid.

"Herr Waldeck hasn't come to see the baby yet. Three days and she still doesn't have a name."

"Do you think he blames the child?" the housemaid asked, shaking out a dress.

The baby's wail grew louder and drew Margaretha's attention away from their hushed conversation. Margaretha lifted a silver rattle over the edge of the cradle. The jangling bells soothed the baby for a moment and Margaretha smiled at her success.

The nursery door burst open. Startled, Margaretha dropped the rattle. The baby cried even louder than before as their three older brothers raced toward her.

"Out of the way, *kliener*," Samuel said, shoving Margaretha away. She fell hard onto the floor and the cradle tottered back and forth.

"You're going to hurt her!" Margaretha shouted. Samuel hammered the rattle against the side of the crib.

Margaretha's eyes pooled with tears at the invasion and she covered her warm cheeks with her hands. As she turned to flee into the corner, she found her brothers had left nursery door ajar. The hall beyond was silent. She longed to escape into the stillness. The nurse was too busy lecturing the boys to notice Margaretha sneak into the corridor.

Outside, the hall smelled like wet river stones. Tall glass windows revealed thick flakes of snow falling outside. Margaretha stepped toward the glass and heard someone clear their throat.

Father stood just a few meters away in a wrinkled jerkin. "Margaretha, what are you doing out here?" he asked in his scratchy, deep voice.

"The hall is quiet," Margaretha whispered, reaching up for him. He seemed to understand and took her small hand in his. They walked to a short wooden bench beneath the nearest window overlooking the snow-covered courtyard.

"Why haven't you come to see the new baby?" Margaretha asked. Father didn't answer. He only looked toward the door with a mixture of fear and sorrow. She gently touched the splotchy skin beneath his eyes.

Father tried to smile but sighed instead. "Mourning doesn't seem to suit anyone in the castle. Least of all me."

"You miss Mama?" Margaretha asked.

"Yes," Father said, pulling Margaretha onto his lap and tucking her black skirt around her legs for warmth. "But we will do our best to remember her."

Margaretha chewed on her bottom lip. He used his commanding voice—the kind he used to prove he was strong. She picked up his hand and played with his fingers, hoping he would use a playful tone instead.

"She knew you before your birth, you know," Father said, resting his chin on top of her head. "I remember how she sat at this very window on a day that was snowy and bright, not dark and blustery like today."

"What was she doing here?" Margaretha looked up, her forehead brushing against Father's whiskers.

"She sat in the sun and embroidered while newborn Henry napped."

Father took Margaretha's hands and pretended to sew up and down through an invisible hoop. "She felt disappointed about having another boy. You see, I had plenty of sons to wrestle and tumble about with. Mama only had Elisabeth to teach the finer arts to. So, as Mama worked, she said, 'Perhaps someday I will have another sweet little girl and her hair will be black like this window frame.'" Father traced the dark painted trim with Margaretha's finger.

"My hair is black," Margaretha said, smiling and pointing to her head. Father gasped and opened his eyes wide.

"Why, you're right." He tugged on Margaretha's thin curls. Margaretha giggled and wrinkled her nose.

"Then Mama said, 'Perhaps her skin will be as pale and fair as the snow outside.'" Again, Father looked down at Margaretha, this time pinching her cheeks in wonder.

Margaretha smiled wider than she had in days.

"But then," Father said, turning serious, "she was so caught up in the beautiful daydream that she pricked herself, and blood dripped from her finger onto the stone sill."

"Was she hurt?" Margaretha gripped Father's thumb, imagining the pain of such a prick.

"No. Mama just laughed and said, 'And perhaps her lips will be as red as the blood on this stone.'" Father hugged Margaretha closer.

"And when you were born, little girl, Mama knew immediately that it was you. You were the child she foresaw in this window."

Margaretha fingered the hem of Father's sleeve. "Windows aren't fortune tellers."

"You don't believe me?" he asked, raising an eyebrow. Margaretha pursed her lips and shook her head. Father checked the hallway before leaning forward and pointing to the stone windowsill.

Margaretha couldn't see anything. Father wiped away the dust covering the stones. Peering closer, Margaretha's mouth fell open in awe as she counted out three faint stains.

"The story is true." Margaretha brushed her fingers over the spots. Mama's trail of bloodstains felt as cold as ice.

"We named you Margaretha after Mama. She thought of you before your birth and, now that she's gone, she left you as a reminder of who she was." Father's voice shook and he held Margaretha like she was the last trace of Mama in the castle.

We named you after Mama... She left you as a reminder...

Was Margaretha like her Mama? The window foreshadowed Margaretha's birth. Did Mama see anything else? Would she ever know now that Mama was gone?

"*Danke* for the story, Father. Please, come back with me. The nursery is warm." Margaretha slipped off his lap and pulled on his hand. Father looked at the nursery door with unblinking eyes, then cleared his throat and stood up.

Margaretha straightened her back and tried her best to walk like a dame. Like Mama used to walk. She squeezed Father's hand as they both stepped back into the confusion of the nursery.

"1. Establish myself as a strong and respectable woman.

2. Suggest his daughters need a tutor or mentor.

3. Become a tutor to Margaretha and guard her against the hatred of her stepmother, Katherina.

4. When she is sent away to live with her uncle, Johann Cirksena, I will accompany her and train her for the Spanish court.

5. When the King of Spain attempts to poison her, I will assist in faking Margaretha's death. We will escape into the rural community, where she will live out the rest of her life in secret."

-Directives from the application of Lilia Vaschenko

CHAPTER
FIVE

W alking through the woods toward the road, Lilia breathed deeply, sensing the fragrance of the pines surrounding her. Lilia's flat took years of sweat and grease to obtain and yet leaving it behind was the easiest thing in the world. Of course, her gadgets were harder to leave. At the last minute she had stashed some necessities beneath her dress: a tin of makeup, her toothbrush, two wire combs to keep her hair in place, and with some sleight of hand, she managed to keep the scalar wire ring by slipping on a glove before The Mirror could see. Hopefully, her keepsake would bring her luck.

The light coming from the mirror behind her dimmed and Lilia finally felt the weight of the moment crash down on her in full force. She was alone. Success was in her hands. She knew Margaretha's case inside and out and wrote the entire mission plan herself. But, despite her preparation, her nerves wouldn't settle. All of this had happened so quickly.

She started down the mountainside, following a rock vein as The Mirror suggested. He claimed at the bottom she would find a road. It was strange that she knew so little about the man who sent her here. She had assumed that talking to him would provide answers to the questions that had built up in her mind over the past few months, but the shroud of mystery was only amplified with greater detail. She didn't know whether to trust or fear him. The mask showed hardly any emotion for her to read.

Though she walked with care, her thin slippers split over the rough stones and briars tugged at her skirts, ripping the hem. At first, she felt dismayed about ruining her new dress. It was the finest thing she had ever worn. She wasn't used to such organic surroundings. Her life was filled with exhaust and cement, not mud and leaves. She envisioned herself stumbling out of the trees in front of Herr Waldeck in a torn dress and mussed hair. It wasn't at all the strong first impression she'd hoped to give. But then she realized how convincing the image would be, and she didn't feel so frustrated as her skirts dragged through the mud.

At the base of the hill, she found a dirt road, just as The Mirror said. She folded her arms and drummed her fingers against her bicep, repeating to herself that she was primed for this. She must keep telling herself that.

Lilia didn't know much about Count von Waldeck. ITTA didn't find him interesting enough to study. She had never found a commission of him, but according to portraits of other counts in the area he would either be so wily and sallow that he looked near death or so plump and red-nosed that it would be a wonder if he were sober long enough to rule effectively. She prepared herself not to grimace at the sight of him.

Pacing back and forth, her skirts kicked up dust from the dirt road. The chirruping birds and the rustling wind through the trees made the world feel muted compared to the roar of engines and shouts of neighbors in Yekaterinburg. The silence revealed a ringing in her ears that wouldn't go away. To distract herself she practiced her introduction in German. Would Herr Waldeck appreciate strength in her, or would he find womanly fortitude offensive? Her fears quickly spiraled into thoughts of all the ways this could go wrong.

No. She could do this. She adjusted her hair and donned the posture of a noblewoman, straightening her back and clasping her hands gently in front of her.

The sound of hoofbeats rounded the bend. This was her moment. A horse galloped down the center of the road and the rider slowed as he approached.

Lilia raised an eyebrow. This man looked nothing like she imagined; neither sallow nor portly. Instead, he was rather plain. His strong posture allowed him to ride with casual abandon. He held no stiff courtly manner like so many of the portraits of his neighbors. His dark tousled hair was thick and his trimmed beard flecked with premature grey. He pulled on the reigns, stopping his horse. A smile lit his face.

"*Schonen tag, Dame*," he said. Even though Lilia spoke old German, he used an accent she didn't recognize. She curtsied politely.

"*Dobryj dyen*," Lilia greeted him in Russian.

The count looked surprised. "What are you doing in the middle of the forest?" he asked.

Lilia sighed in exasperation. "My carriage man cast me aside and claimed my finery. I hoped to find some form of gentry to assist me," she said. She performed the old tongue more naturally than she had assumed possible. Perhaps the costume and the setting made her feel more natural.

"I am sorry to hear it. I would gladly offer you respite at *meine burg* if you would come?" Herr Waldeck held the reins in one hand, offering them to her.

"But what of your journey?" Lilia motioned down the road.

"This was only a casual ride." He hopped down from his mount. On the ground, the count seemed much taller than she expected. He stood eye-to-eye with his massive steed.

He offered the mount to her, keeping the reins for himself. Lilia felt a pit form in her stomach as she looked up at the beast. Horses didn't suit her. Motorcycles, yes, but horses? No.

"You aren't afraid of my palfrey, are you?" Herr Waldeck asked.

"No," she said quickly. He grinned at her lie. She allowed him to take her gloved hand and escort her forward. Before she could prepare, the count easily lifted her onto the mount. This was not at all what she expected. Herr Waldeck turned with the lead in his hand and started back toward the castle.

"So, tell me," he asked over his shoulder, "where do you come from? Your greeting was surely not German."

"I am from Moscow."

"Russia?" He looked up at her in surprise. "That's so far away to be stranded here, of all places."

"I left home five months ago, seeking the traditions and culture of Europe."

"Germany is a wonderful place for you then. Our culture and traditions are a model of civility." His voice displayed the pompousness she expected in a count. Finally.

"Oh, yes. My carriage man was perfectly civil," she said, unable to help herself. Herr Waldeck laughed, a deep cheerful sound. Lilia found herself smiling. She'd hadn't found many opportunities to make people laugh lately. However, she couldn't allow herself to lose sight of her directives.

"I understand you've had a reformation here," she said, turning the conversation. Herr Waldeck's eyes sparkled with zeal at the mention of religion.

"You come seeking Lutheranism? I spent my early adulthood learning from Martin Luther himself."

She remembered his recent conversion from her study but hadn't realized she might be hitting such a powerful way to gain his favor. "I would learn of it," she said. The only doctrine Lilia had ever known was the religion of tools and machinery. She wasn't particularly curious, but if it meant gaining Herr Waldeck's favor, she wasn't against listening to a sermon.

"Beware or I'll make a convert out of you." He laughed again. "Provided, of course, you'll stay long enough to hear the word."

"I accept your offer and your warning." Lilia smiled. At this rate, her first directive to establish herself in Herr Waldeck's household as a respectable woman would be met within the hour.

"It is settled then. I am glad to have met you. Not that I am happy for your circumstances, of course. I admit I know very little of Russian customs. What a wretched man to leave you abandoned in the forest."

The count shook his head. "You are lucky I came upon you. The nights here aren't kind to unprepared travelers."

His words were casual and yet his posture remained respectful. He obviously didn't think women could protect themselves.

"Russian women are strong. We are accustomed to withstanding cold weather and even a bandit or two." She lifted her chin and gripped the pommel tightly, hoping she looked tenacious despite her billowing sleeves.

"And a dishonest carriage man?" the count asked with a suppressed smile.

Lilia frowned. "In Russia, we don't treat our women as frailties. Women are hearty, even allowed to lead the country."

"A woman ruler?" he asked, skeptically. Perfect. She had already introduced her first directive. Now Lilia needed to nourish the seeds she had planted in his mind and prove her value as an instructress.

"Elena Glinskaya recently ruled five years in her son Ivan's stead, waiting for him to come of age." She had studied the history of her homeland in preparation for this mission. Elena's story was one she hoped to model after as she guided Margaretha. A strong tutor could make all the difference in a child's path.

The count shook his head. "I can't imagine it."

"Perhaps Germans don't train their women to be deserving of it," Lilia said.

Herr Waldeck stopped and stared ahead at the road.

She flinched and rubbed the wire ring beneath her glove. Drat her heavy-handed feminism. Those foreign ideas might turn him against her, but she couldn't apologize without proving herself a hypocrite. So, as he looked back up at her, she cocked her head innocently, as if these ideas made perfect, simple sense.

"You are unlike any woman I've ever met," he said, staring at her with curiosity. His gaze felt strong enough to expose her.

"Then you have never met a Russian," she said, looking over her shoulder and arranging her skirts against the horse's flank. He smiled and started on again. Lilia sighed in relief. For a moment, she had feared he might kick her off his horse. But his conversation had been so different from other men. Could he truly be so kind, or would he be like all the rest? They rounded the crest of a hill, and the *Schloss von Waldeck* came into view.

The castle rested atop a picturesque ridge. Its medieval-style stone walls rose into the sky, but she knew that inside sixteenth-century updates spotted the castle; glass paned windows and converted battlements. In a few years, his new wife, Katherina, would pressure Herr Waldeck to completely renovate the castle, reforming it into a modern palace with yellow walls and a black-domed spire.

A wafting breeze blew the fresh scent of the forest past Lilia and her chest swelled with emotion. Could this be real? Here she was, wearing a noblewoman's gown while a count escorted her on his horse to a castle. The nights spent staring at her mildewed ceiling were behind her forever. Assuming she could pull this off...

Lilia didn't know how much time she had to convince Herr Waldeck that she was exactly what his young daughters needed in an instructress. But little time or not, the mission loomed before her, drawing closer with each step.

Philip IV, Count of Waldeck
MARGARETHA VON FRISIA
Ernst
Elisabeth
Samuel
Daniel
Henry IX
Margaretha
Frederick
Anastasia
Esther
KATHERINA VON HATZFELD
JUTTA VON ISENBURG
Elisabeth
Magdalene

-Family tree of Philip von Waldeck, ITTA Master Document

CHAPTER
SIX

"I brought the kitchen tabby's new litter. You may play with them while you wait for Herr Waldeck," the nurse said, setting a basket roughly on the floor. Margaretha's younger siblings rushed forward to investigate. They cooed and pawed at the kittens' feathery fur. Baby Esther had grown in the years since Mama's death. She toddled across the floor and reached in, lifting a mewling white kitten by the tail.

Margaretha rushed forward. "Don't pull on them, Esther." She took the kitten on her lap and helped her baby sister caress its head. Nobody else offered to protect the poor things.

The nurse settled into her chair. "You can name them if you like."

"You should name her Bianka. It means white," her eldest sister Elisabeth said from her window seat.

"It's too Bulgarian," the nurse said, pulling a sugar-coated almond from her pocket and popping it in her mouth before the babies could ask for it.

"I like the name." Margaretha stroked the kitten's back. "Bianka."

Eleven-year-old Samuel flicked Henry's ear.

"Go on, Henry. Go play with the kittens. That's where the babies belong."

"I'm not one of the babies." Henry scowled. Samuel shoved him off the couch and laughed.

"I'm eight years old!" Henry shouted from the rug.

"Margaretha is almost as old as you and *she's* over there." Samuel waved his hand in her direction.

"It's not my fault Margaretha acts like a baby." Henry scowled up at her.

Margaretha pursed her lips and clutched the kitten closer. She knew Henry's accusation wasn't true. Babies pulled kittens' tails instead of protecting them.

"Boys!" Elisabeth shouted. Margaretha looked toward the nurse for help but the woman only settled deeper into her chair. Elisabeth sighed and pushed herself up from her seat.

"You mustn't be so disrespectful," Elisabeth said, helping Henry up from the floor. Samuel stuck his tongue out at her and she scowled back. Henry brushed off the back of his legs then marched toward Margaretha.

"Put that kitten away," Henry demanded, looking down at her sternly. "You're too old for it."

"Someone has to look after them." Margaretha nestled the kitten under her arm. She didn't understand why Henry so often acted like he was in charge.

"Do as I say," Henry said with his eyebrows scrunched up together in frustration.

Margaretha saw the glint of a tear pooling in the corner of his eye. Another mew sounded from the basket as Esther pulled a second kitten's ear. Margaretha paused, realizing that Henry was like the bothered kitten, being prodded and pushed around by Samuel. The babies meant no harm, but Samuel could be malicious. And again, everyone seemed content to let him get away with it. She sighed and set the kitten back in the basket.

Henry turned away. "See. We're both too old for kittens." He paraded back to Samuel with his chin lifted into the air. Samuel groaned.

Elisabeth raised an eyebrow at her younger sister. "Margaretha, you don't have to give in to Henry whenever he bosses you about."

Henry looked ready to argue, but as his lips parted, the door opened. In the entry stood a woman in a foreign dress and long silk gloves. The children all stared as she stepped into the room. The nurse stood, eying the dame whose mysterious appearance the week before made all the housemaids whisper. Father entered next, his boots clacking against the wooden floors.

"Father!" the boys called out, rushing toward him. Margaretha wished she could rush to him for an embrace as well, but Henry's elbows often found her ribs in the scuffle. She couldn't compete with their height or energy. Besides, Father always took time to remember her. She would just have to be patient.

"All right you ruffians, straighten up." Father tousled Samuel's hair. "I brought someone to meet you." He stepped aside, motioning to the regal woman.

"This," Father said, "is Lilia Vaschenko from Russia."

Margaretha wondered what Russia was.

"*Willkommen*," the children muttered.

"I am so pleased to meet you." The woman spoke with a strange accent. Her eyes searched across the room and when her gaze fell on Margaretha, she smiled. Margaretha wished she could hide behind Elisabeth's skirts.

"Are you a traveler?" Elisabeth asked, stepping forward. Lilia stood much taller than her.

"Yes. A traveler and a student of cultures." Even though she spoke to all the children, her gaze stuck to Margaretha. Was there something wrong with her appearance? Margaretha flattened her hands and smoothed them across her skirts.

Lilia turned and glanced at each of them. "I've gained great insight from this castle and your father is so kind. I'm anxious to learn your names." Margaretha's siblings narrowed their eyes and exchanged glances. None of Father's guests ever gave them this much attention.

Henry didn't hesitate to take the initiative. "I'm Henry," he shouted with explosive vigor.

Lilia laughed. "Nice to meet you. Tell me, Henry, what are your passions? Are you studying anything interesting?"

Henry's shoulders sagged. "I study Latin," he said, his face wrinkled up in disgust. Father sent him a warning glance.

"Only Latin?" Lilia asked. "No science or mathematics?"

"Henry is a bit young for further studies," Father said.

"Oh, no," Lilia said, shaking her head. "A child's mind is the best time for instruction. If he learns to reason at an early age, he will be far above his peers when the time comes for university."

Margaretha blinked in surprise. Nobody had ever challenged Father in front of the children before. The older boys looked at each other with worry as Father rubbed his beard.

"Henry," Father finally said, "you've seen Samuel doing his studies. Do mathematics interest you?"

"Oh yes!" Henry said. "I can do anything Samuel does."

Samuel snorted. Father looked at the light in Henry's eyes and turned back to Lilia.

"Perhaps after the death of my wife a few years ago, I lost sight of my children's potential." Father folded his arms and pursed his lips in thought.

"Reasonably, sir," Lilia said, touching his forearm in consolation. The nurse's eyes followed the lady's hand. Margaretha pursed her lips, knowing it would spark another round of gossip among the staff.

Lilia smiled at the older children, but none of them seemed anxious to introduce themselves. So, she crossed to the babies, who also looked away with shy disinterest.

Margaretha felt a pang of pity and stepped forward out of respect. However, she couldn't make herself speak. She stared at the beautiful woman and blinked. Elisabeth came to the rescue.

"This is Mar-" Elisabeth started, but Lilia raised her hand and cut her off. The woman stooped to Margaretha's level where she could watch her, eye to eye. Margaretha's cheeks grew hot.

"Elisabeth can introduce me if she wants," Margaretha said.

"But then I would only know who Elisabeth thinks you are. I want to know who *you* think you are," Lilia said. The room fell silent.

Margaretha hesitated. How would she present herself? She knew exactly what her siblings thought of her. Samuel thought she was a baby.

Henry knew he could boss her about. Elisabeth chastised her for being submissive when she was only trying to be kind.

It was too difficult. A six-year-old could be many things. She could be wild like Henry or sophisticated like Elisabeth.

Oh, if only Mama were here. Mama would know Margaretha's heart. Margaretha closed her eyes and tried to imagine what Mama might have seen through the winter window. She pictured snow, whirling past her, and enveloping her in white.

White, like a blank sheet of paper.

White like the feathery newborn kitten in the basket.

The kitten.

Bianka.

Margaretha opened her eyes and smiled at the lady. "My name is Bianka," she said.

Everyone stared at her in confusion and even Lilia seemed taken aback.

Father furrowed his eyebrows and knelt before her. "Margaretha, you mustn't lie."

"It's not a lie. I'm not very good at being Margaretha. So, I'm going to be Bianka, now," she persisted.

A smile flitted across Lilia's face and she turned back to Father. "It may not be her actual name. But that's not what I asked her for, is it?" Lilia held out her hand for Bianka to take. "What a pleasure to meet you, Bianka."

Bianka's family looked at her in surprise and for the first time, she felt a rush of pride. Margaretha was her mother's name. But Bianka? That was something of her own making.

"...I doubt I'll find my second wife, Katherina, so easy to love as my Margaretha. I take comfort, however, that my children will once again have a woman to care for them. The boys are wild and the girls solemn. Surely, a stepmother shall bring some well-needed tenderness to the home."

-Letter written by Philip von Waldeck

CHAPTER
SEVEN

K eltson scanned the monitors for Lilia's next appearance, but the day passed and she didn't return. He exhaled, trying to release the weight from his chest. Hopefully, her absence meant success. He scanned forward through the surveillance and found her one week later, appearing through the forest. Lilia wore new clothes, which meant she had not only arrived at Herr Waldeck's castle but had become an accepted guest.

She perked up as his mask appeared in the mirror.

"I did it!" She clasped her hands together. "He introduced me to his children."

"Does Herr Waldeck considered you a royal guest or a charity case?" he asked.

Lilia sniffed and waved her hand in dismissal. "Royal guest, of course. In fact, it's rather interesting. Philip welcomed me as an investigator of Lutheranism…"

"You don't call him Philip to his face, do you?" Keltson interrupted. "You should know better than to be so casual with him."

She blushed. "I'm on a first-name basis with the entire family. In fact, Margaretha introduced herself as 'Bianka' and refuses to respond to anything else," Lilia said, changing the subject. "Everyone is quite surprised by it and nobody knows why she chose the name."

"I don't like any of that information." Keltson frowned. "Even the smallest variances can leave a trail for ITTA to pick up."

Variances were Keltson's greatest bane. ITTA scanned the Master Doc every thirty minutes to see if history had been tampered with. If only Keltson could find it and change its contents, he wouldn't have to stick to small-scale jobs. But no matter how often he'd hacked into ITTA's system, the Master Document vault location remained a secret.

Lilia stiffened, the cords in her neck standing out. "It's common for children to experiment with names. It's just a phase."

"You better make sure of it. If new records pop up with the name Bianka, ITTA might get suspicious. You need to be deliberate about every move, Lilia." Keltson tapped his finger on the desk, awaiting Lilia's response. She set her jaw and glared at the mirror, flexing her gloved fingers, and refusing to speak.

The woman had a strong personality, that was for sure. While it would serve Margaretha well to have such a strong guardian, Keltson realized he'd have to adjust his coaching tactics. He did his best to soften his voice.

"You're doing well, Lilia. Most people need my intervention long before now."

She nodded with a hint of a satisfied smile. He'd have to remember to mix in compliments with his instruction. He might be in charge, but disappointed clients meant no payday.

"Continue with your third directive. Become a mentor, but don't let your guard down. Don't get comfortable. Try to solidify your position in the house and I'll see you in another week."

Her smile wavered. "Sneaking away is difficult. Phil... Herr Waldeck isn't fond of me wandering alone in the woods. He might find my ideals and personality strong, but he finds women generally insufficient when it comes to protecting themselves."

"Hmm. I'll see what I can do to make the mirror more accessible." Keltson made a note on his scratch pad. "These first meetings are crucial as we get you established. Eventually, we should be able to narrow them down to every few months."

Lilia still looked concerned but nodded.

"I will see you in a week." Keltson cut the transmission and marked the mission log. He was genuinely impressed that Lilia hadn't needed any major corrections.

He sped through the mirror's surveillance to the next week's transmission, but Lilia didn't show up. Maybe she needed some saving after all. Or maybe she simply ran late. It was highly possible if Count Waldeck gave her trouble. Keltson scanned forward and the days in the woods spun by faster and faster until, one month later, Lilia showed up.

Keltson activated the feed and leaned forward. Lilia struggled to maintain eye contact, and her posture was far too stiff and defensive. Something was wrong.

"What happened?" he asked.

Lilia set her jaw. "Herr Waldeck won't let me leave," she said. "I only came now because he is away on business."

"Do I need to ask why he is acting so territorial of you?" Keltson formed a fist, hoping his suspicions were wrong.

"He's not territorial, just... precautious." Lilia glanced over her shoulder and smoothed her hair away from her forehead. Was she afraid someone watched her? Keltson leaned forward and tried to listen to the ambiance surrounding her. He grabbed his utility belt in case he needed to extract her himself.

"Is Herr Waldeck suspicious of you?" he asked. Lilia was either in trouble or hiding something from him.

"No, no, things are going well."

"Then you've become an instructor to Margaretha?"

"I've made great progress." She planted her feet and raised her chin. "In fact, I've just ensured I'll be a part of their lives for a very long time."

Keltson's stomach dropped and he froze. "What did you do?"

Lilia pursed her lips. "Philip is kind to me. Kinder than anyone else I've ever known."

"You didn't marry him, did you?" Keltson asked, bracing himself for her answer.

"No. But he is canceling his engagement to Katherina von Hatzfeld." She gave him a crisp nod. Keltson groaned and dropped his head into his hands. Lilia spoke quickly with increasing confidence. "You saw how that ghastly woman destroyed this family. I came here to save Bianka, but I realize now how all the children will suffer. This way I can benefit Bianka *and* the others."

"Her name is supposed to be *Margaretha*, Lilia!" Keltson shouted. "You can justify this all you want, but if you make such a drastic change, ITTA *will* send an agent to investigate. We either have to fix this or I have to pull you out before they extract you themselves."

Lilia fixed him with her gaze. "How do you know they'll catch on? Katherina died seven years after she married Philip and she never bore him any children. It won't erase anyone in the future. It's possible this doesn't change anything. ITTA may not notice."

"Lilia, this can't happen." Keltson's voice radiated his solid resolve.

"Please," she whispered. And for just a moment, the protective barrier she held around herself broke and Keltson saw her emotions plainly. She loved Waldeck. It was easy to see how lost and vulnerable she looked. Keltson groaned and paused the feed.

He ran his fingers through his hair, contemplating Lilia's justifications in his mind. Her argument was well crafted. If Lilia took the harsh stepmother out of the equation, Margaretha's family life would undoubtedly improve. However, Keltson suspected Lilia's hidden motivations. Lilia came from nothing, so becoming a countess obviously appealed to her.

This all went against Keltson's one, firm rule—clients shouldn't go back for themselves. Self-interest made for sloppy judgment.

He ought to extract her now and drop her right back in that moldy Russian studio he found her in. He closed his eyes.

He needed those codes. Those tantalizing order codes Lilia held. He shook his head at his own hypocrisy.

If Lilia married Herr Waldeck and her variances became traceable by ITTA, then he'd put a stop to it. If not… he'd have to address his selective morality later.

Keltson stood and crossed to his digital library that covered an entire corner of the cellar. Its shelves contained records of every variance he ever produced. He pulled open Lilia's digital application. Inside, he found a letter from Herr Waldeck that discussed his upcoming marriage to the Countess von Hatzfeld. Herr Waldeck spoke of political gains that would never be realized and a heart-wrenching thought that his children might have a mother again—a mother who sent his children to live with relatives, shredding the family to pieces.

Lilia had a point; Bianka's siblings also suffered under Katherina's hand. He pulled out his copy of the Master Document and scanned it for variances.

He found a big one.

If Lilia married Count Waldeck, they remained married into their eighties. Herr Waldeck never married his third wife and therefore never had two more daughters. That fact alone meant over 1,200 people disappeared in the present day.

Keltson rubbed his forehead and looked above his shelves at a large digital timer that showed the countdown before ITTA ran the next variance scan. The last scan ran five minutes ago. If he didn't clean this up in the next twenty-five minutes, ITTA would see the flag and send out an agent. He scrawled a few notes in his log, then returned to his transmission with Lilia. She waited, with pleading eyes.

"If you're going to do this, you have to promise me you'll follow my exact directives. If you ignore me, you *will* be arrested by ITTA and imprisoned for life," he said.

Lilia looked up at him, blinking back grateful tears.

"You have seven years with him. Then you have to leave."

-Sketchbook of Dorothea Wild

CHAPTER
EIGHT

The servants wheeled in the new mirror, wrapped in fine furs and secured with thick cords. Lilia swallowed and gripped Philip's hand a little tighter.

"What is it?" Elisabeth asked as the servants set the delivery into the corner of the dining hall. The wrappings were removed, revealing the mirror set in a silver-gilt frame. The children gasped with wonder as it was set upright.

"It's taller than Father!" Henry shouted.

"It's a beautiful engagement gift, Lilia. Thank you." Philip's hand lingered on her waist as he planted a kiss on her forehead. She closed her eyes, feeling uncomfortable now that The Mirror watched her. Lilia didn't like this device placed in plain sight. Now that he could survey the family dealings, she felt like a teenager assigned a chaperone.

Philip took her hand and admired the treacherous mirror. It wasn't like she had planned on falling in love with Philip. Lilia hadn't believed in romantic love at all until she met him. Men in her experience only offered catcalls and crass humor. But Philip quickly proved that he belonged to a different class, one that had likely become extinct in her modern age. At first, she'd fought against his gentility and manners. She'd worked her whole life to prove she didn't need anyone to support her. That strength is what she meant to give Margaretha. But somehow, he had needed her strength too, and softened her just enough to let him in.

Now, however, the servants worked diligently, setting up a reminder that her relationship had an expiration date.

The Mirror demanded she only had seven years. Seven years to think of a plan.

Elisabeth admired the smooth glass, running her finger delicately along the fragile surface. "There's hardly a flaw." She tilted her face this way and that, admiring the different angles of her features.

"I've never seen all of me at once." Henry paraded forward. He was instantly shoved away by his older brothers.

"No fighting. You will all get a turn," Lilia chided gently. As the children rotated through, each getting a chance to study themselves, Lilia noticed that Bianka stood firmly rooted behind a chair. Over the last few weeks, Lilia had poured in a special effort to help Bianka. Philip admitted that his endearment for Lilia had been confirmed when she gained the trust of his quietest child.

"You don't have to be scared, Bianka. Come." Bianka obeyed, carefully making her way forward. However, when she came close enough, she grasped Lilia's skirts.

"My dear, are you afraid of yourself?" Lilia asked. Bianka's eyes widened and she shook her head. Lilia wrapped her arm around Bianka's shoulder and walked her toward the mirror. "Then see how beautiful and kind you look."

Bianka stumbled to a halt before it. "It's going to swallow me up," she whispered.

Philip laughed, but Lilia only looked at Bianka curiously. Could the girl sense The Mirror staring back at her? She closed her eyes and prepared herself to deliver The Mirror's next instructions.

"You know, Philip, I believe I have an idea."

"What is it?" he asked, reclining against the wall and watching Henry unsuccessfully attempt to parade past the mirror. Each of the children had such different reactions to their own reflections—and each one spoke of their flaws. Elisabeth's vanity flounced before it, Henry's desperation to stand out strutted in the corner of its reflection, and sweet Bianka's anxious insecurity hid from it.

She lifted Bianka's hand and patted it. "I believe the children ought to take regular estimation of themselves in this mirror."

"But could that not lead to the 'mother sin of pride', my dear?" Philip asked, raising a skeptical eyebrow. Lilia smiled, remembering Pastor Hefentreger's recent sermon. Many of the preacher's lectures felt naive and contrived, but she loved that Philip clung to such utopian ideals.

"It could," Lilia said, hesitating. She pressed her fingers against her lips in thought before continuing. "So, perhaps *we* could place them before the mirror, regard their successes, and instruct them on improvements. It would be a monthly approbation, hosted by their parents."

Philip smiled even wider, most likely at the word "parents". Lilia felt a flush of color rush to her cheeks. The wedding was only a few weeks away and she felt awkward knowing that The Mirror currently analyzed her romance. She turned back to Bianka.

"For example, if you look here, Bianka..." she said, reaching into a pocket she had instructed the seamstress to sew into her newest skirt.

"Has your dress ripped?" Elisabeth interrupted.

"No, it's—" Lilia paused and looked up at the mirror nervously. "It's a pocket."

"In a lady's dress?" Philip asked.

Lilia swallowed. Women didn't wear pockets in this century. It was probably best to keep them quiet, but it was such a commonplace thing in her old life that she hadn't thought twice about revealing it. She reached inside and found the silver pocket-watch she carried. The entire family watched with curiosity now. Lilia flipped open the latch, revealing a puff of rouge and a mirror that lay where the clock face should have been. Elisabeth giggled.

"That's not a watch," Henry said, pointing an accusing finger at Lilia's self-made makeup compact. She blinked, realizing it was yet another thing The Mirror would find inappropriate. Lilia sighed and wiped away the powder from the small mirror and held it up in front of Bianka. "Look. If you place this mirror in front of the other, it reflects itself..." she struggled to aim the face of the glass just right.

Bianka gasped as an infinite number of compact mirrors appeared within the reflection.

Lilia pointed to the girl's face, multiplied time and time again. "So, when you stand in front of a mirror, you may see all the hundreds of possibilities you hold. Just like this."

"Are there hundreds of me, too?" Bianka asked.

Lilia laughed.

"Be careful, my dear, or you will convince us all that you're a woman of invention." Philip's smile slowly built until his eyes shone with mischief. Before Lilia could enjoy it too much, Elisabeth's voice broke through the moment.

"But she is, Father! Have you seen her other contraptions?" Elisabeth never took her eyes off the mirror.

Lilia's heart fell into her chest. "My ideas are mere trinkets."

"An inventor like Leonardo da Vinci," Henry said with wide eyes.

A chill ran through Lilia. If The Mirror watched now, he surely wasn't happy. She couldn't afford to gain such a reputation among the family. That would certainly draw ITTA's attention. From now on, she would try to keep her gadgets to herself.

"Well, I think this approbation idea is wonderful, Lilia. We shall begin as soon as we are married." Philip stepped forward and took Lilia's bare hand. She had abandoned her gloves only days before. Philip's engagement ring had replaced the scalar wire ring she wore during her arrival, though she still kept the wire in a locket around her neck. Lilia felt a wave of comfort at Philip's touch and she looked around at the children. There was so much to be nervous about—the wedding, The Mirror's directives, becoming a mother. It was all daunting. But, as she looked at the people around her, she realized how much she longed to be a part of all this. This home, this family. The boys were quietly whispering, undoubtedly planning some sort of vandalism. The younger children patted the surface of the glass and giggled. Elisabeth gently swayed her skirts in front of the mirror, admiring herself while Bianka watched from behind. Then, of course, the man who held her hand. Yes. This was exactly what she had been missing in her cinderblock tower.

"It will be good for the children to face themselves in the mirror. We shall build up their confidence where needed and deal out a dose of humility to those who need it more," Philip said, lifting Elisabeth's chin with his finger. She blushed and stopped swishing her skirts.

Lilia glanced at the mirror, wondering if the man inside was proud of her for getting Philip to accept the approbation. Now he could monitor the children regularly for variances. But perhaps he would be too angry about everything else to be thankful. She wouldn't know until she met with him here.

Tonight.

THE CORRIDOR WAS silent and chilled as Lilia snuck through the castle. She shivered, partially from the cold, and partially from the chill of fear running through her veins. In the dark, it felt like the halls grew, stretching on into an eerie eternity. She didn't carry a candle. She needed the option of hiding in the shadows if necessary.

Now that The Mirror had seen her with the Waldeck family, what would he say? Had she done enough to stay? She pushed through the dining room doors and locked the latch behind her. The mirror loomed ahead of her and, before she reached it, a haze grew in the center, forming into the familiar mask.

"I have to admit," Lilia said once its features were clear, "this *is* easier than sneaking into the forest to meet."

"I doubt you would have been able to explain to Philip much longer why you kept running away," The Mirror said. She couldn't tell from his emotionless mask if he was reprimanding or agreeing with her.

"You have my next directives?" She crossed her arms protectively in front of her.

"Do you remember why I sent you there, Lilia?" he asked, ignoring her.

Lilia swallowed and shifted her weight. "To stop Bianka from being sent away. To save her from being killed."

"And do you know what will happen if you get caught by ITTA?" he asked in the same even tone.

Lilia knew the risks. "I'll be extracted, arrested, and live the rest of my life in prison." She shuddered.

"Yes. But that's not all. This timeline will return to its original state—a place where you never arrived, where Philip marries Katherina, and where *Margaretha* dies. Every mistake you make, you put *her* life on the line. Are pockets and compacts really worth that?" he asked.

Lilia flinched. "No." She looked down into her hands.

"Likewise, if you stay with Philip for more than seven years, he will never remarry, and his two children with Jutta will never be born. That alone will prevent exactly 1,213 people from being born in today's world. Do you know how big a variance that is?"

"It sounds bad," Lilia said flatly. She didn't like thinking about Philip's *future* children with another woman.

"Well, exactly six minutes ago, all of those people disappeared because you won't leave him. Either you change your mind right now before ITTA's computers run their regular scan, or you'll have a time travel agent breathing down your neck before you wake up."

Tears threatened to jump from Lilia's eyes. "Fine. I'll follow the directives. In seven years, I'll leave. I'll jump to Spain just in time to rescue Bianka from the Spanish court and Philip will think we're both dead. Happy now?" Her voice broke as she said it and she couldn't quite convince her heart to mean it. Closing her eyes, she told herself it was better to have Philip for only seven years of her life than to never have him at all. The Mirror didn't seem satisfied.

"When it comes to it, do you mean it?" The Mirror asked.

Lilia's temper flared. "I have lived in so many different shades of misery! I have been given this one chance to escape. I will take what I can get."

The Mirror narrowed his eyes. "If you don't follow through, I'll come out there and extract you myself. Immediately. Do you understand?" he said.

Lilia pressed her teeth together. He was forcing her hand. She couldn't give this all up now, but maybe she could later. She straightened. "I understand," she said.

Portrait of Margaretha von Waldeck
Age: 14
-ITTA Master Document

CHAPTER
NINE

A dark blizzard howled outside the window while Bianka waited in the corridor for her monthly approbation. Though it was already late April, winter seemed ferociously determined to swallow up spring entirely. Henry stood inside the dining room with Father and Lilia. She hoped he didn't need too much of a reprimand today so she could enter the warm, firelit hall. The tall wooden door stood open a crack, allowing her Father's muffled voice to pass through.

"Henry, you are a dutiful student. But there is a difference between being a good student and an insufferable pupil. You mustn't contradict your tutors. Ask questions, but don't try to entrap them."

Bianka smiled and looked down at her hands. Henry still consistently tried to prove himself equal to his older brothers, focusing solely on academics now that they were off attending university. She looked down at the windowsill and caressed the three stains on the dark stones. Her chest tightened as she thought about her mother—the first casualty in her fragmented family. So much had changed in the last few years. Elisabeth died only weeks after her own wedding. Samuel and Daniel left to university in Muhlberg and Bianka hardly heard from them. A few months after their departure, her youngest sister Esther died. Only four of the children remained at home now. Father and Lilia's approbations sometimes felt like the only thread holding the family together.

The door opened, spilling firelight into the corridor.

"Bianka, you may come in now. Henry is finished," Father said. Bianka straightened and put on a pleasant smile, one she practiced many times in front of the mirror.

Henry stepped out the door, his chin held high. He brushed past Bianka without looking at her. Bianka picked up her skirts and walked into the dining room. Lilia stood near a wooden pedestal covered in intricate, golden vines that rested before the mirror. The silver frame's pristine appearance had faded over the years; bits of tarnish crept along the edges.

"Here you are." Lilia stepped forward to arrange Bianka's skirts around her. "My goodness, you have grown. Your skirts don't reach the floor. I'll have a new dress tailored for you."

Father stepped forward to measure her against himself. In truth, she stood taller. Though she still didn't even come close to Father's towering stance.

He turned back to Lilia. "She is the height of a true lady."

"She could bring any man to her aid with such slender beauty," Lilia said. Father didn't seem to like that idea. Her parents complimented her beauty often enough, but they never teased her with adult matters.

Bianka blushed. "I'm not yet fifteen."

"Yet, you are certainly the fairest in all Weilburg." Lilia smiled. Bianka's smile faded at the familiar words.

"What is wrong, Bianka?" Lilia asked. Bianka pursed her lips, unwilling to speak. Lilia narrowed her eyes. "Bianka, you must learn to speak your thoughts if you are to be a diligent countess someday."

Bianka hesitated, struggling to form a cohesive sentence. "I wondered..." she said. "I'm not complaining, but—Henry often tells how his approbations are filled with interviews and speeches on morality. My meetings are filled with very little instruction and a fair number of compliments on my appearance. I wondered why I don't also have the welfare of my character checked so often."

Father laughed and placed his hands on Bianka's shoulders. "My dear, your brother needs so much more refinement than you in matters of character. Your spirit is as pure as any lily. You are kind and charitable. You need no correction, for you are constantly refining your own morals. Lilia and I wish to build your confidence. We do not praise your younger sister Anastasia's beauty, for her vanity is already inflated. You, however, need a dose of pride from us."

Bianka relaxed. She turned and looked at Lilia for confirmation.

Before Lilia could respond, the doors burst open and a messenger ran inside. "Herr Waldeck, I have an urgent message from your son." He thrust a letter into Father's hand.

"Samuel?" Father asked, reading the front. Gripping the letter, he broke the seal. Lilia stepped forward, grasping his arm. As Father read, Bianka's heart fluttered with worry.

"The Holy Roman Empire attacked the Lutherans in Muhlberg. Samuel lies wounded and captured," Father said. He looked up at Lilia with determination.

"At least wait for the storm to pass," Lilia pleaded. Father leaned forward, kissed her, and strode out the door. Lilia remained frozen for a moment before turning to Bianka. "You may retire," Lilia said.

Bianka stood, immobile on the pedestal, unsure of what just happened. She wished she could run after Father and read the letter for herself. Did the desperation in Father's departure mean Samuel might die? Her family couldn't bear to be broken again. Impatiently, Lilia ushered her with a firm hand from the room. When the door closed behind her, Bianka froze, overwhelming fear for her brother rushing over her.

First Mother, Elisabeth, Esther, and now Samuel?

She couldn't imagine shutting herself in her room. Overwhelming anxieties already threatened to close in around her. While she stood indecisively wondering which way to turn, she heard voices through the closed doors behind her. Turning her head, she placed her ear against the crack. Lilia muttered something and a man responded. Perhaps the messenger? Though she knew better manners, Bianka lay down on the cold marble and peered through the crack beneath the door. She needed to hear what news he had. Inside, Lilia paced back and forth in front of the mirror. There was a man's voice in the room, sure enough, but Bianka couldn't see him.

She shifted her view and saw a light hovering near the mirror while Lilia spoke in concerned tones.

"You've stayed too long, Lilia. Eight years now. You agreed to leave after seven."

"And I have eight more years before he has to remarry. I won't go yet."

Confused, Bianka shifted her view again. Her blood froze in her veins.

A white face hovered inside the mirror, casting a pale light across the floor.

For years, Bianka stood in front of that mirror's glass, never realizing there may be someone lurking on the other side, watching her. The mask's mouth moved, forming strange words as if they were magical incantations. Lilia muttered back at him.

What was this magic?

Was Lilia a witch? This woman she trusted for so long? Years ago, Lilia appeared in the woods with such a vague explanation of where she came from. She entranced her father in such a short amount of time. The servants still murmured about their marriage. Everyone viewed her gadgets as a thing of curiosity, but what if they were something else? What if they were...

Magic.

She looked up at the floating mask and felt her fears confirmed. How else could this be explained?

"Something is wrong," The Mirror said. He looked down. "Variances are appearing as we speak. Right now, Lilia!"

Bianka fell still, feeling pins prick the back of her neck. Lilia cast her eyes around the room and her gaze fell on the shadow Bianka cast beneath the door. Bianka pushed herself up from the floor and broke into a run, fear tearing through her chest as the doors behind her crashed open and firelight spilled down the hall. Lilia's body cast a shadow down the corridor that seemed to grow larger as Bianka ran.

"*Local lore claims a witch rode out of the forest, enchanting Herr Waldeck with her beauty. After their marriage, she revealed her magic little by little, spooking the servants and his children. Herr Waldeck remained blind to her powers. These rumors are attributed to the fall of the Waldeck's influence in spreading Lutheranism through the region.*"

-First unaccounted variance from the Master Document

CHAPTER
TEN

Lilia stood frozen in the doorway, watching Bianka run down the hall with her secret. One mistake and everything she had done to keep The Mirror concealed for the last eight years became worthless.

Lilia slammed the door and gripped the latch behind her. "She heard us."

The Mirror sighed long and deep. "Do you know how tired I am, Lilia?"

"What am I supposed to do?" she asked, reaching her hands toward him.

"I haven't slept since you walked through my mirror. For the last day, you have given me eight years' worth of grief. I barely clean up one mess in time before ITTA notices, then something else happens. You throw variances out like sweets. And every half-hour when ITTA scans the Master Doc, you come closer to hitting noticeable limits."

"Don't pretend I'm the only one who needs to clean up my act." Lilia pointed her finger at him. "You need my codes or you won't survive. If someone like me could discover your orders, how long before ITTA found you themselves?"

"It's time for you to leave, Lilia," The Mirror said.

"I won't. Not yet. Tell me how to fix this. I can do this."

"How to fix this? You tell me, Lilia. This little chat Bianka overheard created over a thousand new variances in the timeline."

"A thousand?" Lilia said, feeling all the air deflate out of her. "What kind of variances?"

"Oh, you know, the fall of Lutheranism in your region, a few missing names aboard the Mayflower, a witch-hunting mentality in sixteenth-century Germany, and congratulations, you are my first client to ever create new folklore!" Though The Mirror's mask remained perfectly calm, the voice on the other side surged with unmistakable frustration.

"What do they say?" she asked.

"Are you kidding me? It doesn't matter. In twenty-seven minutes, when ITTA runs their next scan, they'll see this. There's nothing I can do to reclaim your future from this point. The only way is to backtrack."

"How far?" Lilia asked.

"I'm going to pull you out at seven years like you agreed."

"You can't pull me! My life here can't end like this," she shouted.

"May I remind you this is about saving *Margaretha*? It's not about you living out some fantasy. This is not about *your* happiness, Lilia. This mission is about a girl's life."

A spear of anger filled Lilia's chest. She knew why she was here; to save an insufficient little girl who was destined to die because she wasn't brave enough to stand up for herself. Lilia didn't need that kind of protection. She survived through the years without parents at all. And now, Bianka was the reason Lilia would lose everything.

"Goodbye, Lilia," The Mirror said. The transmission cut.

Lilia braced herself. Could she do anything to stop him from pulling her out of this timeline? Would everything she knew for the last year disappear?

She fled to the front hall to spend her last moments with Philip but found he had already left for Muhlberg. Wandering to her room in a daze, she expected everything around her to fade into the walls of her Russian flat.

Minutes went by and nothing happened. How long before he reset her timeline? Hours? Minutes? Any second she could find the entire last year in the Waldeck castle erased.

As the hours passed and the evening turned to night, Lilia found herself hoping The Mirror met some unavoidable obstacle, or that perhaps she escaped his extraction, preserving the life she loved.

What could have stopped him? Perhaps ITTA found him and arrested him before he could remove her from her timeline. The thought both thrilled her and terrified her. Without The Mirror, she could live out the rest of her life with Philip. She could be rid of the mirror in the dining hall and live like a normal family—with no expiration dates and no dictation every month telling her what she should do.

But, if they arrested The Mirror, did ITTA know about her as well? If she caused a variance as horrible as he claimed, then ITTA must know where to find her. She straightened up in her bed, looking at blue moonlight pouring through the snow-frosted windows.

ITTA may already be here.

"People tell me I'm lucky to live in modern times. And it's true. Throughout history, achondroplastic dwarfs, like me, have been treated as less than human. European courts considered us pets or eternal children. In Rome, they heralded tall gladiators as heroes and dwarf gladiators as a comedic act. We both fought to the death, but people only laughed at us. As an ITTA agent, I was restrained from doing anything about the mistreatment I observed. But, with you, I can change all that."

-Application of Ammond MacBarran

CHAPTER
ELEVEN

K eltson ended the transmission with Lilia and scanned backwards through his surveillance feeds. He needed to find the appropriate moment to extract her. If she didn't exist when Bianka spied their conversation then…

Bianka? When had he started calling her that? Keltson rubbed his eyes. Lilia had called the girl Bianka so often the last few hours, his fatigue made his thoughts blur. He tapped the display on his stopwatch that marked the beginning of his shift.

18:32:26.

Eighteen and a half hours? No wonder he was making mistakes. He couldn't remember the last time he'd worked so many consecutive hours. His clients usually failed or died in a way that didn't leave a variance for ITTA to pick up on. If there was nothing for them to notice, he could clock out and return to the job at his leisure. Lilia filled his day with so many emergencies, he didn't have a moment to stop and rest.

The disposable cell phone on his desk rang.

He stared at it in confusion for a few seconds before looking up at the clock.

3:00 pm.

He cursed under his breath.

10:00 am Eastern Standard Time.

He picked up the phone and ran toward his gear.

"Hello?" Keltson asked, then winced. He usually made it a point never to speak first, but he was so tired and unprepared that everything was muddled.

"This is Ammond," the American said.

Keltson tucked the phone between his chin and shoulder as he clipped on his utility belt. He couldn't believe this. There were still portions of Ammond's case to prepare. Lilia's overwhelming timeline put everything else on hold.

"Do you have the payment?" Keltson asked, looking around for the second duffel bag. Luckily, he'd thought to pull Ammond and Lilia's clothes at the same time.

"Right here, on the table in front of me," Ammond said.

"Hold for thirty seconds." Keltson dropped the phone to the ground and grabbed his travel vest, slipping it over his shoulders. Next, he attached the extension cord to one of the two remaining portable mirrors, completing his quickest suit up on record. He set the coordinates for the Pause and pressed the ignition.

The confines of the cellar disappeared and Keltson found himself in the center of a grand American estate. The room felt muted through the shadowy chill of the Pause, yet everything sat in a clean and orderly fashion. A dreadful wash of exhaustion hit Keltson and he considered taking a nap right there on the floor. If not for the cold, he would have. The icy air bit into his skin worse than normal and he realized he'd left his gloves and beanie at home. He needed to get out of here fast.

Ammond sat at a dining table, staring at the cell phone in front of him with his fingers interlocked beneath his chin. The former ITTA agent had shoulder-length, blond hair, and thick, commanding eyebrows. The most important feature of Ammond however, was his stature.

Ammond had achondroplasia, a common form of dwarfism. Keltson glanced around the room; the furnishings were all built to full-sized adult standards. Keltson smiled, thinking of a line from Ammond's application. "I might have taller mountains to climb than most, but I'm capable of anything they can do and more."

Seeing him in person brought another wash of excitement over Keltson. Ammond's impressive application included twenty years of work as an ITTA time travel agent, and his mission statement proved he was the most assertive vigilante ever to join Keltson's ranks.

As a little person, Ammond went places in history that no one else could. Medieval culture shamefully mistreated dwarfs, but Ammond exploited that mentality. He sat at the feet of kings, stole artifacts from nobles who merely laughed at him for being so mischievous, and observed inner court politics while no one thought twice about his presence. But during his missions, Ammond met others who desperately needed his help. With ITTA's intense rules against interference, Ammond had turned to Keltson.

Keltson carried the mirror to the corner, unplugged it, then dropped the duffel bag gently next to it. Both of the objects fizzled out of the Pause.

"Oh, I almost forgot," Keltson said, noticing the metal lockbox on the table. He activated his photovoltaic transmitter and pulled the box into the Pause. Inside, Keltson found a neatly stacked arrangement of digital currency code bars. Each bar held a partial code. Ammond had the other half of the codes memorized.

"I'm not going to have any problems with you, am I, Ammond?" Keltson asked, hearing the tired catch in his throat as he spoke. Taking on another client was just about the last thing Keltson needed right now. But since Lilia's payment offered no monetary value, he needed Ammond's funds to keep things running.

Keltson pushed the return ignition on his vest and, as the cellar materialized around him, he smiled at Ammond's reaction through his surveillance monitor. The crackle and the materializing mirror startled Ammond. Keltson enjoyed the fact that his inventions could surprise even a seasoned time traveler. Keltson activated the mask and Ammond walked over cautiously.

"I've never seen anything like that before, kid," Ammond said.

Keltson raised an eyebrow. "What makes you think I'm a 'kid'?" he asked.

Ammond smiled and folded his arms. "Obviously you've got some new kind of tech here that ITTA doesn't know about. Obviously, you're new gen. You kids have inventions running through your veins. It's just, usually, people like you come running to *them* for a quick sale instead of going indie."

Keltson blinked. His expectations about Ammond shattered. He'd expected some middle-aged, military guy, and instead, he got a casual American with a hint of a southern accent. What if all his other assumptions about Ammond were wrong too? He already struggled with Lilia. Keltson didn't know if he could handle another client with compliance issues.

"So, I've got a mirror now. I'm assuming it does something?" Ammond scratched his chin, looking unimpressed.

Keltson shook his head, trying to clear his mind and wake himself up. "It's a transport as well as a communicator."

"Hmm. ITTA usually issues flesh packs, fiber-optic screens, that sort of thing." Ammond motioned to a spot on his arm.

"My attempts at silicone fabrication all come out looking like boils."

"And you think this draws less attention?" Ammond said, gesturing to the mirror.

"Hey, look. You're not working in Kansas anymore," Keltson said in annoyance. Ammond laughed heartily, then stooped and unzipped the duffel bag. Keltson felt as if he missed a cue.

"These clothes are good. I'm impressed." Ammond pulled out a bland linen tunic. He slipped it over his modern clothing, holding up his arms in front of him. The sleeves dangled past his fingertips.

"Blast," Keltson whispered. He hadn't had time to make alterations. So far, he'd failed at proving his competence to this veteran.

"It's an easy fix," Ammond said. "Later though. I'm feeling restless. Let's get me out of here." Ammond rolled the sleeves up to his elbows.

"I have a portal established in the woods about forty paces from the safehouse. The abandoned cottage should fix up alright. Especially once you complete your first few missions and have an entire crew to assist you."

Ammond laughed again. "You don't know these people like I do. Half of them were pampered, spoiled, and mistreated by royalty their whole lives. Work and discipline are foreign to them. But they deserve to be treated like human beings, not like pets. So, if they'll come, I'll teach them. The other half... Well, all they know is work and survival. And I think it's about time they get a day off."

"Well... then... all that's left is your cover. I have some digital documents prepared for you to drop around the house for investigators: some flight itineraries for India, research on ashrams and guru's..." he trailed off as Ammond politely nodded. "What?" Keltson asked.

"Your cover is great. Really creative..."

"But..." Keltson asked.

"I already launched my yacht two hours ago and arranged for it to be commandeered by pirates in the Gulf of Aden." He shrugged. "But you should definitely use that cover for your next client." Ammond gave him a thumbs-up and winked.

Keltson did his best not to scowl. Clients never showed him up like this.

"Well then. All that's left is for you to step through the mirror." Keltson activated the display. The mask faded away on the glass and the woods outside Ammond's cottage appeared. A smile lit up Ammond's face and he grasped the frame. He turned, glanced around his home one last time, then slipped through the rippling glass.

Ammond and the mirror both transported to the safehouse clearing, cutting Keltson's feed to the American manor and replacing it with a view of a clearing in the woods of Germany. As Ammond stepped out of the frame he inhaled through his nose, seeming to enjoy the fresh forest air. Keltson pulled up the top page of Ammond's digital file and printed it out.

"I have a list of directives for you. The targets you wish to rescue are spelled out in order. I'll meet with you in one week after you've taken a decent inventory of the place."

Ammond didn't turn around immediately to respond. When he did,

Keltson was surprised to see him rubbing tear trails from his cheeks. "Thank you," he said. Ammond seemed seasoned and prepared; he didn't expect him to get emotional.

"You don't know what this means," Ammond said. "All these years, I've been so helpless. ITTA didn't allow even the most microscopic changes to the timeline. Someone could be drowning and they expected me to just watch. Then they'd talk about what I'd seen with disturbing interest. Like they believed it was only a TV show. They didn't understand how real life is back here."

Keltson smiled in relief. Ammond wouldn't be anything like Lilia.

He leaned forward, softening his expression. "This is the first time I'm attempting to extract individuals from their own time and bring them to a safehouse. It's definitely the most ambitious case I've ever taken on. You have a good cause. Better than most."

"I'll make good use of this opportunity, sir." Ammond pressed his hand against his chest. Keltson smiled and let the newly printed list of directives fall through the portable mirror. It landed at Ammond's feet, five-hundred years in the past. Ammond picked up the list and looked over it carefully.

"Get out there and explore your new home." Keltson nodded, and Ammond didn't wait for a second invitation. He darted down the hill toward the clearing where the cottage lay.

Keltson ended the transmission and yawned. The clock on the wall beeped, snapping him out of his tired stupor.

The variance timer reset ten minutes ago.

No.

Lilia's timeline was a mess and ITTA had undoubtedly found the new variances. All one-thousand of them. He ran over to his bookshelves and grabbed the Master Doc and the most recently uploaded electronic booklet. He linked them together and a discrepancy between the texts popped up. ITTA *had* picked up on the variance and Lilia's story *had* changed. It spoke of Herr Waldeck's wife being an enchantress, just as before. But this time, it had a different ending.

"As persecution mounted against the Waldeck family, a huntsman

became convinced of her guilt and chased the witch into the woods. They never found her body."

A huntsman?

Keltson ran his palm across his forehead. It must be ITTA's investigative agent. They never found the body... Was Lilia in ITTA headquarters right now being questioned? Did she know enough information to lead them to him?

No. His tracks were well covered. But she could give confirmation that he existed. He needed to go back and...

The doorbell upstairs rang. Keltson stiffened, glancing at the front porch security camera. It was only Baigh. He couldn't deal with another distraction right now. The timeline was set. ITTA had his number and the clock was ticking. The doorbell rang again and Keltson's stomach sank. He couldn't have Baigh hanging around to get mixed up in everything. Baigh just got off parole. Keltson couldn't do that to his brother.

Baigh reached in his pocket and pulled out a set of keys.

Oh, no.

Keltson darted toward the ladder. If he didn't get up in time, Baigh could unknowingly trap him down here and they'd both be at risk if investigators came. He scurried up the ladder and pushed the water heater up from its base. Keltson opened the closet just as the front door opened. He lowered the heater and poked his head out from behind the door as if he were inspecting something in the closet.

"Didn't you hear me knock?" Baigh asked, stepping inside. He stopped short. "You look death, Kelts. What happened?"

"You can't be here right now," Keltson said, slamming the closet door. He grabbed Baigh by the elbow and led him back to the front door.

Baigh wrenched his arm free and turned to face Keltson. "You're in trouble?"

"I need you to go." Keltson stared hard into Baigh's eyes. The lack of sleep and mental strain caused Keltson to waiver on his feet.

Baigh reached forward to steady him. His brown eyes glistened in a fierce, protective kind of way. "Talk to me. I know what it's like. Crime swallowed me up and I just spent the last few years in jail because I thought I couldn't get out. Let me help you."

"Three days off of parole and you're already trying to dive back into trouble?" Keltson asked. This was always Baigh's way: to return and immediately break the law in the name of providing for his little brother.

"I don't want to be your wingman. I want to help you *get out*. Whatever you're doing, it will catch up with you, just like it did to me." Baigh gripped Keltson's sleeves and looked into his eyes with an intensity Keltson had never seen before.

"It's too late to get out of this one, Baigh. I just have to solve it."

"It's never too late," Baigh said.

Baigh had always refused to let Keltson join any crime gangs to help support the two of them. If only Baigh knew what Keltson was doing. Would he be proud, or disappointed?

"Come on, let's sit." Baigh tilted his head toward the couch. He looked around the room. "Where's my case of Vibe?" he asked, heading toward the kitchen. A few cans still sat in the cellar, but Keltson just pinched his mouth to the side and shrugged.

"You didn't drink it all, did you?" Baigh asked, his eyes wide.

"It was a rough night." Keltson shook his head, trying to deflect the question.

Baigh pressed his hand against his forehead. "You drank an entire case? No wonder you look horrible!" Baigh darted around, opening kitchen cabinets until he found a cup. He filled it with water and handed it to Keltson. "You can't abuse your body like that, Keltson. One or two is fine, but a whole case in one night?"

Keltson slammed the cup down on the table, splattering water all over the floor. "Baigh! I can't handle this right now. I have things—pressing things—that need to be taken care of."

"Like what?" Baigh folded his arms and planted himself in the center of the kitchen.

"Like a client who left too many fingerprints behind. She'll rat me out in a heartbeat now that she's been arrested. Plus, there's a kid caught up in it all."

"This sounds all too familiar, Kelts," Baigh said. He didn't have to say anything else for Keltson to know he was speaking about their Da.

Baigh's comparison hurt. Keltson didn't remember much about their father other than his whispered meetings with other grim-faced men in the living room around a poker table. The last time he saw Da's face it was illuminated by the blinding blue lights of the Polis cars as Baigh pulled Keltson down a dank alley.

"I don't want to hear it. You can't be here now, Baigh. You just got off parole and I might be pulled into a firefight soon. I don't want you mixed up in the debris."

"You know," Baigh held up a finger, "a few years ago, I would have tried to make some grand scheme for you. But right now, my only advice is for you to find yourself somewhere safe. I mean, if she's ready to snitch, you gotta get out of here."

Keltson let out an exhausted sigh as every remnant of energy he had dripped out of his limp body. Running wasn't a bad idea. But leaving behind everything he worked for stank too much of defeat. He wouldn't consider it just yet.

"Thanks, Baigh," he said.

Baigh nodded, seeming to understand. He turned toward the front door and stopped with his hand resting on the doorknob. "If you do end up leaving, shoot me a note. I've got no ties here. I'll join ya if you like."

Keltson smiled, but inside he knew he could never make Baigh an accomplice in the most condemning crime in modern existence. He couldn't sentence his brother to a lifetime in prison. He stepped forward and gave Baigh a hug, possibly the last. Baigh seemed uncomfortable like he knew what this meant. Keltson waved goodbye and as soon as the door closed, he turned back to his cellar.

HUANG: The Variance Department doesn't believe the timeline change was caused by one of our agents.
SHAZAD: Is an agent failing to report?
HUANG: Everyone is accounted for. But just because we haven't seen an unaccounted variance before doesn't mean it's impossible.
SHAZAD: Then you think this was alien manipulation?
HUANG: Interplanetary interference seems a bit far-fetched, ma'am.
SHAZAD: ...Why do you even work here?

-Private interview between ITTA Director
Banu Shazad and Variance Director Aiguo Huang

CHAPTER
TWELVE

Bianka pressed her clammy hands together and knelt inside the bright, stone chapel. It was one of the few places she felt safe during these torturous days. The gothic archways lining the room felt like a council of stone giants guarding her. She knelt on a stiff cushion in front of an altar rail while Pastor Hefentreger rested on the other side. His kind face reminded her of the moments spent with Father on the pews, listening to weekly sermons.

It took all her courage to approach him for this confessional. But being that Father wasn't here to direct her, perhaps the newly balding pastor would be a sufficient surrogate.

"Reverend, I beseech you to hear my confession," Bianka said as quietly as she could. She didn't want her voice echoing through the empty chamber.

"Proceed, child." He nodded politely toward her. While she heard him speak often in sermons, this was the first time she ever approached him herself. He knew who she was, of course, but he still treated her with a distant respect.

Bianka paused before speaking up. "I've struggled the past few days with a decision, so I've come to you for guidance. I stumbled upon a secret that, should it be revealed, would damage the name of someone I trust—trusted. To guard their lie feels sinful. But to reveal it feels disloyal. Please, guide me."

The pastor tapped his pointer fingers together, creating a steeple with his hands. "A secret that could destroy the name of someone you trust— A question fit for Solomon. Perhaps, dear daughter, the decision lies with the strongest consequence? Will revealing this secret destroy your friend, or will keeping the secret destroy you? We must each work out our own salvation, child. Pray for guidance. God be merciful to thee and strengthen thy faith. Amen."

Bianka's hope sagged. She wanted a clear, moral answer, not this confusing response. And she needed to decide before Father came home and she faced the decision of telling him what his wife was. The pastor's advice didn't help her one bit. The weight of Lilia's secret still rested solely upon Bianka's heart. Lilia's witchcraft made her tremble, but could she deliberately cause Lilia's downfall? Would this secret destroy her? When the pastor completed his invocation and stood, Bianka felt more alone than ever.

With Father gone away to rescue Samuel, Bianka had no one to comfort her. Lilia remained aloof and nervous, refusing to speak to Bianka. Everyone assumed she feared for Samuel, but Bianka knew the secret that caused her fretful mood.

Bianka wished she could forget the magic. The last witch in town, Gertraud Muck, met a swift demise just a year before Bianka's birth. People still mumbled about her trial and execution. She couldn't bring such swift retribution down on her own stepmother, could she?

Bianka turned toward the chapel entrance and retrieved her cloak. As she fastened the clasp around her neck, the front doors burst open. A boy who looked about seventeen, with dark skin and eyes, entered. He wore a thick leather vest and a white linen shirt beneath it. His working pants were worn at the knees and a bit too short for him. A traveler perhaps? He reminded her of a caravan of traders that came through every summer and brought fine spices from India. Perhaps he owed his darkened complexion to days spent working in the sun?

"Preacher, I brought back another deer. You must bless the meat!" the boy shouted, his voice echoing through the empty chapel. He paused as he noticed Bianka and sent her a cheerful smile.

"Charul!" The pastor moved through the pews toward the boy. "Not so loud. I told you, I bless the meat after its preparation, not after the kill, my son." The boy held the pastor's hands, bowing his forehead to the man's fingertips. The pastor awkwardly smiled as he removed his hands and tucked them under his robe. He backed away slowly, nodding. Bianka used the moment to sneak behind them toward the door. But as she stepped into the winter sunlight that lit the steps outside, the boy also turned to leave, forcing her to acknowledge him. He smiled at her.

"Hello." She tried to look friendly, although the turmoil inside her threatened to send her running back to her chambers.

"You must be Herr Waldeck's daughter." The boy leaned against the stone rail. "I'm Charul."

Bianka raised her eyebrows at his casual stance. "You greet a pastor with respect and a countess with informality?" she asked.

He laughed and straightened up. "I toy with him. He treats me like a foreigner, so I pretend to practice odd customs." The boy took a step back and bowed to her properly this time.

"Why haven't I seen you before?" Bianka asked, politely clasping her hands in front of her.

"Do you know all your servants and subjects?" Charul teased, tipping his head to the side and raising his eyebrows.

"I think I'd remember seeing *you* in the castle before now." Bianka looked up at him through her eyelashes. As she stared, her mouth grew dry, and she wished she could take back the words.

The apprentice grinned and looked down at the ground. "It's not uncommon for me to struggle to blend in." He stomped his boot into the snow to pack it down.

Bianka wanted to clarify, but didn't think it appropriate to explain how she would remember him for his handsome eyes and intriguing smile. The longer she stared at Charul, the warmer his gaze grew.

"I've only been here a week," he said. "The Huntsman took me on as an apprentice. I am your newest, though not your humblest, servant." Charul spread his arms wide and bowed his head.

It seemed odd for the huntsman to take on a neophyte from outside their own town. Hunting was an admirable profession, one that many within the village would likely be jealous of.

"Where are you from?" she asked.

"A caravan left me in Weinbach as a child. A farmer raised me and trained me as a farm hand. But he cast me away when he found me practicing my aim in the duke's forests." He shrugged and looked around. "My skills eventually landed me here, catching you enough dinner for the week in one afternoon."

She narrowed her eyes. "You must be skilled to have taken down so much meat on one of your first days."

"I'd never admit to it, but I've had lots of practice. Lots." He winked at her.

Bianka blinked in surprise. Was he admitting to poaching? His sly smile made her doubt his sincerity.

She pursed her lips, trying to suppress her own smile. "Careful, or you'll make me turn right back around to confess that I'm harboring another secret."

"Is that why you were inside?" Charul asked. "What could someone as lovely as you have to hide?"

Bianka felt herself blush. "Sometimes the loveliest rose holds the bitterest thorns."

She immediately felt foolish. And yet, she felt so desperate for someone to talk to and his eyes seemed so kind. He seemed to analyze her words with intense curiosity, trying to figure out the mystery she spoke of.

"Will I be having venison tonight, Huntsman?" she asked, trying to change the subject.

"Of course, Your Highness," he said with a slight bow.

"And tomorrow?"

He thought for a moment, pinching his lips playfully to the side.

"Duck." He gave her a short nod.

She curtsied and as she started down the steps toward the castle doors, she couldn't help but smile. For the first time in days, she felt the weight of sorrow lifted from her chest. Perhaps her confession granted her this gift. She cast one last glance over her shoulder at Charul and saw his gaze follow her. She blushed and stepped through the castle door.

Lilia stood with folded arms, waiting for her. "Who is that boy?"

Bianka clenched her hands behind her, nervously. Lilia spoke as if nothing happened between them three days ago. However, pinched lips and rapidly blinking eyes were uncharacteristic for her stepmother.

"The Huntsman took on a new apprentice," Bianka said, shuddering. Lilia's eyes narrowed and Bianka expected a reprimand for speaking to someone so lowly.

"How recently?" Lilia asked.

Bianka blinked in confusion. "It is the first I have seen him."

Lilia's gaze cut toward Charul abruptly and she stiffened. "I prefer you stay away from him until we know who he is. His appearance seems peculiar. I don't like that a stranger arrived on our doorstep and was instantly admitted into a position of rank. I should like to investigate if I can."

Bianka felt heat rise into her cheeks. Lilia disliked Charul for no reason other than he was new to the kingdom?

"He killed a stag," Bianka said, saying the only detail she knew to defend the boy.

Lilia paused, and Bianka could almost feel frantic, pleading words pass through Lilia's gaze. Bianka swallowed and nodded, too nervous to contradict her further. Still, something about the way Lilia looked at Charul made Bianka worry for him.

"An odd phenomenon occurs when time travelers repeat a timeline. The synapses in the subject's brain are pruned to a most basic form. Whatever motivation the traveler bore during arrival becomes the dominant causeway linking neurons together. This highly unstable cognitive distortion is commonly known as 'splitting'. Therefore, we propose an amendment to travel laws that prevent agents from repeating a time where the individual already existed."

- Report from ITTA scientific research center

CHAPTER
THIRTEEN

L ilia spent the torturous days wondering if every step she took in the castle was her last. At any moment, The Mirror could erase the last year of her life and she was helpless against him. She couldn't bear the thought of returning to her old concrete-encrusted flat.

She looked down at her soft hands. They didn't resemble the hard-working hands of a mechanic anymore. But as the days passed by and The Mirror refused to respond to her, a new fear settled in. What if ITTA caught on to their efforts here in the Waldeck family? Part of her wondered if The Mirror had abandoned her so she would take the blame when ITTA arrived. Could there be an ITTA agent here already? Every new face in the courtyard made Lilia anxious.

The Mirror didn't even offer her an escape plan. She tried to push her way through the dining room mirror, but the glass remained solid. She hated him for abandoning her in such a horrible moment.

But then Lilia remembered something tucked deep into her memory —the mirror in the Weilburg Forest. Perhaps it was still there, waiting for her. If it was, maybe he would speak to her. Perhaps she could reason with him.

She called for her riding clothes and cloak. As she walked past the chapel on her way to the stables, she passed the huntsman's new apprentice. Lilia couldn't help but suspect him. However, she doubted ITTA gave teenagers responsibility in time. Especially someone who stood out so profoundly with his tanned skin and foreign manners. ITTA would certainly send someone who blended in. So, she watched for anyone else suspicious as she passed into the stables and gathered her horse.

Riding to the rock vein that marked the path to the mirror, Lilia followed the trail as far up the hill as her horse could carry her, dismounting when the terrain became too rough. She climbed between the rocks and found the mirror still stood upright in the center of a large circle of stones. Snow-covered ivy grew around the metal border and sheltered the glass. She pulled the ivy away, revealing her reflection.

"Mirror," she said. "Mirror, answer me!"

How could he do this to her? The moment she needed him most he ignored her! Desperate to gain his attention, she grasped the frame, rocking it back and forth. Nothing happened. She growled, stepped back and saw another face staring at her from over her shoulder. Whirling around in surprise, she found the huntsman's apprentice standing behind her.

"*Guten tag, Dame,*" he said.

She felt a chill run down her spine despite his pleasant tone.

"Why did you follow me?" Lilia moved behind the mirror. The air between them felt charged with deadly electricity. Her muscles tensed. Why hadn't she trusted her first impression of this boy?

"This is a strange place for a piece of furniture." He stepped forward to study the mirror.

"You didn't answer my question." Lilia gripped the edge of the frame with both hands and prepared to throw the glass shield at him if he came any closer.

The Huntsman paused, giving her a compassionate smile. Then he pulled out a pair of electric handcuffs from beneath his shirt and shrugged apologetically.

"I am here to arrest you for violating the laws of the International Time Travel Summit of 2043."

Lilia's vision blurred and she wavered. Was this how her dream ended? Adrenaline shook her into action. She planted her feet and tipped the mirror on its side toward the boy. He jumped back as the mirror fell. Lilia expected a violent crash of glass and electricity, but it held firm as if made of stone itself. Settling into the snow, the glass reflected the coral blue sky and looked like a hole in the ground. Lilia longed to jump through the clear air into a different moment, one without handcuffs.

The agent regained his footing and moved cautiously around the mirror. Lilia gathered her cumbersome skirts and scrambled up the hill. Ten years ago, she would have been strong enough to fight this teenager off, but living in a castle had dissolved most of her junkyard muscle and grit. The agent leapt across the mirror and grabbed Lilia's arm, pulling it behind her at an odd angle. He closed the cuff around her wrist and she cried out.

"Mirror!"

Before the agent reached for her other arm, she brought her elbow back hard into his skinny ribs, causing him to bend over in pain. She turned and punched him in the face, sending him back a few steps. He obviously didn't have much fighting experience. Lilia turned to run further up the hill, hoping to lose him in the rocks. But as soon as she turned her back toward the boy, something sharp penetrated the skin on her shoulder and a ripple of electricity ran down her nerves. The world shimmered through a blue electric field. Every muscle in her body seized and she fell backwards. The trees and the sky twisted above her. But instead of hitting the ground, she kept falling, through a metal frame covered in wires and dials, watching the blue sky tilt away from her. She felt like the hands on a clock, spinning backwards through new dimensions.

Finally, she hit solid ground and shook. The electric current that held her captive wore off and she felt immediate cold wash across her skin. The sky darkened as if a cloud covered the sun and cast eerie shadows over the evergreens. She took a breath and the air stood still.

Her muscles ached from the attack. She sat up and looked at the woods around her. The snow had completely disappeared. Her gaze darted through the rocks. The trees shattered and expanded as her eyes passed over them.

What was wrong with her?

Looking behind her, she expected to see the agent, but the space between boulders where he stood only moments ago was empty. She rubbed her hands along her arms beneath her cloak. She came into the mirror from a snow-filled afternoon, but this cold seeped into her bones faster than any winter chill.

Somehow, the mirror had repositioned itself, standing upright in the clearing. She pushed herself up and ran her fingers over the strange assortment of wires and dials covering the back of the frame. She was a mechanic. There must be a way for her to manipulate the controls and return somewhere safe.

As she looked over the interface, she found the power source was turned off. How had she passed through the mirror without power? Two thin strings trailed out of the mirror's glass and, as she followed their path, she realized they were attached to the taser spines in her shoulder. She winced as she pulled them out and tossed them to the ground. Perhaps the electrical surge from the taser activated this mirror long enough for her to pass through.

She found a display on one of the upper corners.

Location: Weilburg Forest, Germany (50°29′N 8°15′E)
Date: 5 April 1539 - 4:02:25 PM

That was the day she met Philip on the road at the bottom of the hill. Except, instead of the warm breeze that calmed her the first time she stepped through, the air was perfectly still. Did The Mirror know how to pause time? She'd never heard of such a thing. She looked around through the dim light. If it was true, then no wonder The Mirror could stay under the radar of ITTA. He had all the time in the world. And yet he couldn't spare a second to respond to her over these last days? This place had the potential to make him invincible, yet he allowed Lilia to be arrested?

She wouldn't allow herself to be betrayed. With this tool, she could change everything. If she could only go back and stop Bianka from eavesdropping, all her problems would melt away and she could live out the next few years in peace. She could return to her life with Philip. Her heart ached at the possibility.

She tried to change the dials on the device, but the security scan rejected her fingerprint. Sighing, she tracked the route of the wires that led to the digital command panel. If only...

She hesitated, remembering the strand of scalar wire she held in her locket. Pulling out the good luck ring, she used it to bypass the security interface. She tried the dial again and reset the dates. This time it worked.

Location: Weilburg Forest, Germany (50°29′N 8°15′E)
Date: 27 April 1547- 4:02:25 PM

There. Her simple adjustment should take her back to the day of Bianka's approbation, giving her enough time to get back down the mountain and into the castle to stop her from spying. As she activated the command, the world around Lilia warbled and faded into an immobile blizzard on all sides of her. The snow hung in midair and pressed against her skin. She pushed the large wet flakes away and became even more aware of the cold biting into her fingers. Lilia remembered her worry three days ago as Philip went riding out into this blizzard to save his son. She looked for a way to activate the mirror but found no switch. It must be remotely controlled. So, again, she rerouted a few wires, bypassing some key security components of the mirror, then watched as the glass rippled with energy, reflecting a looping scene of the snow on the other side of the glass.

If she could stop Bianka from spying on her, everything would return to normal. She could do this. Bracing herself, she repeated the new directive to herself.

Stop Bianka and life will be made right.

Stepping through the mirror felt as if tiny threads of glass shredded through her body. Every nerve filled with the burning fibers. She screamed and collapsed into the snow. Time travel hadn't felt like this the first time.

Cold, wet snow buried her as she writhed in pain. Bits and pieces of her mind burnt inside her skull. She didn't deserve this pain.

The burning dulled, but instead of losing consciousness, she gained clarity. Her breath became more regular. The pain subsided, leaving hollow pathways inside her head that filled with a warm, consuming liquid. The warmth sustained her. She felt the desire to move again. The need to live. Feeling stronger as each second passed, she pushed herself up from the snow.

As her head cleared of the pain, a chanting rhythm pulsed through her mind as if carried by every beat of her heart.

Stop Bianka and life will be made right.

The thought coursed through her muscles, filling every fiber of her body with the motivation to move. The motivation to... *Stop. Bianka.*

Bianka caused this pain. Bianka created this tragedy. Lilia deserved to be at home. With Philip. She must *stop Bianka.*

Lilia stumbled down the hill to where she had left her horse. However, when she arrived at the correct spot in the barren woods, she only found howling torrents of frozen water. Her teeth chattered as she realized her horse wouldn't be in this part of the woods for three more days. The castle was at least a mile away. She longed to be in front of a warm fire.

Bianka put her out in this blizzard. Bianka probably sat in front of Lilia's fire herself. Her eye twitched as snowflakes clung to her lashes.

Stop Bianka.

For what felt like hours, Lilia trudged through the miserable snow-storm. As long as she moved downward, she'd find the road. She shivered uncontrollably on her way back to the castle. She must *stop Bianka.*

Lilia reached the castle wall and knocked against the front gate with fists that felt like shattering. The door creaked open and a gatekeeper peered out. He looked down at her with a critical eye.

"By the forbidden *schnee...* Who goes there?"

"Let me in, gateman." Lilia's voice wavered, though she tried to keep her tone firm. For a moment he seemed suspicious, but after studying her face, he jumped back.

"My lady!" he shouted, pulling the door open wide for her. Why had he taken so long to recognize her? As she stumbled inside, the gateman removed his own cloak to throw around Lilia's shoulders. She pushed him away.

Only her directive mattered. She must get inside and *stop Bianka* before she spied on her conversation with The Mirror. She couldn't be late.

"Don't tell anyone of my arrival," Lilia said, harshly. The gateman fumbled nervously with his hat, then nodded. Creeping through the blizzard to a side door near the kitchens, she pulled her hood down low over her face before she stepped into the empty entrance. Lilia crept through the halls. Her clothes grew heavier as the snow melted and soaked through her skirts. She must reach the corridor before Bianka ruined everything. *Stop Bianka.* Lilia only hoped she wasn't too late.

She turned the corner into the corridor just outside the dining hall.

Bianka stood in the hallway, hesitating by the entrance to the dining hall, probably about to peer through the crack beneath the door. She heard Lilia's approach and stepped back in surprise.

"Lilia!" Bianka muttered, looking at her from head to foot. Lilia stood upright, towering over the girl. This was exactly the right moment to *stop her*. This was the instant Bianka ruined everything. How dare she? How dare she ruin everything Lilia worked so hard for?

"Coming to spy, are you?" Lilia seethed.

"Spy?" Bianka asked.

"Your disloyalty ruins everything," Lilia said. The girl must know what she had done. Bianka must feel the weight of her betrayal.

"Milady?" Bianka asked again, backing away. Lilia pressed closer, her soaked clothes dragging on the stones beneath her, her body shaking from the cold, and her nose flaring with her labored breathing.

"Stay away from my mirror," Lilia said. Bianka took another step backwards.

The latch on the door behind Lilia clattered and Lilia whirled away, leaving Bianka shrunken against the wall. Warm firelight spilled across her terrified face.

"Bianka, whatever happened to you?" a voice asked. Lilia froze, recognizing Philip's deep timbre. Lilia longed to reveal herself, to run to him, but instead, she pressed herself against the wall where he couldn't see. Bianka looked back and forth between the soaking Lilia to her father with confusion and terror. She ran toward Philip, disappearing around the corner.

A new memory hit Lilia as if someone slapped her in the face. It competed with an old memory that already rested in Lilia's mind. The new image slowly edged out the original, becoming more real and vibrant with every second.

Three days ago, when Bianka came in for approbations, she refused to speak. She wouldn't tear her eyes off Lilia. Just before Philip pulled an answer from her, a messenger arrived with news of Samuel's capture and injury. Philip asked Lilia to take care of Bianka, but as he left, Bianka fled from the room in fear.

But as before, Lilia summoned The Mirror to discuss Samuel's injury and Bianka's odd behavior. And again, he warned her that strange variances were popping up.

Bianka still spied on them from beneath the door.

The memory released Lilia. She panted, exhausted and chilled to the bone. If she waited behind this corner, she could *stop Bianka* when she returned.

But footsteps from down the hall approached her hiding place. Deep inside, Lilia knew she couldn't be seen. So, she retreated toward an alcove where she could hide. Lilia gripped the wall. She'd failed. Everything she went through was in vain. Her frustration felt like it would kill her. The cold, the weight of her dress pulled her to the floor. She needed a new plan. Perhaps if she changed out of these clothes she could think better. She fled to her chambers, all the while the words beat in the back of her head... *Stop Bianka.*

Stop Bianka.

"The Pause has a nasty habit of making organic material shatter when I focus on it. The best I figure is that shattering is nature's way of showing potential variances. Maybe it's a glimpse into some alternate reality. I'm not a theorist. While I'm working in the Pause, if I stray too far from my mirrors, things multiply, making my path back impossible to recognize or get through. So, I've installed a beacon at the top of each mirror that is only visible in the Pause. That way, if I roam too far, I can find my way back by looking into the constant sky, while using my periphery to guide me."

-Logbook of Keltson Grammar

CHAPTER
FOURTEEN

B ianka sat at her bedroom window, watching the front gates, and hoping her father returned early from Muhlberg. Footsteps sounded through her door and Bianka whirled around with wide eyes. It was only her lady-in-waiting, Agnetha, carrying a tray of food. Bianka glanced at the untouched breakfast laid on her bedside table. Agnetha stomped her foot in frustration.

"Milady, your mother won't stand for this. You must eat or she will come here herself to…"

Bianka grabbed one of the stale biscuits on the plate beside her and bit into the crumbly bread. Agnetha stared at her in confusion. Bianka had refused to eat more than a few bites of food the last three days but she would do anything to keep Lilia away.

Her stepmother haunted Bianka. One moment, she walked regally about the castle, then the next lurked around corners with dark rings under her eyes, tangled hair, and a poisonous snarl curling her lips.

The only reason Bianka dared leave the safety of her chambers anymore was to dart across the courtyard to the chapel where she offered up fervent prayers against Lilia's magic. How could one body hold such contrasting countenances? Bianka couldn't abide being confronted by those sunken eyes again.

She took another bite of the biscuit and showed Agnetha. Her slow chewing appeased her lady-in-waiting enough that she left. Bianka relaxed, then perked up when she saw Charul walk through the front gates. Today he carried no meat for the castle. He kicked at the slushy snow with his hands tucked inside his pockets. Over the last few days, speaking to Charul became her only solace. He lingered outside the chapel after she emerged from saying her prayers and listened as she spoke. Without his kindness, she may have gone crazy.

Bianka grabbed her cloak, refusing to look into her dressing mirror on the way out. She peeked into the empty hall, then darted past her siblings' rooms, taking a back set of stairs into the courtyard. Charul sat on a bench across the cobblestone way, tightening his crossbow. She approached so quietly, he didn't look up until he saw the hem of her dress.

"*Guten tag,*" she said. Charul looked back down at the ground and pinched his mouth to the side. "Has something upset you?" she asked.

"Today's catch proved more elusive than I anticipated." He pressed his foot against the crossbow to stop it from slipping as he cocked the string.

"I'm sorry."

"Do you often check on the emotional well-being of your father's subjects?" he asked, looking up at her playfully.

Bianka blushed. "Do you prefer I don't?"

He set the crossbow on the ground then stood. "I like that you talk to me. But it's also frustrating. You never speak your mind. You hint at things, but I know you don't trust me. Otherwise, you would say what bothers you."

Bianka backed away. She wanted to tell him, of course, but could he understand the complexity of what was going on? How could she tell him her own stepmother was a witch? She wanted for someone else to understand how much misery this secret caused her. Bianka longed to express the fear she felt every time she stepped around a corner.

The door to the castle behind her burst open.

"Bianka!" Agnetha shouted.

"I'm sorry. I must go." Bianka lifted her hood and darted behind the church, away from Agnetha's voice. She couldn't bear to be locked in her room another moment.

Seconds later, Charul fell into stride beside her. "What are you hiding from?" he asked.

Bianka shook her head. She couldn't tell him. They entered a cluster of houses and found an alleyway to hide in. Charul leaned against the wall next to her with his arms folded. His eyes searched her face and Bianka felt heat rush to her cheeks. He stood so close. His warm brown eyes studied her and she wondered what he was looking for. Perhaps... Perhaps she could tell him pieces of what she felt.

"I fear someone is..." but her words were cut off.

"Bianka!" another voice cried from down the street.

"Here." Charul clutched her hand and pulled her along with him. Her fingers tingled with his touch. Following behind him, he smelled like pine needles and sun-warmed leather. He led her through the crowd, keeping his protective grip on her hand until they reached a cart laden with hay and hitched to two mares. Charul turned and stared into her eyes for an immeasurable moment, then handed the horses' lead to Bianka and gave them a hearty slap, clicking his tongue twice. They moved toward the front gates.

"Guide them through the gate and I'll meet you on the other side." He darted away, leaving her to carry on. Why was he leading her outside the castle wall? She had never gone out there alone before. She imagined leaving Lilia's walls and the memory of magic behind and running into the forest where only God's nature could find her. Perhaps the weight on her chest would lighten and she'd be able to breathe.

However, the gateman at his post ahead would surely recognize her face. She didn't know how to stop a cart and the horses seemed confident in their march. She'd make a spectacle by trying to turn the animals around, so she gripped the ropes and followed them.

Peasants loitered around the walls where a company of merchants had spread their wares along the ground. Perhaps with all the bustle, she could walk through without being noticed.

But as she approached the gate, the merchants parted, leaving a perfect channel for the seated gateman to take notice of her. She stiffened, preparing herself to be caught, when she heard someone to her right singing a bawdy tavern song. She peeked over the horse's side as Charul tramped out of an alleyway with the crossbow slung over his shoulder.

"Headed out again, young master?" The gateman sat up and pushed his hat out of his eyes.

"Aye, a second round, for a second round!" Charul shouted, boisterously. Bianka walked only a few meters away from him, but he'd skillfully garnered all the man's attention.

The gateman leaned over in his chair, resting his forearm on his knee. "You seem in a different form than when you returned empty-handed earlier."

"A pint warmed my spirits and my resolve is..." Charul paused and inhaled through his nose. "You shall feast on fresh meat tonight!" He stepped in circles as he passed through the gate, following Bianka's cart.

The gateman chuckled and leaned back against the wall.

Bianka couldn't believe it, the charade worked! The cart easily passed through the gates and soon the forest loomed ahead. Charul walked at a quick pace toward the tree line. He motioned for her to follow him. She dropped the horses' lead and tiptoed across the muddy road to the untouched snow. Charul stopped and smiled warmly, offering her his hand again. Bianka didn't hesitate to accept it. It felt so reassuring to be with him.

They stepped further into the woods, leaving the road behind. For an instant, deep inside, Bianka felt a rush of concern. This was the first boy outside of her family she'd ever been alone with. But the chance to have a few moments away from magic and Lilia's hateful spying was too much to resist. Perhaps it wasn't concern she felt, perhaps it was excitement.

Charul let out a long breath and the cold wind carried it away. "This is the best place for quiet thoughts," he said.

Bianka pulled her cloak tighter around her shoulders. "I've never been outside the gates without Father."

Charul grinned, a single dimple showing, then tucked her hand inside his own coat pocket to keep her close. Her heart thumped within her chest.

"It feels like a different world here. One that I've only peeked at through carriage windows." Despite the warmth of Charul's hand, she shivered. "Sometimes at night, I hear the wolves howling at the gates." Bianka remembered hearing how winter left the wolves half-starved and she suddenly felt worried for the horses she'd left in the road. She looked behind her, trying to catch sight of them.

"There's no need to be frightened, Bianka. There's so much more to these woods than wolves." Charul hung his crossbow on his back. "Look up. The trees are full of birds and glistening snow."

Bianka looked at the scraggly limbs of the dead trees like cracks in the sky. She did her best to trust Charul. A cold gust tugged her cloak against her legs as if begging her to return to the safety of the castle walls.

Charul pressed further up the hill. She didn't want to lose her warm grip on his hand, so she followed him. It comforted her to know that he spent most of his days in these woods. He could protect her with his crossbow if they met any hungry beasts. The snowy path they followed was packed down by a variety of footprints—cobbled, hooved, and clawed. Charul navigated their way around the brush, escorting her across precarious footholds.

"You seem confident out here," Bianka said. She wished there was a place she could feel so self-assured.

"It is one of my favorite places." Charul pulled her hand out of his pocket and guided her forward, holding back an evergreen bough from her path. She held her fingertips shyly to her mouth as she passed. She felt that while most men in the castle were courteous because of her station, Charul's attention meant something more.

"I can't imagine being in the woods by myself." She shrugged her shoulders and waited for Charul to resume guiding her.

"But you were so desperate to escape the castle?" Charul asked.

Bianka paused. She feared being alone in the woods, yes, but she feared being alone in the castle as well. Was there no safe place for her? "There are wolves inside the walls too."

"Thorns... Wolves... Will you ever just tell me what you mean?" Charul stepped closer, leaving very little air between them. "There are no ears out here besides mine if you wish to speak your heart."

Bianka swallowed. "It would tarnish the name of someone very close to me."

"Do you trust this person?" he asked, raising his eyebrow.

Bianka bit her bottom lip. As soon as Bianka had uncovered Lilia's secret, their entire relationship disintegrated. They couldn't speak to each other, and Lilia eyed her hatefully.

"No. I don't," she answered.

"Yet you guard their confidences?" Charul asked. "What makes you think they are so generous to you?"

"What do you mean?"

Charul continued up the hill casually. "Only that someone in the castle might not be guarding *your* secrets with as much care."

"What?" she asked, pulling her hands into her cloak to warm them.

"Is it true your name is really Margaretha?"

Bianka stopped mid-step. "Yes, but I haven't gone by that name since I was six-years..."

"Who changed your name?" He asked, pushing forward through the snow. She struggled to keep up with him as he stomped down a narrow gulch lined with boulders the size of carriages.

"I did." She furrowed her brow.

"Why?"

"I didn't feel like the name fit me any longer. I don't see why you should think that such a scandal." The path became slick and wet from the melting snow and Bianka rested her hand on the boulders to keep herself from falling.

"I also heard you were frightened of your own reflection as a child," Charul said.

Bianka felt her face redden as she gave him a flinty glare.

"What does that have to do with..." She stopped in her tracks.

There, in front of her, stood a mirror identical to the one in her dining hall. Withered ivy and heavy snow covered the frame. The mirror looked so foreign and mysterious in the cluster of boulders.

She'd wanted to escape magic and Charul led her straight back to sorcery. Her hands shook and her eyes refused to blink. Had Lilia sent him? Bianka heard the snow crunch behind her and whirled around to see Charul a few meters behind her.

"How did you..." she murmured. Her voice caught in her throat. Was Charul magic as well?

"I didn't believe the hints at first, but you, Bianka, don't hide your emotions well." He pulled a pair of shackles from beneath his shirt.

"I'm here to arrest you, for breaking the laws established at the Time Travel Summit of 2043. I already have your mother in custody. All traces of you in this timeline must be explored and variances removed. The authentic Margaretha von Waldeck will be found and restored to her rightful place as Countess of Weilburg. You will be questioned and if you are found withholding any pertinent information, you may be subject to additional sentencing."

Bianka blinked in confusion. Charul spoke with so much authority and yet he made no sense.

"Who told you these lies? I *am* Margaretha von Waldeck!"

Charul sighed. "I've gathered evidence against you all week. There are plenty of rumors and people inside this castle that like to talk. Your story is all too clear. Lilia Vaschenko appeared and you immediately changed your name to Bianka. She tried to hide you, her daughter, here in the past, but neither of you did a good job covering your tracks the last few days. I already took Lilia in and she did not come peacefully. It wasn't very pleasant for her. I don't recommend resisting." He stepped forward and reached out as if he expected Bianka to come without a struggle. Bianka backed away and stumbled across a root hidden in the snow. She fell backwards, landing in a drift beneath the mirror.

Charul knelt down in front of her.

"Come with me, Bianka. Your mother brought you here. This isn't your fault. I can help you." The corners of his mouth turned down in regret as he stared at her. He leaned in closer and when he spoke again, his voice was softer, less confident. "Maybe an exception could be made. I know the director of ITTA. You're a likeable person. I'd vouch for you.

You belong in your own time." He reached out, offering her his hand again.

She stared at him in disbelief. "Someone told you horrible lies about me. You offer me mercy for a crime I never committed. A crime I don't even understand."

His eyes followed her as if she were a deer he didn't wish to scare away. She feared if she moved too quickly, he would attack, like the hunter he was.

Her hand felt behind her, searching for the frame of the mirror. Perhaps she could use it as a shield... But instead of finding the smooth surface, her fingers passed through something cold, like the air turned to ice behind her. She glanced down and saw her fingers pass through the glass. Her heart constricted at the magic. A flickering thought passed through her mind that perhaps the mirror was trying to rescue her.

Accepting magic went against everything she believed in, but when faced with Charul trying to capture her and a mirror beckoning her to step inside, she took the chance.

Charul's eyes widened as Bianka fell backwards into the mirror's embrace. He shouted and reached forward as the sun and the air around Bianka turned cold. She fell onto her back. The snow crackled like ice beneath her.

The air stilled and everything darkened to a mere shadow of what it had looked like before. Even the mirror changed, odd strings and magical, glowing symbols covered the frame. Bits of blue lightning spurting from the colorful strands sounded like dragonflies buzzing. She looked at her surroundings. Large rocks encircled her and the forest behind them seemed faded and dark.

Alone in the forest, her gaze rested on a fallen tree and it shattered into shards of glass that flew into the air around her. As they swirled above her head, the fragments folded in on themselves, forming three separate versions of itself—one fallen, one healthy, and the last a burnt hollow. She flinched and looked away, but a shrub fell into focus and shattered, multiplying as well. The world expanded around her at an infinite rate. She looked up to stop the plant from closing in on her and saw a bird, hovering in mid-air. That was the worst mistake of all. A fragmenting crowd flocked around her head. She screamed and ran, covering herself.

The forest changed and expanded as she moved through the woods. She had to find a way out.

Stumbling up the mountain along the frozen ground, Bianka couldn't remember which direction she needed to go. The branches of the trees above her split—some drenched in springtime flowers, others with aging red and yellow leaves. As she ran, the snow disappeared in patches, revealing thorns and sharp stones that tore at her clothes. Roots of trees appeared and tripped her. Puddles splashed around her ankles, then froze again into snow and ice. Tears flowed as her cloak snagged on a bush that grew to twice its size. She stumbled into the path of a woodland stag. The deer shattered and multiplied into a herd, some with horns missing, others with moss growing on their velvety antlers. Bianka fell to her side, expecting a stampede to overwhelm her.

She closed her eyes, covering her head. How could she escape this horrible place? Even if she found the mirror again, Charul stood on the other side, his hand outstretched, ready to capture her.

Perhaps…

Perhaps the mirror in the castle held this same magic? Keeping her eyes closed, she tried to calm her breath and think of the direction she needed to go. The only course she knew was down the mountain, past Charul and the first mirror. She shuddered but felt determined. Following the slope of the hill, she tried not to scream as animals and plants startled her.

Things began to look familiar and she hurried her pace back to the castle, away from Charul, and out of this horrible place. But when she found the path leading through the boulders, she stopped in her tracks.

Ten yards down the mountain, stood a man. A white porcelain mask covered his face. She stared at him, in fear. Was this the realm of the masked figure Lilia spoke to? Though her eyes lingered on his form, he didn't splinter like everything else. His clothes were thin and clung to his body. He wore tools around his waist like a craftsman.

Then he moved.

She screamed and stumbled back up the pathway. The man followed her as she darted off the path and into the brush. He rummaged through the bushes above her head calling out her name. She buried her eyes in her hands so nothing around her could multiply and give her away. Shaking with the cold and her fear, she listened to him search for a few more minutes, then finally, return to his mirror.

Even though he had withdrawn, Bianka shook. How would she get home now that the masked man blocked the path? And, if she got around him and returned home—what would stop Charul from searching her out? Charul claimed he had already captured Lilia. She looked up at the sky, desperate for heaven's guidance to direct her, when she saw a pillar of light ascending from the forest where the mirror rested.

She turned, looking to the sky above the castle. A similar pillar rose there as well. She pulled her fists close to her chest and spun in a circle. Down the road, above the tree line, a third ray of light shot into the sky. If the other two mirrors had light marking their way, then could this third one also be a mirror that could transport her away from this magic?

Perhaps, if she found a way there, she could escape the masked man, Charul, and Lilia. The cold darkness seemed to close in around her at the thought. She would probably find things more terrifying than she already faced, but the third beacon offered hope. Safety. She started forward following the slope of the hill, doing her best not to let her gaze linger on the plants around her.

Before long, she found the road leading back to the castle. As tempting as it was to turn back, she fled down the road toward the light. She passed a cart laden with hay, and the man driving the wagon became an entire host of toothless and bedraggled farmers, staring forward with deadened eyes. Turning away, she tried not to imagine them following her as she ran further down the road. She tried to keep her focus on the beam in the sky. The light became her one constant, the only thing that didn't multiply on the horizon. She raced forward, determined to make it.

"When Count Waldeck returned home from rescuing his son in Muhlberg, he found his daughter, Margaretha, had run away with a huntsman's apprentice. Despite searches throughout the neighboring villages, they never found the young Countess. Herr Waldeck's wife went mad with grief and never recovered from her mental strain. The servants feared her until she died at the age of eighty-two."

-Second unaccounted variance from the Master Document

CHAPTER
FIFTEEN

K eltson climbed down the ladder to his cellar with newfound resolution. He felt the cost of failure pressing against him. Too many people depended on him for him to give up. Baigh just got off parole; he couldn't abandon him. Bianka didn't deserve to be kidnapped by ITTA. And although Lilia deserved it, he couldn't allow her to be captured either.

If ITTA got enough information out of her, it could lead them to Keltson. Once they arrested him, they would erase all he worked for the last five years. All his clients would be extracted and his fingerprint on history wiped away. Every life he saved would return to their original dismal fate. His whole empire would crumble.

Lilia needed to be removed from Bianka's timeline. At his desk, he pulled up the surveillance feed. All he had to do was override the conversation Bianka overheard. To Lilia, it would be like the first conversation never happened. He could influence the past without having to go back there himself.

He activated the transmission. Or at least, he tried to. Nothing happened except an error buzz. Confused, he checked the connection. It should have worked. Trying again, his transmission failed to go through.

He ran a diagnostic scan, which came back normal. He ran his fingers through his hair in frustration. This could not be happening right now.

Perhaps if he tried activating a different transmission. He jumped to the fateful conversation Bianka overheard. But again, the old transmission ran its course. He listened as Lilia flung open the doors and found Bianka, standing frozen with fear before she turned and fled down the hall.

Keltson paused the feed. Perhaps he was tired, but he didn't remember seeing Bianka when Lilia opened the doors the first time.

No, she definitely wasn't there. He remembered Lilia explaining what she saw in the hall. Why did this small detail change? He watched the surveillance feed again to see if anything else was different.

The moment Philip initially opened the door for Bianka's approbation, Bianka seemed terrified. She pulled away from Lilia any time she even glanced at her and darted from the room at her first opportunity. Keltson leaned back in his seat. What happened to make Bianka so nervous around Lilia?

His stomach sank. *He* hadn't changed anything. Could ITTA already be there, investigating and making changes? Is that why his tech failed to respond? Did ITTA have a way to lock down the timeline or disable his equipment?

He sped forward to see what Lilia's future held. Things initially panned as normal, however, three days later, the entire castle sank into commotion. The servants gathered in the dining room for an emergency meeting.

Bianka was missing.

"Oh no."

Keltson ran to the library, flipped open the newest variance record and found a new story claiming Bianka ran away and Lilia "went mad". Slamming the booklet shut, Keltson ran to the computers and scanned forward through the next week. Lilia appeared in front of the mirror as scheduled, standing on the pedestal to speak with him. The skin beneath her eyes sagged with dark circles as if she had recently suffered sleepless nights. She wavered a moment on her feet. He tried to activate the transmission and sighed in relief when this time, the commands worked.

"Lilia, what happened?" Keltson asked, leaning forward in his chair.

"I caught a cold and nearly died," she answered with an uncharacteristically raspy voice.

Keltson wrinkled his brow. Did she think her cold was worse than Bianka disappearing? "I'm sorry for that, but where is Bianka?"

"She's gone," Lilia said.

Keltson caught an odd glimmer in her eye. Perhaps a tear? "The new legend says she ran off with a huntsman. Is that true?"

"An apprentice. A guard saw him leaving, alone, but she disappeared the same day, so rumors are flying." Lilia sniffled, sounding bored.

Perhaps she wasn't worried because she expected him to fix it. After all, he often appeared in time to warn her of upcoming disasters. He picked up his pen and scrap paper. "I can fix this, Lilia. I just need you to tell me what happened."

"Why would I want you to fix this?" she asked through tight lips. The veins in her neck stood out as if they could hardly take the pressure the thought evoked.

"You... Wait. You *don't* care that she disappeared?"

"If she remains, I lose everything!" Lilia shouted. Startled, Keltson paused the feed. Something was very, very wrong.

"Please, no," he muttered under his breath, as he pulled up the dining room mirror travel log. Everything looked normal. No record of anyone passing through without his guidance. Then he checked the Weilburg Forest mirror.

Output: 27 April 1547
Input: PAUSE

His throat tightened. He never sent clients to the Pause. Had someone messed with his controls?

He turned back the Weilburg mirror surveillance track and watched as Lilia stumbled out of the mirror on April 27, 1547. He stared in shock as she fell to the ground, screaming and writhing in the snow storm. His frown deepened as he watched her, still trembling in a time where she already existed, safe and warm inside the castle.

Lilia split.

He closed his eyes. So much of him wanted to deny it, but this irrefutable evidence spoke against her. Her pain seemed to subside and as she pushed herself up from the ground, her appearance changed. Dark circles formed around her eyes and her skin became ghostly pale.

Keltson slammed his fist down on the desk. Didn't she know the consequences of her actions? Repeating a timeline was against the law—a law Keltson happened to agree with. When the first-time ITTA agents revisited times where they already existed, they experienced what was now known as a split. Splitting caused unnatural synaptic pruning, a process that killed healthy neurons and unstable synaptic connections attached themselves to a singular, obsessive motivation. In Lilia's case, apparently, the consuming thought must have turned her against Bianka.

And losing her mind wasn't the only risk. If Lilia somehow prevented her original self from going back in time to split, that meant she didn't complete the loop and there would be two Lilias co-existing in the same timeline.

He looked again at the new legend.

...The queen went mad with grief and the servants feared her until she died at the age of eighty-two.

If the split Lilia still lived in the castle, what happened to the sane one? Did Lilia dispose of her? Or worse, did ITTA have her locked away? He returned to his conversation with Lilia and resumed the transmission.

"What did you do with the other Lilia?" he asked, his fists tightening with anger.

A grin spread across her face. "She got the fate I avoided," she said. "If Lilia remained countess, I'd have nowhere to go. *I* belong here."

"And Bianka?" he asked, rubbing his wrists. His stomach churned in dread.

Lilia sneered and leaned back with folded arms. "This castle thrives on rumors. All I had to do was drop a few false hints among the staff and now that ITTA agent thinks Bianka was just as guilty as me."

Keltson leaned in, his avatar's mask growing menacingly large in the display. "You sacrificed the girl you came to rescue to ITTA?"

"*You* didn't cover my tracks well enough. So, I convinced their little agent that, not only did Lilia replace Katherina von Hatzfeld, but she brought her own daughter, Bianka, to replace Margaretha."

Keltson set his jaw. He should have known Margaretha's name change would come back to haunt him.

He shut off the transmission and grabbed his utility belt to fix this whole mess once and for all. With the Pause compromised, he'd need his mask, in case he ran into Lilia there. He strode over to a shelf and pulled down a dusty porcelain mask he used in the early days of his career before he programmed his avatar.

Moments later, he pressed the ignition on his vest and appeared in the Pause. Before him stood the Weilburg Forest mirror. He found no sign of Lilia. However, bursts of energy sparked from the frame.

"No, no, no." He stumbled forward and fingered the severed wires. This is why his commands in the cellar didn't work. Lilia bypassed his remote command and manually input the directives. He pulled at Lilia's foreign wire that bypassed his security interface and the free-flowing electricity shocked him.

He sucked on his stinging fingers while he analyzed the damage. His security interface wasn't the only thing she had tampered with. He looked over the mirror, resetting all the misplaced cables. Exposing a scrapper mechanic like Lilia to his inventions was probably the worst thing he could have done to himself.

Keltson prepared to jump back to his office for more tools when he heard something. With his mask still in place, he turned around, careful not to focus on anything.

He heard the sound again, a whimpering sob.

Was Lilia still in the forest? He didn't know how the Pause worked with other people here. Keltson started up the path, trying to focus on the sound. He heard the rustle of fabric and the soft thump of a body falling to the ground.

And then, Bianka appeared at the top of the hill, staring down at him.

At first, he felt relief. ITTA didn't have her like Lilia thought. But before he could speak, she screamed and darted back through the woods, in the opposite direction. He went after her.

He called her name, but she didn't respond. After searching through the multiplying shrubberies, he gave the effort up as hopeless. There were other ways to save her: like stopping her from coming here in the first place.

How long had the poor girl been here? It could have been hours or days. He had no idea. He hated spending more time than necessary in the Pause. His mind couldn't wrap around the idea of a prolonged stay here.

As he jumped back into his cellar, a full wave of exhaustion hit him. He looked at his stopwatch: 20:02:54.

Twenty straight hours.

He scanned the forest mirror log and found the moment Bianka fell through the glass. The girl had courage to jump through technology she didn't understand in order to protect herself from the agent. If Keltson changed the input/output to transport her to the dining room mirror instead of the Pause, she would land somewhere familiar and avoid being trapped.

He had reversed Lilia's manipulation, but the controls still refused to respond. He tried, over and over again. But nothing worked. All the while, the sane Lilia probably sat in some ITTA interrogation room, spilling details about Keltson's operation. Maybe Baigh knew best. Maybe he should pursue the safehouse option. At least then he could take his time to work all this out.

"The cottage isn't so bad. There are a few mushrooms growing on the ceiling and the beds are moldy. But I think after two weeks of work, I should have the place tidied up enough to bring people home. I look forward to reuniting with the friends I made during my ITTA surveys."

-*Journal of Ammond MacBarran*

CHAPTER
SIXTEEN

I t was time to make some money for a quick getaway.

Keltson pulled up the feed for Ammond's mirror. The safehouse cottage stood only three kilometers from the Waldeck castle. Clustering clients like Lilia and Ammond so close together might have seemed irresponsible, but once Keltson found a genuine blind spot in ITTA's research, he worked without fear of discovery.

Ammond stood in the forest, wearing a tattered cloak that pooled around his feet, and he hobbled oddly.

"You look taller, Ammond," Keltson said.

Ammond revealed a pair of stilts beneath his robes.

"I don't know how tall people keep their balance. This is more leg than anyone can manage." Ammond struggled on the slight incline.

"You'll attract less attention if you wear them, but it's up to you." As he spoke, Keltson pulled up a remote diagnostic on Lilia's mirrors to see what kind of materials he needed to purchase to fix them.

"They'll notice my short arms and I won't be able to run if anything goes wrong," Ammond said.

"You think anyone's going to chase an old beggar man?" Keltson asked, scanning his diagnostics again to figure out what could be causing the disconnect to his other mirrors.

Ammond squinted his eyes. "I'm not that old," he said.

Keltson winced. He needed to be careful to stop dropping hints about his own age. Especially with ITTA investigating.

"You understand your directives?" Keltson asked, changing the subject.

Ammond knocked on the glass in frustration. "I wrote them, kid."

Keltson could imagine the thoughts running through Ammond's mind. *Young and inexperienced.*

"Remember, if things go wrong, return here and explain what happened. I'll coach you through the pitfalls. Don't do anything desperate. Fail if you must, but don't break any rules."

"This isn't my first jump, kid," Ammond said. "Get me to work. I've wanted this opportunity for years. I'm not going to screw it up."

Keltson sighed and activated the mirror. Ammond stepped through to rescue his first target and the mirror disappeared from the clearing. Two seconds passed and the frame returned as a hand reached back through the mirror, testing the air on the other side. Two unfamiliar little people stepped through and rubbed their eyes, astounded by their surroundings. Ammond followed them through and clapped the older man on the back.

The first man stood an inch or two taller than Ammond, with dark hair and a scraggly, pointed beard. The second, a boy of perhaps twelve, had blond hair and bright, rich clothes. Ammond turned to face the mirror, revealing a short, greasy beard. He no longer wore the tattered cloak or stilts, but Keltson saw them poking out of his pack.

"You've succeeded already?" Keltson asked.

Ammond laughed. "Already? It took me three weeks to get these guys away from their masters."

Keltson couldn't keep the surprise from his face.

"I would rather do this once perfectly than twice haphazardly."

"You didn't break any rules?" Keltson leaned in, tapping his fingers anxiously against the desk.

"Nobody died, as much as I was tempted," Ammond said. "You forget my background, Mirror."

Keltson smiled. He treated Ammond as any other client, but the fact was, Ammond had far more experience with time travel than Keltson did.

Keltson looked back at the directives. "I thought you went back for three people?"

"Ethel didn't want to come. She's happier than when I knew her and seems to have fallen in love with one of the kitchen servants. I won't force anyone to leave." Ammond turned to the dark-haired man next to him. "Urig, however, couldn't resist my offer to leave."

"What is this magic?" Urig asked, staring up at the mask's reflection.

"It is nice to finally meet you, Urig," Keltson said. The man nodded without smiling. Keltson turned his attention to the boy. "And you must be Gunther."

The boy nodded, transfixed by the face in the mirror. Keltson had never transplanted anyone from their own timeline before. Often the individuals they targeted lived out their new and improved life without even realizing they'd been affected.

Keltson smiled and shook his head. "Get some well-deserved rest. When should we meet for the next mission?"

"Two weeks. Those blasted stilts gave me blisters," Ammond said.

"Of course." Keltson scribbled down the note on his scratch pad. "I'll send you some moleskin for the next mission."

"Moleskin?" The twelve-year-old wrinkled his nose and looked at Urig. Ammond snorted.

"Thank you. I'd appreciate that." Ammond turned to leave but paused. "Oh. The code is 9x45."

"What?" Keltson asked.

"The first payment code."

Money never came this easy. Ammond could be the most efficient client he'd ever dealt with—likely due to his ITTA experience. Keltson turned to the box of Ammond's digital currency and punched in the code. One of the bars flickered to life, activating the money. The amount wasn't enough to take Baigh's advice and run to a safehouse, but it was a decent start. Perhaps, if Ammond completed his other directives this easily, Keltson could finish the missions and salvage this situation.

Keltson gave a slow bow of his head. The mask copied the movement perfectly. "Thank you, Ammond. And to the rest of you, welcome to your new home."

Keltson cut the transmission and rolled back in his chair. If he was going to keep working to earn himself a decent chunk of money, he needed more Vibe. And another song.

"Agent Charul Shazad apprehended Lilia Vaschenko in the year 1547. She attempted to escape through a full-length mirror thought to be imbued with illegal time travel technology (further investigation of the mirror is pending). Lilia agreed to offer full disclosure in exchange for a plea deal in her upcoming court date. Rumors of a hacker known only as 'The Mirror' were verified and investigators dispatched."

-Investigative report, ITTA agency files

CHAPTER
SEVENTEEN

WALDECK CASTLE, WEILBURG, GERMANY
30 MAY 1547

W ithout Bianka in the castle, the voices in Lilia's head were silent. She could finally enjoy her dinner in peace. Now she only bore the sniffles of Frederick and Anastasia as they mourned their wretched sister. Those sounds would also die down in time.

The staff arrived with dinner and placed food before Philip. He looked at his plate and declined with a solemn wave of his hand. The servants turned toward Lilia, who nodded. They placed a chunk of mutton on her plate. Philip looked at her with frustration.

Lilia wanted to roll her eyes. She tried her best to be sensitive to Philip's concern over Bianka, but Lilia didn't feel the same about the child's disappearance, and she didn't think it fair of him to demand the same melancholy emotion from her. However, she hated seeing Philip in pain.

Fine. If pretending to care would make him happy...

She forced a tear, letting it slip down her cheek. Just as Philip began to soften, she couldn't maintain the act any longer and a manic sort of giggle escaped her throat. The servants looked at her in concern. She knew they thought her mad. Let them. She couldn't help herself.

Ever since she had fixed The Mirror's horrible mistakes, she felt an immense pleasure with her accomplishment. Everything she ever wanted in life lay before her. And now with his hijacked equipment, she didn't worry about him pulling her away from her beloved life.

And Philip. Her dear Philip.

She looked at him as she flicked the tear away from her cheek. He met her gaze with confused horror. Losing interest, she sawed into her mutton. Glancing at the mirror in the corner of the dining hall, she smiled as she bit into the meat. What would The Mirror think if he could see her now, if he knew what really happened that day?

Before making Bianka disappear, the ITTA huntsman carried away the second Lilia as well. She hated to think about her other self being questioned and imprisoned sometime in the distant future. She didn't deserve to be punished. Nobody loved Lilia more than herself. But there couldn't be two of her running around the castle. So instead, she looked at the ceiling and daydreamed about all the adventures her other self might be having. Maybe the young agent protected her from the law and helped her run away. She didn't like to consider that some version of herself might be paying for her crimes. She didn't deserve thoughts like that.

Perhaps one day, she would go see what happened to her and rescue her, if needs be. But for now, Lilia ate across from Philip, where she could watch his handsome face for years to come. Though why he seemed so upset was a mystery.

Directives:
1. Urig
2. Gunther
3. ~~Ethel~~
4. Rusha
5. Mathilda
6. Cenric
7. Volker
8. Aiantes
9. Pelagon

-Targets to rescue, Application of Ammond MacBarran

CHAPTER
EIGHTEEN

B ianka's face stung from the salty tears that dried on her cheeks. This forest surrounded her in hundreds of reaching branches, sudden infestations of woodland creatures and nightmarish shadows that would haunt her for the rest of her life. She kept the pillar on the horizon in her sights and pressed onward. Bianka didn't know how long she spent in the eternal forest, but she felt hunger beyond anything she had ever experienced before.

The pillar grew closer, finally appearing over the crest of a hill. Stumbling across a snowdrift, Bianka found the mirror resting in the heart of a clearing. The glass reflected springtime within its frame. Her skin ached for the warmth and color of the real world.

She studied her surroundings. Only trees and brush surrounded her. There were no humans in sight. Stepping through this mirror might be safer than stepping through the others, but she couldn't be sure.

One question troubled her—why *was* there a mirror here? There must be someone close by who used its magic; someone as untrustworthy and deceitful as Lilia and Charul. She shivered uncontrollably and knew that whatever danger lay on beyond this mirror, she couldn't brave this frozen land much longer. Reaching out, she pressed her hand through the mirror, stepping through to the other side.

A strange sensation trickled through her entire body, like numb skin thawing beneath warm water. The sun soaked into her face and hands and, while it relieved her tense muscles, her shivering didn't stop. Her lungs savored the warm, humid air.

Before her stood a tree covered in maturing buds of bright green. It remained firm, solid, and singular. A bird flew past her, piercing the air with its song. Instead of snow, soft ivy covered the stony ground. No trace of the late spring storm remained in the woods. Did magic change the land beneath her, or had time passed while she fled through the terrible frozen land?

She turned and looked at the mirror, her own ragged reflection stared back at her. Brushing her hair away from her blue lips, she shuddered at the memory of the shattering forest. She never wanted to go back there and never wanted to see the masked man again.

As she took her first step away from the mirror, pangs of hunger hit her with such ferocity that she worried she might faint. The hem of her dress hung heavy with snow and mud, making every step difficult. Stumbling down a narrow path, she noticed the trampled grass along her way. Bianka shivered. She didn't want to meet any more people involved in the mirror's magic.

She slid her wet cloak off her shoulders and wrapped it into a sodden ball in her arms. Emerging from the thickest portion of trees, she stopped. Ahead of her stood a lone cottage in a clearing. No smoke rose from the chimney and the crumbling walls were infested with birds' nests. It looked fairly abandoned. However, new cedar shingles pocked the roof where someone had recently patched a few holes.

Bianka hesitated. Who lived here so far out in the woods? If they owned a mirror, she may be better off running to the nearest village, rather than approaching.

Her stomach howled in protest. She needed food and there may not be another village nearby.

She couldn't just stand there, frozen in terror, waiting for the mirror's owner to discover her. Bianka forced herself to take another step forward to inspect the cottage and see if it held anything of worth for her. With wavering strength, she picked up a branch from the woodpile to use as a weapon if needed. Even as she raised the club, her body ached from running through the eternal forest.

Pressing on the door, Bianka flinched as the hinges creaked. Bianka waited a few seconds to see if anyone noticed the rush of sunlight she unleashed inside. She didn't hear anything, so she peeked in further.

In the main room stood a long dining table with rough-hewn benches. A goose hung over a wooden tub next to the hearth. On the table sat a basket with cheesecloth draped over the top. In the corner, a ladder led to an upstairs loft.

She darted toward the basket and found two large loaves resting underneath the cloth. Taking up one of the loaves, she tore a chunk from the end. Despite never having eaten bread so coarse, she enjoyed the rough texture. She longed to sink onto the bench and rest her legs for just a moment, but she couldn't afford to be discovered.

While hunting through the room for anything else she could take with her, Bianka found an empty sack on a hook near the door. Pulling it down, she shoved the bread inside, followed by a thin blanket and length of rope. In the corner, Bianka found a variety of short staves, clubs, and spears. Imagining wolves howling through the trees, she selected a spear.

Pulling off her bloodstone ring, she placed it on the table as payment. The ring probably didn't pay for all she took. She'd never purchased her own goods so Bianka couldn't be sure of their worth. She debated also leaving the thin golden strand she wore around her neck, but her hands were full and she needed to leave. Perhaps they wouldn't mind. The room bore no finery so her ring might be a welcome treasure. Bundling everything in her arms, she turned just in time to see a short, dark silhouette block the front door.

She froze.

More silhouettes gathered in the blinding sunshine. Bianka stood two hands taller than any of them. As her vision adjusted to the light, she recognized that the people were dressed in a confusing array of clothing. Some wore sweat-stained togas, holding crude metal helmets with frightening masks emblazoned on the front. Others wore peasantry clothing, carrying large packs on their backs. Height seemed to be the only uniform thing about the group.

A man stepped forward and Bianka gasped, dropping her armload of supplies, including the spear. His forearms were covered in scrapes and bruises and he had a swollen eye like an overripe summer blackberry.

"Who are you?" he asked.

Bianka choked back a whimper and backed up against the wall. The dead goose hung near her head. A cold sweat broke out beneath her wet clothes and her chin quivered. The group of men pressed forward, but the blackberry-eyed man held out his hand in warning.

"She's a thief, Ammond," a dark-haired man whispered, glancing at the goods scattered around Bianka's feet.

"I left a ring..." Bianka tried to whisper, but her lips refused to move. She couldn't form a single coherent word.

"She looks ill," a soft voice said.

The exhaustion, the fear, and the hunger overcame Bianka. Her eyelids fluttered and she fell to the floor.

WHEN BIANKA AWOKE, she felt woolen blankets scratching against her chin. She peeked one eye open and found herself lying in a bed tucked into an alcove of the main room. Two little men sat near her bedside, speaking in hushed tones. One of them whittled sticks into a fine point as he mumbled. Two others sat near a now blazing fire, one sewing up a gash on another man's arm.

A woman no taller than the bedpost pushed her way toward where Bianka lay. "Out of my way, she's waking up." She leaned against the edge of the bed and spread a cool cloth along Bianka's forehead. "Now you tell me, little squirrel, why were you stealing bread and a spear?"

Bianka stiffened, pressing her feet on the footboard and knocking her head against the wall. Everyone stared at her. They were each shorter than anyone she had ever met—half as tall as Father. The man with the blackberry eye washed his hands and face in a corner wash-basin, then stopped, patting his skin dry and wincing as he touched the bruise. Another woman hid behind a coat rack, fingering the fabric of Bianka's cloak. She wore Bianka's bloodstone ring. A young boy perched on a ladder that led into a loft.

Bianka swallowed.

"It's obvious, Rusha," the man with the black eye said, tossing down his hand towel. "She's running from something."

"In these shoes? Really, Ammond?" Rusha held up one of Bianka's travel-worn slippers.

The blond-haired boy jumped from the ladder to the ground. "If she's running, then she needs protection."

The man—Ammond—narrowed his eyes and walked toward Bianka. "What's your name?" he asked.

Bianka gulped. Did he know the man from the mirror looked for her?

"Well... Come on, child," Rusha said. "I've cleaned your clothes and given you my bed for the last few hours. The least you can do is give us your name."

Though the woman was undoubtedly kind to give her such things, Bianka still didn't trust her. She couldn't reveal who she was. Casting about in her mind, she remembered an uncle with a poetic last name.

"Cirksena. Bianka Cirksena," she said. Her chin quivered with the lie.

The woman clicked her tongue and leaned forward, brushing Bianka's tangled hair away from her face. Bianka hadn't felt such a warm gesture in days.

"Enough coddling the thing." Ammond placed his hand on Rusha's shoulder, and Rusha politely stepped back. His intense gaze made Bianka shrink back into the bed. "Where are you from, Bianka?"

"I..." Bianka stopped and shook her head, refusing to answer.

"You don't want to go back?" he asked.

Bianka nodded and the woman clicked her tongue sympathetically.

"How did you find this place?" Ammond's voice transitioned to a smooth, tired tone.

Bianka narrowed her eyes. "Why do you care *how* I found you? Are you worried someone else will find your mirror too?"

The entire room fell still.

Ammond put his hand on his hip in frustration. "What do you know of mirrors?"

Bianka stared at him with icy solemnity. "I stepped into one."

The others in the room cast curious glances at each other.

"Did The Mirror send you to me?" Ammond asked, straightening. Some of the men whispered, but Ammond threw his hand out to silence them without losing eye contact with Bianka. It seemed like he expected her to say yes. Perhaps she could use this to her advantage.

"Yes. He wanted you to guide me to the nearest village. When I found no one here, I knew I couldn't waste any time. I decided I'd go by myself."

Ammond and Rusha glanced at each other. The men behind them rubbed their beards.

Rusha spoke first. "You should eat. We'll speak of these things when you're feeling stronger."

"No, I must go. I can't..." Bianka tried to pull her legs off the side of the bed, but they didn't respond. Her muscles felt so fatigued from running through the eternal forest, she lacked the strength to move.

Ammond watched her struggle then chuckled. "I'll have a word with The Mirror. Keep an eye on the girl, though I doubt she'll be going anywhere."

He strode out the front door, not bothering to close it behind him. Rusha smiled gently, then stepped away to tend to her half-cooked meal. Everyone turned back to their original tasks, occasionally casting curious glances at Bianka.

She clutched the blankets to her chin, wondering how long until Ammond returned with the news that she had lied.

"The Pause regards every second as a different location. Two people could stand in the same room in the Pause and never see each other if they weren't programmed for the same moment in time."

-*Journal of Dorothea Wild*

CHAPTER
NINETEEN

K eltson tossed another digital currency bar onto his desk. It was Ammond's fifth payment in just a few hours and Keltson's best payday ever. Though Keltson couldn't take all the credit. Ammond's detailed research and proficiency made it all possible. By working together, the woodland cottage now housed an entire pack of grateful runaways.

Keltson watched the latest return mission. The troupe gathered around the mirror, welcoming the newest members of the family— Cenric and Volker. The gladiators were intimidating, yet Rusha warmed them with a motherly hug and insisted on guiding them home.

"Ammond, I have a proposition for you," Keltson said, stopping the man before he made his way down the hill.

"What is it?" Ammond asked. The poor man looked tired and had the worst black eye Keltson had ever seen.

"What if I adjusted the interface on the mirror so you had access to program the coordinates yourself? You're nearly finished and…"

"Is there something wrong?" Ammond asked, planting his fists on his hips.

"No. I trust you. I think you can handle it."

Ammond narrowed his eyes. Keltson didn't think the man was

fooled. The truth was he only offered so if anything happened and Keltson had to leave abruptly, Ammond wouldn't be stranded. That and a faint inkling that he might need backup if this whole scenario continued to spiral.

Finally, Ammond nodded in confirmation.

"Sure. Thanks," Ammond said, then he turned and started down the hill with his comrades.

Keltson leaned back in his chair. He had hoped Ammond would view the proposal as flattering. But it seemed that Ammond never failed to spot Keltson's weaknesses. Perhaps that's what he got for taking on a client with more experience than himself.

He ran a quick update, authorizing Ammond's fingerprint to program coordinates on the mirror's interface. He scanned forward through the surveillance and was surprised when only an hour later the camera picked up movement. Keltson scanned the screen in curiosity. Ammond had returned. He activated the transmission. But before he could speak, Ammond folded his arms and huffed.

"You never asked me if I wanted to babysit."

Keltson blinked in confusion, his face as blank as his avatar on the screen. "What are you talking about?"

"Why'd you send me the girl?" Ammond demanded.

Keltson's heart jumped out of his chest. "Girl? You mean Bianka? She's there with you? Is she alright?"

"We found her looting our house when we returned with Cenric and Volker. Her feet were as cold as ice. Where'd she come from? And what's the trouble that made you send her here?" Ammond drummed his fingers on his bicep impatiently.

Keltson's fingers flew across his keyboard, pulling up the coordinates of the Weilburg Forest mirror in relation to Ammond's safehouse. "She's from Weilburg," he said, answering the beginning of Ammond's question.

His mind trailed off and he mumbled to himself. "The Weilburg mirror is over three kilometers from there. How did she end up with him?"

Ammond squinted his eyes. "You mean, you didn't send her?"

Keltson snapped to attention. "No, and I want her home as soon as possible."

"So, do it," Ammond said.

Keltson paused. He couldn't tell Ammond that another client had hijacked his mirrors.

"It's not that easy," he said. His fingers flew madly over his keyboard, trying to pull up surveillance at the Waldeck Castle mirror. His screen fizzled with grey static. He knocked his fist against the desk. Lilia had likely commandeered that mirror as well. "Just let her stay with you while I figure this all out."

Ammond sent him a glare that told him exactly what he thought of the idea.

Keltson leaned forward and spoke with as authoritative a voice as he could muster. "This isn't a diversion. Your next mission will still happen on schedule. Keep her safe. I'll get her out of there as soon as I can. I promise." Keltson cut the transmission.

With Bianka out of the Pause, history likely had changed. Keltson ran back to his research corner and pulled out a current doc.

"Twelve years after her disappearance, Margaretha emerged from obscurity, dressed as a woodland peasant. Count Waldeck received her home with a great celebration. However, his wife grew violent during the reunion and when guards were sent to detain her, she disappeared into the walls. She was never seen again. Philip remained protective of his daughter afterwards, insisting she stay within the castle at all times. He began renovations on the castle. Some said it was to find his enchantress wife who he believed still lived inside the stones."

Keltson sighed. This history looked more and more like a folktale than fact. Fortunately, Bianka found a way to correct the course of her own timeline. Essentially, Lilia's objectives were fulfilled. Bianka still lived by ousting the stepmother who threatened her. It didn't solve his dilemma with ITTA, but at least the girl ended safely back at home.

Meanwhile, Lilia could be anywhere. She most likely jumped through the dining room mirror, causing the tale that she slunk into the walls.

The thought made his stomach churn. A split woman with access to time travel couldn't end well. Thankfully, Bianka was at the safehouse while he sorted this all out.

He threw on his vest and set his dials to the Weilburg Forest. He needed to bring the forest mirror back to his workshop for repairs before ITTA came to retrieve it themselves. Plus, he didn't want Lilia to use it again. But, as he pressed the ignition on his vest and the Weilburg Forest appeared in front of him, Keltson blinked in shock.

The mirror that should have been nestled between the boulders was gone.

He set his vest coordinates back to an earlier time, but no matter where he jumped, the mirror never appeared. He pinched the bridge of his nose. How was this even possible? Bianka ran through the glass only moments before.

Perhaps it had to do with the Mirror being part of the Pause and real time? All these years of manipulating time and he still didn't understand the laws of how things worked. When he was the only one making changes, it was easy to keep track of where things were. But now that Lilia also ran around inside, he didn't know what to expect.

-Sketchbook of Dorothea Wild

CHAPTER
TWENTY

That night, Bianka slept in a fit of nightmares. The eternal forest swallowed her whole, splitting her body into millions of shards. Each sliver formed into a child and darted into the woods. She tried to gather them, but so many pieces of her were lost that she couldn't move properly. Bianka tried to wake up but felt as if her body were dead, lying in a heavy sleep she couldn't rouse from no matter how hard she tried. Bianka feared she would never escape the dreadful eternal forest.

When she finally opened her eyes, the morning sun shone high above the tree line and streamed in through the open door. Her skin felt swollen and tender. Her damp clothes clung tightly to her ribs when she tried to move.

Rusha stood by her side, cup in hand. "You poor dear. You ran hot as a hay fire last night." She held out a steaming wooden mug. "Here, drink this tea." Bianka accepted the cup and drank slowly. Hints of cinnamon and lemon myrtle mixed on her tongue.

Rusha smiled at her. "You make me miss bits of my old life. I was a nursemaid for my previous master. He considered me a playmate for his children, but they were like my own babes." She gently pulled Bianka's sweaty hair away from her neck and tucked the blankets underneath her legs. She paused and inspected Bianka's fingers and wrists. She clicked her tongue. "Though I would never have allowed them to be covered in so much dirt and muck. I've drawn a bath for you. The boys are all outside, so you'll be fine."

She helped Bianka toward the warm stove where a wooden tub waited with warm water. As Bianka soaked away the sweat and the mud, she began to feel more like herself. Rusha fed her breakfast and Bianka's weakness faded along with the weight on her chest.

Rusha gave her some clothes to wear while her own dress was being washed. The skirt ended just below Bianka's knees and the peasant top was made from scratchy, ill-spun linen. Bianka tried to hide her ankles but failed, so she sat on the bed with her feet tucked underneath her in an unladylike fashion. Lilia might have scolded, but Rusha didn't look twice. Bianka relaxed her shoulders and allowed herself to sink into the bed. It was the first time in days she hadn't felt scrutinized.

Outside in the yard, Bianka caught glimpses of the men building furniture and provisioning food. Once the bath was drained, they traipsed in and out of the cottage, leaving ledgers, tools, and vegetables scattered over the kitchen's long wooden table. Rusha didn't seem to mind them as she went about the house, tending to the fire and washing clothes. Rusha thankfully never asked Bianka any questions. Once Bianka's dress had dried, Rusha brought it inside for her.

"This dress is much too hot to be wearing in the spring. I'll see that we make you a linen smock for this warm weather." Rusha picked up a bobbin of spun flax and twisted it in her hands, her mind likely envisioning the dress the threads would make. Bianka held her breath. Was Rusha planning on keeping her?

"Come outside now dear, the sunlight will do you well," Rusha said, setting down the flax and waving Bianka toward the door. Bianka swallowed and stood, eager to leave.

Outside, the men stood around a worktable, crafting weapons, while two of them sparred with a pair of Roman short swords. They all stopped to look at Bianka as she approached. Ammond stood near the tree line, splitting firewood. His muscles rippled angrily as he threw a final swing, anchoring the ax in the chopping block.

"You're looking much healthier today," Ammond said.

Bianka ran her fingers through the ends of her tangled hair. How horrible must she have appeared yesterday, covered in filth and half starved. The woman with Bianka's bloodstone ring clapped her hands behind her back and mumbled something that sounded French, though Bianka couldn't understand her.

"I spoke to The Mirror about you," Ammond said, leaning his elbow on the knob of the ax.

Bianka's heart froze. She prepared to flee if anyone moved toward her. "I'm not going back in there."

Ammond shook his head. "He wishes you to stay with us for a while."

Rusha smiled and clapped. "Heaven knows I've missed my duties! Taking care of a bunch of ruffian men is nothing like caring for a child."

"When you spoke to The Mirror, did you find out who she *really* is?" a dark, surly man asked Ammond, not seeming to care that Bianka stood right in front of him.

Ammond rolled his eyes and sighed. "Whoever she is, she's important. The Mirror wants her protected."

Bianka raised an eyebrow. Protected?

"Why should we care?" the dark-haired man asked.

"Because, Urig, The Mirror never does anything for himself. If he asked me to keep her safe, it's for a good reason. He sees things we can't. He knows better than any of us what is right. I trust him." Ammond stepped away from the chopping block, crossed toward a bucket and dumped a ladle of water over the back of his head.

"You trust magic?" Bianka asked. Her bare toes pressed against the sun-warmed dirt beneath her.

"I've seen opportunities for a better life in his mirror." Ammond wagged the ladle at her, before setting it back into the bucket. "I know magic gets a bad rap *nowadays*, but everything can be used for good, missy."

Bianka stepped backwards, blinking rapidly. "I've been inside that mirror. It is a frozen, shattering wasteland with no light, no warmth, no life. How could something so fearsome be used for good?"

Ammond peered at her, pursing his mouth in thought. "I've never seen the things you speak of."

Her mouth fell open. He brushed past her trauma as simply as if he were shooing a fly.

"Have you ever stepped inside a mirror?" She needed to see in his eyes if he had ever visited that horrid place.

He shrugged easily. "Plenty of times. All of us have. It took me to England to retrieve Gunther and Urig, then France for Mathilda..." Ammond motioned to the woman with Bianka's ring.

Bianka stared at him in confusion. "Why would you choose to travel such great distances in that wretched place?"

Ammond tilted his head to the side. "It's not like traveling at all. It's only a matter of a step."

"No. It's not." Bianka said, her throat tightening and her voice tense. She paused for breath, then continued. "A few steps take an eternity. The world splits apart at every glance and the light casts ghostly shadows before it freezes you into ice." She turned to look at each person listening in the clearing. They all seemed confused. Bianka raised her hands, pleading with them to agree with what she had experienced. "Nothing moves, nothing breathes. Everything felt dead as if I was the only living thing."

Ammond watched her, stroking his bottom lip while he thought. "Perhaps there are things we don't know. But rest assured, you don't have to go back there if you don't want to."

Bianka's shoulders relaxed and she exhaled a shaky breath.

"Do you want to stay here?" he asked

Bianka swallowed. Going back meant facing Lilia and Charul. It meant waiting for Father, afraid of the news he'd bring back of Samuel. But staying here meant that she was in the power of The Mirror. These people obeyed him. Just like Lilia. Was either option better than the other?

"I don't know," Bianka said.

Ammond turned toward the others. "Then, until I receive further instructions, she is part of the household. She'll carry out duties and support herself, just like I ask of you."

Bianka wrapped her arms around herself, watching each of them give Ammond an understanding nod. Only the dark-haired man hesitated to agree.

The mistrust went both ways.

Rusha called everyone in for stew and as Bianka followed them inside, she made a decision—if she could gain her strength, she would set off on her own to see how to make things right. Bianka took a bowl from Rusha and watched the strange assortment of foreigners, studying them.

She would wait for the right moment. Then she would go.

"Once, as a child, I found a portrait of my mother covered with a linen cloth in the spare room above Father's study. I think he put the painting away after he married Lilia. If I find my way back to the castle, I am going to retrieve her likeness and hang it in the great hall, so it won't be lost."

-Journal of Bianka Cirksena

CHAPTER TWENTY-ONE

B ianka's hands burned from the lye soap. Rusha sat across from her peeling vegetables while she oversaw Bianka's attempts to clean the men's clothing. Mathilda sat a close by, spinning strands of flax with a drop spindle. The men were all off scouting a gold vein.

Rusha clicked her tongue. "You must use your arms, Bianka. You'll never release their dirt and sweat with such a meager effort."

Bianka grimaced at the dirt-caked trousers she washed but didn't try any harder. "The water is so muddy and brown. Even if I had arms like Cenric I wouldn't be able to get these clothes clean."

"You'll have to do a second wash," Rusha said. Potato and carrot shavings covered her shoes. She turned another yellow-fleshed potato over, checking for any remaining spots of skin before dropping it into a bucket, splashing water across the hem of her dress.

Bianka groaned and lifted her red, wrinkled hands from the suds.

Rusha cleaned the peeling knife on the edge of her apron. "Bianka, these men are hard workers. We women must make an equal effort to dispel their troubles from their clothing." She leaned forward, resting her palms on her knees as she stared gently at Bianka. "Clean clothes are a gift. We wash away the memory of their toil against the dark earth, soften it in the wind, and brighten it in the sun. We lift their weary souls with our offering."

Bianka pursed her lips. "My father would never approve of such hands," she said.

Rusha huffed and turned back to the vegetables. "It's a crime you never learned such skills."

Bianka pulled the stopper from the bottom of the washbasin and watched the murky water rush down the hillside into the creek below. "I never knew *living* required so much effort. In the castle, clothes were merely taken away then brought back clean and folded."

Rusha laughed. "Our tasks become easier the more we focus. You're like an infant in the way you work."

"I'm a dutiful student when it comes to needlework, writing, and the finer arts. But these skills require forceful hands." Bianka massaged her red palms.

Rusha dropped another potato into the bucket at her feet. "I don't blame you for resisting change. Coming here was hard after living in the nursery. But freedom makes the work worthwhile." Rusha looked lovingly at her new potato while she peeled away the dirty brown skin.

Bianka narrowed her eyes. Hearing Rusha speak about freedom struck a nerve. While Ammond's crew didn't have her under lock and key, she knew they watched her. The Mirror wanted Bianka to stay. She distrusted her sense of freedom. What would happen if she tried to run away?

"What is wrong, *liebling?*" Rusha asked. Bianka flinched at the pet name. It meant that Rusha felt some kind of ownership over her. Perhaps like she did over her nursery children.

Bianka stared into the washbasin filled with sloppy mounds of clothing. "When do I get to see my family again?"

Rusha stopped peeling but didn't look up at Bianka. "The Mirror thinks you'd be in danger if you went home now. He's trying to work out your safety."

"But how does he know?" Bianka asked.

"I don't know how the magic works. All I know is I trust him." Rusha shrugged and dropped the last potato into the bucket. She stood, gathering the stray shavings for the garden mulch. "I was skeptical like you when Ammond first introduced me to The Mirror. But over time, I've come to know that he only speaks the truth."

Bianka narrowed her eyes. She didn't like that the only answer she ever received was to blindly trust. Hadn't she trusted Lilia and Charul? They both proved false in the end. No. Bianka needed to confront the mirror herself. Summoning the magic on her own terrified her, but she needed to know if Rusha and the others were manipulating her. She couldn't bear to be lied to by these people as well.

"Now that you've finished draining, go fetch more water. A second round will rinse out the mud and soap."

Bianka sighed and picked up the water buckets, then headed down to the creek. Dunking her arms into the cold river washed away the burning lye on her skin, relieving the sting for a moment. She closed her eyes and listened to the sound of the water rushing across the smooth river stones.

Perhaps she could sneak away without anyone knowing and speak to The Mirror herself. Bianka shivered at the thought. The darkness of the woods terrified her. She glanced back at the cottage and saw Rusha carting the bucket of potatoes inside. This might be her only chance. She steeled herself against the dark woods, then dropped the buckets and crept toward the trail that led to the mirror.

All too soon, it rose before her. For a moment, she imagined herself running back down the path. She set her jaw. This was the only way for her to know. No longer could she assume that others had her best interest at heart. So, she stepped into the clearing.

Her reflection seemed unrecognizable. Her cheeks were red from spending so much time outside and Rusha had pulled her hair into a simple braid instead of coiffing it like Agnetha usually did.

She looked like a peasant.

Her reflection quickly faded into darkness. A white sunrise bloomed in the center of the blank glass, forming into a mask with a furrowed brow. The Mirror's masked features moved as if he were made of skin and muscle. However, the eyes Bianka wished to study for their sincerity were merely blank holes filled with shadows. Bianka stumbled back.

"Why are you here?" The Mirror asked. Though he spoke German, his voice carried a strange accent.

Bianka swallowed. "They say you only speak the truth," she said. Her years of practice in front of the mirror during approbations gave her the courage she needed to speak. "I've come to speak to you myself."

"If you're wondering if you can go home, you can't. It's not safe yet and I have larger problems to deal with at the moment." His face remained emotionless and uncaring.

She felt a rush of angry heat rise through her body. "More important than fixing this? Your magic brought me here. It should take me back as well."

"That is not my job. I leave that type of task to my clients." The Mirror's voice sounded tired.

"I don't know what that word means, *clients*." Bianka waved a hand in front of her. "All I know is that you help Lilia, Ammond, Charul, and everyone at the cottage. And yet, you refuse to let me leave. I know just as much about you as they do about your magic. I ran through your blasted forest!"

The mask stared at her with his empty eyes, but when he spoke, she was surprised by the amount of frustration in his voice. "First of all, I never spoke to Charul. Second of all, I don't take orders from twelve-year-old kids."

She flipped her long braid over her shoulder and lifted her chin. "I'm fifteen now, thank you very much. I had my birthday a few days ago in this exile and no one knew any better. Rusha made me eat fish. On my birthday."

"You're still not going home."

All of Lilia's training came rushing at Bianka, and she straightened her back, clasped her hands together firmly in front of her, and put on her most commanding tone.

"I am a countess and you will listen to me. I don't deal with magic lightly and I didn't choose to be cast into that horrible world of yours."

The Mirror looked upwards in exasperation. "It's also not my fault you trusted that huntsman and followed him into the woods. I thought Lilia taught you better than that."

"Charul was kind to me. I never suspected he..." Bianka stopped and looked down at the ground in confusion. How had she not seen the hint in his eyes? She came here to judge The Mirror's character, and yet he had just proven to her what a terrible judge of character she was. "I'm scared to think that people can be so different from what they seem."

"It's a fact of life, kid. People are going to let you down. Sometimes you just have to trust yourself."

"But how can I trust myself when I so easily misjudge the character of others?" Doubts seeped into her heart, rushing like a trickle of water, threatening to burst through a dam. Her chin quivered. She felt bare in front of him like everything she ever believed about herself had been stripped away.

The Mirror watched her, then began laughing. "I knew I shouldn't have spoken to a teenager."

Bianka scowled. "I am being genuine. I thought Lilia strong and kind, but in the end, she threatened me with sunken eyes. Then I met Charul, who seemed an honest friend, but tried to capture me and take me away. If others around me prove so false, then what kind of person am I?"

The mask looked away for a moment, then turned back to face her. "The truth is a fluid thing, Bianka. Lilia's kindness may have been genuine one minute and her menace certain the next. Charul might have actually thought he was helping you." His voice softened and carried with it a hint of compassion, though it was still muffled beneath the overarching monotone of his countenance.

"But how can one person be two different truths?" She lifted her red, raw palms toward him, pleading.

The Mirror chuckled. "Can't you see that in yourself? You stand before me in peasantry clothing and yet you are a countess, are you not?"

Bianka rolled her eyes in frustration. "A countess and a peasant aren't the essence of a person. It's merely their exterior."

The Mirror nodded and pinched his mouth to the side in thought.

Bianka thought the motion made him feel quite human. "I feel like a fraud sometimes. Others tell me I remind them of my mother. I was named after her. But how can I live up to the name of someone I don't remember?"

"You were never like her," The Mirror said. Bianka looked up, intrigued that he might know something about her mother.

"Your family said you reminded them of her all the way back when you were a baby. How much can an infant resemble their mother? Perhaps you looked like her, but nothing more. Beauty means nothing. To be like her is to be forgotten in the pages of the world. Not even a single painting of her lives through history to carry on her story."

Bianka's breath hitched as she tried to speak. "How could you be so harsh?"

"You asked for the truth."

As angry as she felt, Bianka also sensed the honest tragedy in his words. She had seen it herself. The entire castle forgot her mother. Only three fading blood stains hinted at her existence. "My mother died young. Perhaps she never had a chance to prove herself."

The Mirror tilted his head to the side. "That wasn't a problem for you."

"What?" Bianka asked, confused.

"I have seen what you become, Bianka. And I am working hard to prevent your own early demise. A demise that people will know about for hundreds of years, unless you help me stop it. I need you to trust me. I am acting in your best interest."

Bianka had never considered The Mirror might be a soothsayer as well. "You can see what might be?"

"Yes. And if I don't like what I see, I change it."

"You didn't like what I became?" Bianka asked.

"No. I didn't like your fate at all. Aside from dying tragically, you never really amounted to much. Sure, your great genetics ensured your portrait was appealing enough to hang above the fireplace after you died, so you didn't suffer the same oblivion your mother did. However, being ripped from the lap of luxury isn't the worst thing I've seen happen to you. In fact, you may be better off here, learning some work ethic from Ammond and his troupe."

Bianka's mouth dropped open, and she swore she could see a hint of a smile flicker in the corner of the mask's otherwise stoic mouth. How dare he speak to her like that? Bianka felt hot tears prickle behind her eyelids. She straightened, trying not to let it slide down her cheek. "You are wicked."

"If you came here hoping to hear you're still the 'fairest in the land', and you are brave and strong and the ultimate feminist Lilia wanted you to become, that doesn't do you any good."

"I am the daughter of Philip von Waldeck and..."

"You can't claim his legacy as some accomplishment on your part. You said so yourself. A title is not the essence of who you are."

Bianka froze. This moment felt like an approbation. However, The Mirror's brutal words hit her harder than any examination her parents ever offered. For so many years, she looked in the mirror and heard every fault turned into potential. Every beautiful trait became amplified. Yet, The Mirror quickly tore down all that false confidence with his truths. She felt like a little girl again, worried that the mirror would swallow her up into a stagnant, frozen world where no one could hear her, or see her. A world where she bore no consequence.

"You speak the truth," Bianka whispered, defeated. She hated considering The Mirror wasn't wicked, but honest. "He only speaks the truth," they had said.

Bianka didn't want to hear any more truths today. Before he could utter another word, she turned and fled down the path toward the cottage. She didn't feel like crying or sulking. She only felt... numb. Blank. Like a sheet of paper without words.

As she neared the creek, she heard Rusha calling for her. The empty buckets waited near the creek's edge. She filled them and stumbled back up the hill toward the cottage.

"There you are! I was afraid you'd run off," Rusha said, still wringing her hands.

Bianka stared at Rusha, not knowing what to say. She shrugged. "The wash isn't done."

Rusha smiled and shook her head. "Well, it's generous of you to return to your duties. It's more than I can say for Mathilda," Rusha said. The abandoned stump where Mathilda sat earlier was surrounded by a mess of linen fibers.

The Mirror said she had no work ethic. She would learn and prove him wrong. "I could finish there, too, if you'd teach me," Bianka said.

Rusha raised an eyebrow. "That's kind of you dear." Apparently, suspicion wasn't enough reason to reject the offer. However, as Bianka walked back and forth, pouring the buckets of water into the washbasin, Rusha continued to watch her curiously. Bianka hadn't hidden her animosity toward chores the last few weeks.

Bianka looked down at her raw hands. Washing clothes was a gift, Rusha said. A kindness.

"I can be kind," Bianka whispered to herself.

While The Mirror thought she was "a coddled little thing who never amounted to much", her natural inclination always leaned toward kindness. She clung to the realization, swallowed, and tried to focus on scrubbing all the dirt, sweat, care, and toil from the shirt's fibers.

Mirror 1: Cellar- Active
Mirror 2: Ammond's Clearing- Active
Mirror 3: Weilburg Forest- Missing
Mirror 4: Waldeck Castle- Unresponsive

-Equipment Report

CHAPTER TWENTY-TWO

L ilia looked down from her bedroom window toward the main gate. Her joints ached from the tense fury she bottled inside. A small army rode into the courtyard and the soldiers did nothing to stop it. She'd heard rumors of the advancing troupe for weeks. Now they walked peacefully through the front door, invading her home.

At the front of the rabble hoard rode a group of miniature warriors on horseback. The little men rode their mounts with frustrating dignity. In the center of it all rode Bianka. She wore an ostentatious gold crown that glittered upon her raven hair in the sunlight. Lilia couldn't bear the sight. How dare Philip's full-grown daughter ride back to claim her place in the family.

Lilia growled and turned to Agnetha. "Get my commander," she said.

"But your majesty, if it is truly the countess…"

"She is not welcome here!" Lilia screeched. "She must not enter this home. Do you understand?"

Agnetha fled and Lilia turned again, watching as soldiers in the courtyard saluted the wretched girl. Not one of them tried to stop her.

Stop Bianka.

The pulsing words rose into her mind once more. For years, Lilia lived in peace without the thoughts. Any mention of Bianka triggered the thrumming in the back of her head, so the mere memory of the girl had been banished from the castle. Now a force awoke inside her heart, pumping the chant throughout her limbs, her head, her core.

Lilia flew into the hall and glided down the stairs in a fury. The girl wanted to take away everything Lilia worked for. Her peace. Her sanity. Her family.

She ran, holding her skirts as she stumbled into the armory. She grabbed a bow and arrow and turned to the window facing the courtyard.

Bianka stood inside the gates now.

Stop Bianka.

People cheered around her.

Fools.

Did they know they welcomed a fiend?

Stop her.

And then, the most horrendous sight of all. Philip—her very own Philip—rushed forward. Tears streamed down his cheeks. Did he even know what the girl had done so many years ago? Lilia couldn't stand it any longer.

"You must stop her," Lilia whispered to the head of the arrow. She fitted the nock to the bowstring, aimed through the window, and released.

Her gaze followed its path hungrily.

Stop her.

Her poor skill caused the arrow to fall short of Bianka. It clattered against the cobblestones and slid in the girl's direction. The horses whinnied with discomfort and the crowd looked up at the window. Lilia glared out, showering hatred down on the lot of them. Why didn't they *stop her*? This was Lilia's home. She would defend it. Even if she must kill them all. Some of the men pointed at her and six soldiers darted up the stairs toward the castle entrance.

These foolish peasants thought they could stop Lilia. They didn't understand her power. She could do more than merely defend her castle *after* an attack. Lilia could prevent Bianka from ever coming back in the first place. The mirror in the dining room was long since programmed to respond only to her touch. It sat dormant for ten years. But today, it would serve its purpose.

She dropped the bow and pulled a dagger from its place on the wall. As she fled, Lilia heard the footfalls of the knights behind her. She smirked and threw open the doors to the dining hall. Men shouted behind her. Let them see her power. Let them witness the control Lilia wielded on the universe. She stepped up to the mirror.

This time, she wouldn't just *stop Bianka.* This time, she needed to *end Bianka.*

She pressed her hand against the glass and as the first guard ran into the room behind her, she stepped through its surface.

This time, Bianka would die.

-Sketchbook of Dorothea Wild

CHAPTER TWENTY-THREE

B ianka held the pommel of the wooden long sword and let the tip rest on the ground. Her arms ached from wielding the weapon for so long.

"You missed another opportunity, Bianka!" Cenric shouted from the fence. Volker swiped his own wooden blade through the air, aiming for her side. Bianka blocked the blow, using the momentum to spin herself around him. He blinked, his view was now obscured by the sun. He tried to regain his position, but she defended her place well.

"Good. Now press the advantage you just gave yourself!" Cenric instructed. Bianka parried as Volker brought his sword in a wide streak toward her hip.

"Will you louts get in here and eat your supper?" Rusha called from the cottage. "Gunther will eat the whole pot if you don't come soon."

Bianka and Volker shared a glance, then simultaneously dropped their swords. Volker smiled—a rare gift. "Your weapon isn't as balanced as a metal sword would be, but you wield it well," he said.

"She doesn't deserve a metal weapon," Cenric said, scowling.

"Stop pouting, Cenric," Volker said. "This is the first time Bianka didn't lose. You should be happy."

"I accept the draw," Bianka said, wiping a sweaty strand of hair away from her face.

Cenric harrumphed. "You could have won if you took the offensive. Why do you hang back so often?"

"Attacking wouldn't be kind, Cenric," Bianka said, fluttering her eyelashes innocently.

Cenric pulled his blond curls over his eyes in frustration. "You are such an infuriating student."

"You used to be so exuberant about training me. What happened?" Bianka asked, smiling as they walked back to the cottage. Cenric only rolled his eyes.

The moment they stepped through the door, Rusha dished up dinner into bowls. "Ah, finally. Mind the bread, Bianka."

Bianka crossed to the hearth and threw on another log, spitting ashes across Bianka's carefully shaped loaf of bread.

"Blast," Bianka whispered.

"Did you burn another hole in your hem?" Rusha asked, glancing over her shoulder.

"I'm not *that* clumsy anymore, Rusha."

Rusha chuckled. "You hardly need me nowadays. I'm afraid Ammond will call me out to the mines with the men because you are so efficient around the house."

"If only I could get her to be so efficient with the sword," Cenric grumbled.

"I defend myself perfectly," Bianka said, wiping her hands on her skirts.

"But there's more to fighting than defense. You have to attack for once!"

"I'll defend myself, but I'll never attack," Bianka shook her head as she sliced through the hot loaf.

"And why is that, child?" Volker asked, massaging his fist.

Bianka's grip on the bread knife tightened. "My stepmother raised me to become a strong dictator who could order people about. I don't want to be anything like her."

"So, you decided to *let* people attack you?" Rusha asked.

Cenric pointed to Rusha in agreement. "Enemies quash nice people. Give them an inch and they won't hesitate to give you gaping wounds." He pointed to the scars on his shoulders.

Volker shook his head and placed a calm hand on top of Cenric's pointing finger, tucking it into a fist. "Fighting was our life, my friend. It spared us both from death. Bianka is not in an arena."

"But she does hope to return home. Kings don't reclaim thrones by being 'nice,'" Cenric said.

Bianka laid the knife next to the cutting board and placed the sliced loaf into a basket. "I don't want to come charging in with flame and sword, burning the home I love and killing the people I care for."

The conversation was interrupted by heavy stomping entering through the front door. Urig came first with the telltale sign of dirt on his cheeks and carrying a bag filled with gold from the hills. He placed it into a concealed chest next to the hearth. Mathilda followed him, fingering a golden nugget close to her face. She preferred to be off with the men, sorting through rocks for shiny bits of gold, rather than at home scaling fish or plucking hens with Bianka and Rusha. Ammond entered the cottage last. He seemed exhausted, stooping to unlace his boots.

"What's wrong with you?" Bianka asked while arranging the plates on the table.

Urig shook his head as he sat at the table. "This man works twice as hard as he should, picking at the mountain."

"Every ounce of gold brings us closer to buying our comrade's freedom. I'm anxious to be off." Ammond used the back of his hand to rub his whiskery chin. He crossed to the small table next to the door and laid his tools atop its surface.

"Once we bring them back, there won't be room for us all. We'll have to build another cottage." Rusha set her hands on her hips.

"Well, perhaps we won't stay here much longer." Ammond said. The room froze and all eyes turned toward him. He stretched his back, then turned to face them.

"Bianka is seventeen, my friends. How long are we going to wait for The Mirror to reunite her with her family? Her training is sufficient. She can at least protect herself now. I think once we purchase the freedom of our comrades in Greece, we will have enough support to restore Bianka to her home in safety."

Everyone looked at each other in surprise.

"Do I- get to live in her castle?" Mathilda asked in broken German, though it didn't hide the hope in her voice.

Ammond smiled and rubbed his neck. "I'm sure we'll work out details later, Mathilda."

"Why are you doing this?" Bianka asked. "The Mirror doesn't think it is safe for me to return yet." She never expected Ammond to go against anything The Mirror said.

"After this next rescue, I'm through with what I set out to do here." Ammond straightened and stepped toward Bianka. The determination in his eyes glinted in the firelight from the hearth. "You are one of us, Bianka. And you deserve to have your own life set right, just as any of us have."

Bianka couldn't help but smile. "I've received nothing but kindness from you all."

"What if she must fight?" Volker asked. "We have no true weapons, and the only metal we have to forge is gold."

Cenric snorted. "A golden sword? You might as well attack with butter."

"Perhaps we can make her something golden for battle, nonetheless," Rusha said.

"A crown," Mathilda whispered, glancing up from the table with excitement, spinning a dirty nugget in her fingers.

"A crown is a good idea, Mathilda." Ammond pressed a knuckle against his lips in thought. "Bianka needs more than just her own arm to defend her. Perhaps, if she is recognized as Herr Waldeck's beloved daughter, the people of the province will support her."

"But what if the people hate Herr Waldeck?" Volker asked. "We can't reveal her if they wish to depose him. And what of the Countess and the Huntsman? What if they still have a vendetta?"

Ammond raised his hands to quell further questions.

"Bianka and I will go to the village tomorrow for supplies. People won't recognize the young woman she's become. We can gather information about Herr Waldeck, then plan how best to rally support. If we get a large enough force around her then she will be protected against Lilia and Charul until she reaches the count."

"And, if you go to the village, you could purchase some new sewing needles!" Rusha said, clasping her hands in front of her, practically pleading.

"And sugar," Mathilda said.

Gunther pressed his lips together and rose up on his toes, barely holding his tongue from expressing his own desires. Ammond shook his head and laughed.

"We cannot make any promises about novelties. But I do hope, Bianka, that we can make some useful allies to get you home. Even without The Mirror's help."

Bianka smiled. "Thank you Ammond."

She couldn't believe it. She had long since given up dreaming about the day she could go home. The old ache she suppressed so long ago returned, filling her heart with memories of her home, her family, her life.

Finally, it was her turn to be liberated.

BIANKA AND AMMOND stepped through the forest with pouches of gold tucked inside their packs. Ammond stopped outside the village to put on his stilts.

"Why do you insist on wearing these?" Bianka asked, arranging his robes around the wood so he could practice walking over the rough terrain.

"You may be used to my size, Bianka, but I assure you, I'll attract every gaze if I walk into the village. People don't think twice about staring at something they're not used to."

"How rude."

"We change the world one step at a time, Bianka. But it's not for my sake. I can't risk *you* being recognized. Especially if people don't support your father. So, I'll wear these and try to blend in... for now." He winked.

The trees thinned and a country road came into view. Bianka felt a rush of butterflies in her stomach. She had lived with the troupe in solitude for so long that she felt nervous about meeting people outside of her safe haven.

"If anyone asks, I'm your father," Ammond said. He wobbled as he stepped on a stray stone on the dusty road.

"Or my grandfather, the way you're walking." Bianka smiled as she caught his arm.

"I hope the village isn't too far. I've endured more than my fair share of blisters from these stilts."

As she helped Ammond down the road, Bianka fingered the piece of wood in her pocket that was inscribed with the troupe's wishes. She hoped to repay their kindness with gifts from her visit to the market.

Within minutes, they reached the small village of Weinbach. The center square rested at the base of a forest-covered hill, surrounded on the other side by flat expanses of farmland. She paused, feeling a tight knot in her stomach. Seeing the carts, people, and shops made Bianka realize how much she missed the castle courtyard—the cobblestones beneath her feet, the noises of animals and people bustling about.

As they passed the first cottage on the outskirts of town, a man repairing a broken length of fence straightened to watch them. Bianka felt short beneath his towering height. It was the first person in two years who stood taller than she did.

Cottages grew closer together the further they walked. Soon they entered the main square and found a line of pavilions topped with faded flags that fluttered in the breeze. She glanced around at the stands selling meats, trinkets, and other gifts for her friends. She touched the list in her pocket and smiled in anticipation.

Ammond hobbled about, speaking to men about Herr Waldeck and trying to gain information, leaving her to scour the market. Bianka watched others haggle over goods and questioned her own ability to barter. She didn't know the fair amount for things. But soon enough, her sack was filled with household luxuries and she still maintained a variety of gold nuggets in her pouch. Perhaps the shopkeepers swindled her in some cases, but Bianka recognized the need in their eyes. She handed them payment, hoping the gold blessed their families.

Bianka turned to find Ammond and walked past a blacksmith's shop. Swords and tools lined the cedar-planked wall surrounding the fire and bellows. The man did not look up as he hammered a red-hot iron rod into nails atop an anvil. She noticed a single, precious long sword hanging above the shop opening and imagined Volker handling the weapon, teaching her how to use the blade. She had more than enough money to purchase the sword. However, she could only imagine how fast rumors might spread once a strange girl asked to buy a weapon of war.

Perhaps once she established her presence in the village she could think about such things. Instead, her eyes rested on a pickax. Urig always complained of their primitive methods of extracting gold from the rocks. She smiled to herself, imaging the men squabbling over something as common as a pick.

She made up her mind and stepped forward. But with the blacksmith's back turned to her and the sound of his hammer, her shouting did nothing to draw his attention. Instead, an old woman poked her head around the corner of the window. Streaks of white speckled her thin and wiry hair. Her face seemed wrinkled by cares rather than by the sun. She gave Bianka an eager smile.

"Purchase, my dear?" she asked. She held out a piece of detailed leather in her hands, motioning for Bianka to examine it.

"Oh, no, thank you. I came to inquire about a pick."

The woman shook her head. "No, no, no." She limped around the counter to the front of the store where Bianka stood. The blacksmith continued to hammer, ignorant of their transaction.

The woman seemed like someone who looked beautiful once, but now was bent and skittish. In her hands, she held a bodice made of stiff leather with intricate embellishments etched into the surface. She held it forward, showing Bianka runes and winding curls that moved around the masterful seams.

Bianka reached a hesitant hand out and ran her fingers over the patterns. "It's beautiful," she whispered.

The woman's dry tongue clicked against the roof of her mouth as she spoke. "Once, I dreamt of a woman warrior, riding on black horseback surrounded on every side by soldiers who bowed in allegiance. She wore no armor but a thin dress draped her body as she rode into battle. A long sword rested at her side and she wore a crown of delicate gold. Can you imagine how inspiring it was? But when the moment came for her to claim her glory, a single arrow pierced her ribs and she fell."

Bianka blinked at the sudden end to the story.

The old woman stroked the leather. "Something so precious as life must be protected. So, I made this armor and prayed for the warrior who needed it. All for a price of course. I can't be a philanthropist, even for a vision."

The talk of riding into battle made Bianka think of how the thick bodice could protect her during sparring. Besides, she didn't know what kind of reception she would have when she returned home. Would she have to fight her way back? If so, a bodice like this would be imperative.

The old woman sighed, her knobby knuckles cracking as she turned over the leather, admiring her own handiwork. "But alas, the maiden warrior has never arrived to claim my work."

"I will buy the vest from you," Bianka said. The woman looked at her in surprise. Then she burst out laughing.

"You are the fairest warrior I have ever seen. You have a battle to win my dear?"

Bianka blushed. She hoped this woman didn't enjoy spreading rumors around the village.

"Oh, no. I..." Bianka began, but the woman interrupted.

"But who am I to deny an interested party after all these years? Here. If you have money, I will part with it."

Bianka smiled and pulled a piece of gold from her bag. The woman looked hungrily after the bit of metal.

"Will this purchase the bodice *and* the pick?" Bianka asked, placing the nugget gently into the woman's callused palm.

"Of course, of course. But first, try this on to see if it fits, my dear."

The woman held the leather up. Bianka dropped her pack to the ground and thread her arms through the bodice while the woman laced up the back. It was too large, but she still had a few years left to grow into the tailored leather. Perhaps it was a sign that she needed to wait to return home until she filled out the shoulders and chest.

The woman's hands tugged on the laces, pulling the leather closer to Bianka's skin. While she waited for the woman to finish, she glanced over her shoulder and sensed a familiarity to the old woman's jaw line beneath the drooping skin. A dark feeling settled over her. The woman fastened the last lace and Bianka gasped and spun to face her.

Lilia, old and withered, smiled back at her.

"Lilia?" Bianka asked, stumbling backwards. She felt more and more strange with every passing second.

"You haven't much time, dearie. Run and show them your battle armor." Lilia turned and fled into a darkened alleyway.

Fear gripped Bianka. What did Lilia mean? She struggled to bend down and pick up the satchel from her feet. The bodice grew tighter, making it difficult to breathe. She stepped forward to see if she could find Ammond and felt a pain in her legs as if her bones splintered with each step.

However, as Bianka looked down she realized that her breath wasn't cut short by the bodice growing smaller, but by her body swelling with age. Her stockings fell short, her sleeves stopped above her wrists, and the chest of the bodice pulled tight against her ribs. She reached behind herself, struggling at the laces.

"Ammond!" she shouted, searching up and down the street, trying to spot his brown robe in the crowd. She ran, trying not to draw attention, but desperate all the same. Bianka felt tired, and though her body stopped growing, every step drew strength from her she couldn't explain.

She held up her hands and saw that age spotted her skin. Her veins stuck out as if poisoned. Her aching joints caused her to stumble and cry out. In the back of her mind, she longed for Rusha to hold her and stroke her hair. The memory of the dear woman felt vivid and yet very far away. Bianka looked around at the unfamiliar buildings. She didn't know where she was. What was she doing here?

Each step grew more and more impossible. Her hands grew frail and knobby as Bianka fell against the rim of a village well. People scurried away from her as she struggled for breath. She could see the fear in their eyes. Her strength failed as she tried to push herself up from the stones. Her hair fell around her as white as freshly fallen snow. The last thing she thought of as she closed her eyes was the storm her mother saw before her birth.

"The Countess von Waldeck hired a huntsman to slay Margaretha. He showed her mercy and she fled into the woods. The Countess went mad with anxiety for fear of Margaretha's return and the servants in turn grew to fear her. Eleven years later, villagers found Margaretha dead in a nearby square. Rumors spread about the Countess, suggesting that in her jealousy she sent a curse that withered the girl's beauty and killed her."

-Third variance recorded by ITTA

CHAPTER
TWENTY-FOUR

K eltson sat, studying the new edition of Bianka's future and shook his head. Peasantry lore often distorted facts. He didn't quite understand the curse or the comment about Bianka's withering beauty. But what he did gain from this story was one important truth—Lilia killed Bianka.

Worry pulsed through his chest as he realized she must have split again in order to claim her revenge. He couldn't know for sure since the Waldeck Castle mirror failed to respond to his requests for surveillance. That made two mirrors out of commission. Did Lilia know how expensive those two mirrors she commandeered cost? She likely didn't care.

He needed to focus. Crossing to his sound equipment, Keltson found a song with a deep, steady bass and downed another can of Vibe. The energy surged through his tired body and his blood pulsed with the rhythm. He crumpled the can in his hand and threw it into the corner. He could do this.

If he talked to Ammond, he could get details about Bianka's death and coach him on how to save her. Crossing to the screens, he pulled up a meeting with Ammond from after Bianka died. The man came into focus. His limp blond hair stuck to his cheeks and he paced in front of the mirror.

"Hello, Ammond."

"You have to save her." Ammond pointed his finger into the mirror. "I know she's not on my list of directives, but you have to do something."

"I will. I just need you to explain what happened that day."

"Your blasted live-wire client killed her." Ammond threw his hands in the air and spun in a disoriented circle as he spoke. "She strapped a device on Bianka and aged her to death within seconds."

Keltson didn't have devices that did any such thing. His heart clenched, terrified to think that Lilia invented her own concoction of time travel equipment. "What do you mean by aged her to death?"

"Bianka wore a leather corset wired with photon accelerating tech. One minute, Bianka was seventeen, the next she looked ninety. She died of old age." Ammond stopped, then gripped his forehead in his hands, looking like a wave of guilt was about to crash down on his head.

"Did you see Lilia there beforehand?"

"I didn't see Lilia, but I asked around. Bianka died two days ago around three in the afternoon in the main market of Weinbach."

"I'll check it out," Keltson said.

Ammond wrung his hands in front of him. "Please. Rusha won't stop crying and Volker's about ready to kill me for not looking after her. You have to fix this."

"I will. I'll get back to you." Keltson shut off the transmission. Now that he knew where to find Lilia, he could extract her and prevent her from doing any further damage. Finding the latitude and longitude of Weinbach's center square took some research. He put on his vest and mask and jumped to the time Ammond had given him.

Around the old marketplace, people scattered about the square purchasing goods from the canopied shops. They quivered as his eyes scanned his surroundings, threatening to shatter if he looked too long. He looked for Ammond but couldn't see him. However, he did find Bianka. She examined a sewing needle from a vendor's booth.

Seeing her in person felt different than watching her from the other side of a monitor. Her pasty childhood skin had disappeared beneath days of working outside and her peasant clothing suited her. He didn't care for the styles of sixteenth-century nobility. They

plucked their hairline to make their foreheads appear bigger, for goodness sake.

He stared a bit too long, and she burst into twenty different forms.
He shook his head. Why did she have such an extraordinary number of
variances? He refused to study any of them.

Jumping forward a few minutes, Ammond followed her trail. Again
and again, he jumped through the Pause in small increments, watching
Bianka make her way across the market. Finally, she stood at the blacksmith's, speaking to a stooped woman who held out a patterned leather
vest.

Keltson's stomach twisted at the sight of the repulsive woman. Lilia's
dramatic transformation from her younger, graceful self made it difficult to recognize her. But it was definitely her beneath that haggard
form and the frayed cloak. Her long, wiry hair pressed against her scalp
at odd angles. Any shred of personal dignity she possessed lay buried
beneath dirty and tattered clothes.

He jumped forward fifteen seconds. Lilia spoke to Bianka. Fifteen
more seconds. Bianka allowed her to lace up the bodice. Fifteen more
seconds. Lilia ran toward an alleyway while Bianka fled toward the
village square, her face already changing with age. How had Lilia
invented such a horrible time-manipulating device?

Keltson trailed Lilia as she hobbled down an alleyway. The isolation
of the alleyway made a perfect place to confront her. He jumped back to
his cellar, grabbed the portable mirror, and jumped back to the Pause.

Setting the mirror in front of the woman, Keltson planned to grab
her by the throat and pull her into the Pause. He'd have to be careful.
Too many things could go wrong if he exposed himself in the past. His
detainment or death meant game-over for all of his clients.

No matter how he positioned the mirror, Keltson found he would
need to lean through the glass in order to grab her. It was too risky.
Instead, if he could coax her closer, then he could grab her and dump
her old hide somewhere remote where she couldn't mess anything
else up.

He jumped back to the cellar. At his computer, the mirror trans-
mitted Lilia's form in the alleyway. The last time he saw her, dark rings

circled under her eyes, but this time, so much more lay corroded beneath the surface of her skin. Splitting apparently devastated your appearance as well as tore apart your soul. He activated the transmission.

"Lilia!" he shouted. The old woman stumbled to a halt in front of the mirror. Her eyes grew wild.

"Get away from me. I don't need you anymore," she yelled, casting her arms about.

Keltson leaned forward, pointing his finger at the monitor. "You broke every point of your contract. I don't care if you need me. You..."

"Contract! Since when do contracts matter to you? You put more effort into defending that stupid little girl than you ever protected me." She pushed her sleeves back up her arms and sniffed. "You are a failed guardian. You'll never see a single code from me, you worthless fraud."

Keltson swallowed his anger. She wasn't close enough to the mirror. He scowled, waiting for just the right moment.

Lilia sneered at his silence. "Look at you. You act like you're the one saving these people. You're a mask on the other side of the glass. You can't do anything because you're restricted. Well, not me."

"I can't afford to be reckless. I have people counting on me." Keltson gripped his chair's armrest, squeezing his palms into the leather.

"Counting on you? Ha! You're only concerned about your own skin. You left me to be picked up by ITTA all those years ago. You gave me no way out because you were too afraid of what might have happened to you." She pushed the hair out of her eyes, wavering on her feet. "But I don't share your burden. Do you think I cared when they arrested the weaker version of myself? You think I cared at all?"

Keltson swallowed. "You're right Lilia, I do care. A lot. And, because I care, I can't let you succeed."

"You're too late. Without Bianka, I will return to my home and continue living out my story in peace."

"Your home?" Keltson laughed. "You stole Bianka's life! You cast her out. You became worse than Katherina von Hatzfeld, the woman you went back there to stop. Your mind is warped, old woman."

Lilia stiffened. "I can't grow old when I control time."

"That's a lie. Just look at yourself," he said, then allowed the mirror to reflect Lilia instead of the mask. Lilia peered into the mirror, her nose almost touching the surface. Keltson paused the feed.

Perfect.

He darted around the room, gathering a pair of handcuffs, his utility belt, and a rope. Then, just to be safe, he grabbed a pair of mag-gloves. Once he captured Lilia so she couldn't mess up anything else, he might just be able to salvage this situation, get Bianka back home, get Ammond back on track with his directives, and ITTA off his trail. He put his mask on, took a calming breath, and jumped back into the Pause.

Lilia peered into the mirror with distaste. Would Lilia move once he touched her? Keltson put on the mag-gloves, focused, then thrust his arms through the mirror. The mag-gloves made reaching through the mirror feel like reaching through cellophane. He grabbed Lilia's neck with one hand and her hair with the other. The image inside of the mirror came to life. He tried to pull her in, but she grabbed the mirror frame with strength he never would have suspected could live inside her frail looking limbs. Keltson didn't have much leverage to help him. Lilia's hand flew toward the glass and Keltson saw something buzzing with electricity inside her palm.

"No!"

The gem crackled as it hit the surface of the glass, rippling electricity across the mirror and cutting the transmission. The mag-gloves crushed his hands with searing hot pain. He cried out and fell on his back, clawing at the melted remains of the gloves.

They peeled off, sizzling on the frozen ground. The cold air soothed his red, raw skin. Without the barrier the gloves created, his hands might have ended up sheared off and lying at Lilia's feet when she shut down the mirror.

He yelled at the sky. In the Pause, Lilia now stood with the gem in her hand, surrounded by shards of glass. Lilia's gadget had been enough to claim victory in this game of tug-of-war. The mirror frame grew dark, pulled from the Pause and into Lilia's time.

"That was expensive!" he shouted, wishing his hands didn't hurt so he could punch something. Instead, he pushed himself up from the ground and marched around in a circle, growling.

Lilia already disabled two of his other mirrors and had now broken a third one. Only the safehouse mirror remained functional. Mirrors should have been indestructible. Half of their molecules lay in the Pause, frozen in place, rigid, and harder than stone.

Keltson turned on his vest and jumped back to the cellar. He needed to come up with another plan. Pacing back and forth, he wracked his exhausted brain for any possible way to stop her. Just then, he heard his security alarm. He whirled around, gazing toward his home security monitor. Baigh stood on his front steps with a bag of groceries looped over his arm.

"Come on, Kelts. I've got nothin' else to do. Open the door!"

How many times did he have to tell Baigh? He couldn't handle having him here. Far more pressing things weighed down on him. Baigh continued to ring the bell and his voice faded into the back of Keltson's mind as he continued to pace, trying to figure out what he should do.

"I'll make dinner and be out of your hair in a *jiffy*," Baigh said.

Keltson stopped pacing and looked at the screen. Baigh stared into the camera. 'Jiffy' was their secret distress call and could only be used if something was seriously wrong.

"Of all the ruddy times…" Keltson mumbled under his breath.

Keltson scrambled up the ladder, gripping the rungs with his burning hands. He opened the front door, startling his brother. Baigh pasted on a fake smile and stepped inside the door.

"There you are. Did I wake you from a nap?" he asked, speaking too loudly. Like he wanted to be heard. He shut the door behind him, then dropped the bag of groceries on the floor and grasped Keltson by the elbows, looking at his scorched hands. "Kelts, what's happening to you?"

Keltson couldn't stop them from trembling. "It doesn't matter. What are you doing here Baigh? What's wrong?"

"Somebody's watchin ya, Kelts. I noticed him when I left this morning. He's spent all day out there. Talking to neighbors, spyin'."

Keltson groaned.

"You've got to get out of here. Let me help you," Baigh said.

"I appreciate it, Baigh, but I can figure this out. I can't have you mixed up in my troubles." As much as Keltson needed help, he couldn't bring his brother into any of this.

"At this point, they've already seen my face. I'm affiliated. So, whatever is going on, you're not getting rid of me." Baigh shrugged and gave his best mischievous grin, though it was tainted with undeniable worry.

Keltson looked outside and saw a black car pull up next to one identical to it. "I don't have time for this," Keltson said, pointing his finger in his brother's face. "You're coming with me, but I swear if you for one-second step out of line, I'm going to erase every memory you have of me. Do you understand?" Baigh seemed surprised at the threat but nodded. Keltson darted down the hall and threw open the closet, lifted the water heater, and pointed for Baigh to descend the ladder first. Baigh looked at the hole in the ground with wide eyes before stepping in. Keltson followed, making sure everything closed up behind him. He might not have long before ITTA came to investigate.

Baigh reached the floor and blinked at the sudden light. "What is this?" he asked.

As Keltson made his way down, he made sure the water heater slid into place above him. "Have you ever heard of 'The Mirror'?" he asked.

Baigh turned around in excitement. "You work for him?"

Keltson sent him a serious glance, then turned toward his computer. "If you're going to be down here, you need to be silent. None of my clients can know you're here, but I have to keep working. If I don't fix this, ITTA is going to barge in here and destroy everything."

Baigh spun around in a circle, his wild gaze hardly resting on anything before he stopped, staring at Keltson. "Wait, you mean, you *are* The Mirror?"

"It's a stupid name. I wouldna picked it," Keltson said, then held up his finger for silence. Baigh nodded with wide eyes and backed away, studying the corner workstations.

Keltson took a deep breath. He couldn't believe he just exposed his secret. But he couldn't think about the consequences now. He'd worry about Baigh later. He pulled up a new transmission with Ammond. It happened only moments after his previous one. Keltson needed to gather more details before he knew how to save Bianka.

"You don't care at all for her, do you?" Ammond yelled. Keltson swallowed in surprise. But before he could even question what was going on, Ammond resumed shouting. "We came day after day, waiting for instructions. Waiting for Bianka to return to us. But you never came back. Every day. You said you would save her but you lied!"

"Ammond, I've been gone for three minutes. What are you talking about?"

"I mourned Bianka's death for over a year. You have no idea what that did to us. She's like our daughter. And she died in such a horrible way... I had to get her back."

Keltson's eyes widened. "What did you do?"

"I got her back," Ammond said. For the first time, Keltson recognized the dark circles under Ammond's eyes.

The same kind of eyes Lilia earned after she split.

Keltson slammed his fist down on the desk. "I told you I'd be here! I told you I'd bring her back. You, of all people, should know the cost of splitting!"

"It's a sacrifice I can live with," Ammond said. "I don't regret breaking the rules."

"Of course you don't! Because now you can't reason straight."

"I'm not broken," Ammond said between clenched teeth. His hands curled into desperate fists.

"Did you complete the loop? At least tell me there's not two of you I have to deal with..." Keltson said, offering a silent prayer.

"Of course not. I made my other self go back and save her. We agreed it was better not to have to deal with two of us," Ammond said.

Keltson moaned. "Why didn't you follow the rules?"

"Your entire livelihood is made from breaking rules. Why should you get to be selective about them but not me?" Ammond spread his arms in defiance.

"Splitting yourself violates natural laws, not stupid politician's ideals." Keltson ran his burnt fingers through his hair. "Denying those laws is like saying you don't agree with gravity anymore so you're going to jump down the Grand Canyon. There are consequences, Ammond. I can't believe you gave up your sanity for Bianka! I don't know if I can erase what you've done."

"I don't regret taking matters into my own hands," Ammond said.

Keltson ended the call and dropped his head onto his desk. He sat there for a moment, overwhelmed. Everything had unraveled over this one girl. This one, horrible, twisted case. He stood up to check his research library and nearly fell down in surprise at the sight of Baigh standing right behind him. Baigh looked at Keltson in concern.

"Absolutely none of this makes sense to me," Baigh said. "But, whatever is going on down here... I'm in."

"Margaretha von Waldeck spent her last hours in bed, scrawling out her will. Her hand shook with the effects of poison, leaving a clue and allowing historians to work out her unfortunate demise. The King of Spain's desperation for a political marriage must have run deep if he willingly destroyed such a delicate and innocent creature as Margaretha."

-Record of Margaretha's death, Master Document

CHAPTER TWENTY-FIVE

L ilia fell to the ground in front of the shattered mirror, fighting for breath. Her throat pulsed with the memory of The Mirror's grip. Her scalp burned where he tore out her hair. For years she viewed him as a voice inside of the glass. She shuddered. He was a body of flesh and bone.

She looked lovingly down at her palm where she held her gem. It saved her. She made it to hijack the castle mirror and always wore it on her in case of an emergency. The clear shard rippled with the timeless invincibility of the Pause and an electric current. Because of it, this mirror lay in pieces at her feet.

Good. She needed new scraps. The other mirror had served Lilia well, lining the beautiful bodice. Lilia smiled, unable to resist the urge to check on Bianka, to see the confusion surrounding her death.

Lilia lifted herself from the ground. But when she rounded the corner of the alleyway, she stopped short.

Bianka lived. She stood in the center of a crowd with the beautiful bodice abandoned on the ground with its circuitry still sparking. Lilia's dreams burnt to ash. Victory had been in her hands for only a moment. As she finished tightening the last string on the bodice, she saw time taking effect on the girl.

Next to Bianka stood the little man who would ride beside her as she came to invade Lilia's castle.

Lilia snarled.

End Bianka.

Bianka stole the last few years of Lilia's youth from her. Now she could only dream about her finer days. She deserved to be young and beautiful. That's why the idea for the bodice appealed so much to her. Lilia wanted to see Bianka age, to see her beauty melt away. The Mirror served Bianka because of her youth and beauty. If she grew old and withered, he'd drop her as he had dropped Lilia.

But instead, the bodice placed Bianka in the prime of her youth. Watching the beautiful girl standing in the middle of the crowd, Lilia wished she could burn the image from her eyes. The Mirror must be behind this. But why he chose to serve Bianka over his own client remained an infuriating mystery.

Bianka must die.

Lilia scuttled back down the alley and ran her gaze over the glittering glass on the ground. She'd spent much of her time lately salvaging parts to help her build the bodice. Anyone else would have passed over this collection of scraps. Nobody saw the value of these materials like Lilia. Shattered glass, a motherboard, the wire framing of a mirror. Lilia collected every last piece she took from The Mirror. Everything could be repurposed.

Repurposed to kill Bianka.

She scratched at the skin behind her arms and found herself bleeding again. Her cloak had fragments of glass woven into its fibers, enabling her to travel through time without stepping through a mirror. The digital display lay tucked inside her sleeves for easy programming. Her cloak made for efficient time travel but came with a price.

If she could gather these scraps and transport them back to the junk-yard, Lilia would have everything she needed to succeed in the future. She could create another contraption. But this time, she needed to be subtler. She had to be less brazen and the moment of attack more diffi-cult to pinpoint. But what could she do? She needed something else.

Something less apparent. Lilia closed her eyes and tapped her knobby fingers against her forehead as she thought.

End Bianka.

Her eyes snapped open.

She didn't need to invent a new plan. Someone already succeeded in killing Bianka once. The King of Spain had despised Bianka nearly as much as Lilia and poisoned her.

Poison would work.

-Portrait of Margaretha von Waldeck,
Master Document

CHAPTER
TWENTY-SIX

WEILBURG FOREST, *WEILBURG, GERMANY*
12 JUNE 1558

T he entire walk home, Bianka felt shaky and breathless. Her ribs ached from the tight bodice Ammond had cut from her.

He seemed different. Hardened. Perhaps shaken by what happened. She rubbed her arm as she walked, feeling her tight sleeves pull past her wrists.

"I'm still so confused, Ammond. What happened to me?" Bianka asked, glancing at him.

Ammond's face grew tense with anger. "The leather bodice forced you to grow old too quickly. Every second brought you closer to dying."

Bianka swallowed. His words explained why she felt taller and her clothes felt so tight. Her dress no longer dusted the forest floor as she walked. "But why did Lilia want me to grow older?"

"She didn't want you old. She wanted you dead."

Bianka stopped walking.

"Dead?" Bianka whispered. She stared out into the empty forest. Her heart felt hollow, like a fallen tree. "Lilia raised me. What made her so hateful? How did she grow so old? Why is thi—"

Ammond rushed to her side. "Bianka, take a deep breath." He held her wrists and forced her to look him in the eyes.

"Why does this magic follow me and change the people I love?" Her fluttering pulse inside her chest made her hands tremble.

Ammond sighed, his shoulders sagging. "Very few people can wield The Mirror's power responsibly."

She remembered Lilia's sunken eyes, her haunted stare as she glared at Bianka across the courtyard. "When I was inside the mirror, things shattered as I looked at them. People became dark, grizzled versions of themselves. Is that what happened to Lilia?" She looked at Ammond and swallowed. The skin under his eyes filled with the same darkness, as if he hadn't slept in days.

"Yes. The mirror divided her. By returning to a time where she already existed, her mind split. She grew overwhelmed with a selfish motivation. She lost the beautiful, diverse, and complicated parts of herself that made her human." Ammond looked wistful.

"You seem—" Bianka paused, wondering if she should voice her suspicions.

"I seem what?" Ammond asked.

"You seem changed, too. Though not as frightening as her." She paused, hoping she didn't offend him with her words.

He looked at the ground, his lips pursed. "Bianka, you didn't deserve what Lilia did to you today. Returning to this moment meant you could live."

Bianka widened her eyes in surprise. "You... *split*, too?"

"To save you."

A sour taste formed in Bianka's mouth and she struggled to swallow. She remembered Lilia on that day so many years ago when she appeared soaking wet with wild eyes in the corridor. What if Ammond decayed into the same, haggard condition she found Lilia? She couldn't bear if he tried to kill her as she did. Perhaps if she ran back to the cottage, the others would see. Would they know if Ammond was different? Could she abide losing the man she'd relied on all these years?

Ammond reached forward and grasped her hand. "Bianka, you needn't worry. I want to guard you, not destroy you." He stared at her, with those sunken eyes. Could she trust those eyes? "Not many peasants saw what happened. Word won't reach the castle. Lilia won't be able to find you again."

"How can you know that? She found me in the village. How did she know I would be there?"

Ammond shook his head. He didn't have any answers for her. Instead, he reached behind him and pulled out his pack. The bag was stuffed with goods Bianka purchased from the market. He pulled out the remnants of the leather bodice and brought it forward. Bianka flinched, afraid to touch it. The severed stays flickered with magic as they rubbed against each other.

He dropped it to the ground in front of her. "You trust too easily, Bianka. You can't allow yourself to be tempted by kindness and let your guard down. Do you understand?"

She looked at Ammond with concern. "Kindness is not a temptation, Ammond."

"But it can be a weakness."

Ammond always gave Bianka direction and hope. This didn't sound like him. But then again, Lilia's dream of the woman warrior with no armor had fit Bianka's hopes. Did Lilia know her well enough to fabricate such a story to tempt her? Or did Lilia know her future like The Mirror did?

Ammond knelt, resting his forearm against his knee as he leaned toward her. "Bianka, I'll do everything in my power to protect you. I can gather some men from the village I know to be honest. We'll take you home. Lilia does not deserve to live in your stead."

Bianka still sat undecided on whether or not to trust Ammond, but she nodded.

IN THE CLEARING in front of the cottage, Bianka stood with Cenric as a guard. Five peasants emerged from the woods and Urig grunted behind her. She understood how much he disliked compromising the location of the troupe. But recently, Ammond didn't care about anyone else as much as Bianka. All the work on the gold vein had stopped. Ammond left a guard with Bianka at all times and yelled when he saw her unwatched. Rusha stood next to Bianka and shifted her weight back and forth. No one felt secure in this scenario. The troupe had remained isolated so long that having strangers in their clearing felt unsettling.

"My friends," Ammond said to the peasants, stepping forward and listing each of their names as he took their hands.

"How goes the task?" Ammond asked one of the men. "Have any villages agreed to support the countess?"

The man's eyes flicked to Bianka. "People are not yet swayed, sir," he said. "Convincing people that the countess survives so many years after her disappearance is difficult. Even *I* struggled to trust you. But now that I see her myself, I reason she is about the right age and she looks like Herr Waldeck's first wife. I accept the truth of the story, sir."

"Are you suggesting that the others won't believe unless they see her?" Ammond asked.

Cenric stepped forward protectively and the peasants backed away. Despite his small stature, his strong forearms and stance obviously intimidated the scrawny farmers. "Of course they want to draw her out! They know she is too well protected here."

The first peasant stood straighter, not cowed by a physical threat. "We promise to protect Dame Waldeck. But I speak the truth. The young Countess has turned into somewhat of a myth. Her genuine beauty," he said, bowing to Bianka, "must fulfill the people's expectations. Many of the villages are superstitious."

Ammond nodded and turned toward Bianka. "Superstition often drives people into deeper fervor than truth. Though, she does not have any of the finery expected of a countess. What do you say we start putting our gold toward something useful?"

"It *was* going to be useful, Ammond—the missions," Urig interrupted. Ammond held up his hand.

Worry gnawed at Bianka's stomach and she stepped forward. "I will not forget others with a worse fate than mine, Ammond."

Ammond pointed at her sternly. "You deserve to be rescued, too." The grey rings under his eyes darkened and Bianka frowned. She didn't exactly consider going back home a rescue...

Ammond turned back to the peasants. "I want you to assemble a group of ambassadors. No more people than necessary. Choose only those who will be loyal to Herr Waldeck's daughter's return. Ensure they are influential people in their communities. We'll reveal the countess to them once arrangements have been made. I'll give further instructions then."

The peasants nodded, and each bowed to Bianka. However, as she looked around to the rest of the troupe, all of them watched in worry as the men left. She knew confronting him would only bring a string of defensive words, but she didn't want him making rash decisions because of her. She opened her mouth to say something, but Rusha caught her by the wrist and shook her head.

Bianka said nothing.

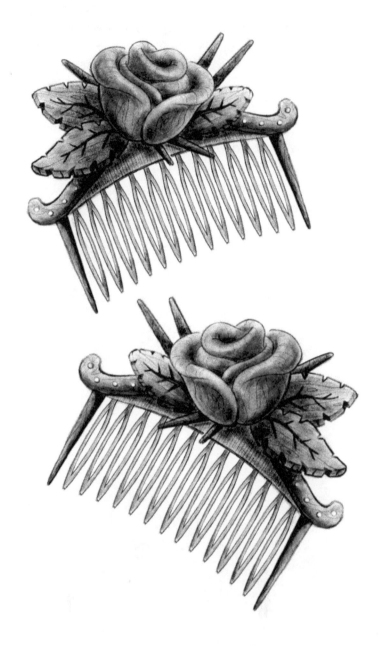

-Sketchbook of Dorothea Wild

CHAPTER
TWENTY-SEVEN

"You look lovely my dear," Rusha said, gazing over her new white linen dress. The girls spent weeks preparing the flax, spinning the fibers, weaving the cloth, and bleaching it for Bianka. Ammond and Cenric embellished the cloth with golden leaves along the hem and sleeves.

Bianka felt it was overly pretentious.

Outside, she heard the murmuring crowd as they waited for a glimpse of "The Countess". According to Ammond, each ambassador would return home and garner support for Bianka's safe passage back home. With a large personal guard, Ammond hoped to shield her from Charul and Lilia until her Father could offer her further protection.

Bianka felt a rush of nerves. What would people think when they saw her? She stood in a homespun linen dress, wearing gold her friends pulled from the dirt of the mountains. She looked older now because of Lilia's magic. For so long she dreamed of returning home, but now she wished to climb under her blankets and wait for everyone to forget about her.

"It's time," Volker said, stepping through the front door, ready to usher Bianka out.

"I can't. I really…" Bianka began. But through the open door she saw the back of a peasant, standing on a stump and shouting to the crowd.

"…the taxes. The roads are littered with bandits. Herr Waldeck has forgotten his own people because of his grief. If we reunite him with his daughter, she can resurrect his desire for justice in the land. She can heal the grieving insanity of his wife that weighs daily on his mind…"

Bianka clutched the front of her dress. Did the people truly suffer in these ways? Did Father miss her that much? Would her return actually help him? It seemed reasonable that Lilia's shattered consciousness might distract her father from his duties.

Bianka took a deep breath and accepted Volker's outstretched arm. He led her through the cottage door and into the bright sunlight beyond. The crowd standing before her stretched into the tree line. The men cheered and the women curtsied. Bianka folded her hands in front of her and shoved her anxiety deeper inside.

Lilia had taught her how to behave like a countess, but those instructions were only a distant memory now. Bianka spent the last three years learning to keep a house and training to fight. She felt stronger and rougher than a countess should be. These people expected beauty and regality. Ever since the bodice aged her, Bianka felt like she wore a stranger's skin. Years and station were supposed to sneak up on you so slowly that you didn't realize the stretching and growth they demanded. But both flew at her now and she struggled to keep her balance with their weight.

She felt too young and insecure for this rollicking crowd. They cheered for all the things they wanted her to be—to save them from injustice, to heal her father's sorrow. How did they know her return would make Father a better count? How could she possibly save others when she needed protection herself?

Despite the torment raging through her head, she graced the crowd with a smile, hoping her expression didn't look too forced. Rusha wasn't fooled. The woman pushed Ammond forward to the stump to draw away some of the attention and grabbed Bianka's shaking hand.

Though Ammond still couldn't see above the crowd, he shouted with a voice that could be heard by all. "Countess Margaretha von Waldeck wishes to return to her home, to end the fearful reign of the count's mad wife, Lilia!"

Another cheer sounded.

"I've had enough of this," Rusha said, pulling Bianka quietly around the side of the cottage. As they sank into the shadows, Bianka felt as if she wore the tightening bodice again, squeezing the life out of her. Rusha led her to the woodpile and Bianka sank down onto the split logs.

"I can't do this, Rusha. Every time I hear the name 'Margaretha' I flinch. That name belonged to my mother. I've never felt worthy of it."

Rusha took Bianka's hand and placed it on her lap. "Bianka, all they want right now is for someone to give authority to their ideals. I don't think it's fair of them, but perhaps your face is all they need. Perhaps you will give them enough hope to fix their own problems."

For some reason, the chastisement of The Mirror popped into her head—another critical voice. He'd warned her about being nothing more than beauty. Beauty crumbled through time and wasn't powerful enough to influence the world. What if she genuinely couldn't give Ammond and these villagers what they needed?

"I am not ready to face them yet," Bianka said. "I need another moment."

"I'll go speak to Ammond. You wait here, dear." Rusha stood and rounded the corner into the bright sunlight. Bianka leaned back and rested her head against the wall of the cottage. But before she could enjoy the relative calm, a voice to her right startled her.

"Oh, the poor dear. She seems overwhelmed."

Bianka straightened and saw two old ladies peeking from behind the house. They each wore white *schürze* and had thin hair braided in a crown around their heads. One had a decorative wooden comb in the shape of a flower tucked behind her ear.

One of them looked embarrassed to be caught staring.

"My apologies, my lady. My sister and I wish to comfort you if we could." She curtsied to Bianka, her entire body shaking with a gentle tremor. The old woman was so wrinkled Bianka wondered how old she was.

"We remember the insecurities of youth and when you disappeared from the crowd, we thought we might offer a few kind words and some confidence for the task," the younger of the two ladies said.

"Your beauty alone is enough to inspire anyone to your side," the elder sister said.

"Thank you. You are very kind," Bianka said.

The elder sister stepped forward, pulling the wooden flower from behind her ear. With a shaking hand, she drew Bianka's thick, dark hair away from her eyes as she placed the comb gently next to the filigree crown.

"Thank you," Bianka said, smiling at the woman's gentle gesture.

"Now, might we escort you back to your place?" the younger sister said, taking Bianka's hand and pulling her along. Bianka swallowed and smoothed down her linen skirt carefully before stepping back into the view of the crowd.

The people immediately surrounded her and she lost her grip on the old woman's satin fingers. Children held out offerings of woodland flowers. Young men attempted to kiss her hand. Mothers held their babes forward to be touched by her. The crowd pressed in on all sides, making it harder and harder to breathe.

She felt as if every person she brushed against might be overtaken by the curse of the mirror; a curse that would leave them shattered by magic. She flinched away from a babe's tiny pink fingers. Tears welled in her eyes and the gazes of the villagers softened in confusion. The noise of their chatter grew. The sun flared above her and she squinted. The faces around her grew grotesque and warped. She flinched away from them. A short man walked toward her, his teeth sharp and stained with blood. Bianka pushed him away harshly and screamed. Her legs stopped working beneath her and she sank to the ground. Pine needles pricked her skin beneath her clothes. The sun grew brighter and brighter. A pair of strong arms cradled her as she slipped into the blinding light.

BIANKA STIRRED IN HER BLANKETS. The cottage was quiet. Opening her eyes hurt.

"You're awake, child?" Rusha asked, dropping her chores and starting over to Bianka's side. She laid the back of her hand against Bianka's cheeks and clicked her tongue. "We feared you wouldn't survive, but Ammond seemed certain."

"What happened?" Bianka asked, carefully. Her throat felt swollen and her breath caught if she inhaled too quickly.

"Poison. That blasted comb. We think Lilia tried to kill you again."

Bianka felt a chill run through her sore veins. She felt burnt from the inside. She struggled to find enough breath to speak.

"Lilia enlisted those women to do that?" Bianka asked.

"No, they *were* Lilia."

"But, there were two of them."

Rusha shifted her weight, licking her lips nervously. "Yes, from what Ammond told us, Lilia became both. I don't understand the magic, but it frightens me."

Bianka closed her eyes again. How long could this go on?

Rusha sank down onto the edge of the bed, her face wrinkled in pain. "When you came around the corner, Ammond burst out of the woods near the mirror, running at you full speed. He wore a disguise, so people didn't realize he was here twice. But we knew it. He pulled the comb from your hair and doused you with a bucket of cold water." Rusha brushed Bianka's sticky hair away from a rather sore spot on her scalp. The same place the comb had rested in her hair. "You only wore the comb for a moment, but the poison's touch was enough to bring you near to death. Ammond said that the first time, her poison killed you. But he hoped you would pull through. He said your convulsions weren't as strong as before and that you originally died within a few—" She hiccupped and looked down at the blankets. "Oh, child... all this. I am so sorry."

"There are two of Ammond now?" Bianka asked.

"No child. He told himself to go through the mirror to save you. There's only one. But it's all so strange, I still have trouble sorting it out."

Bianka stared blankly toward the door. It was closed, preventing sunlight from filling the room. "I'm no longer safe in either of my homes. Was it not enough for Lilia to drive me from my family, that now she threatens my life with my friends?"

Rusha sniffed and rubbed her eyes. Those kind warm eyes...

"Where is Ammond?" If Rusha spoke the truth and Ammond had returned to save Bianka again... A heavy weight settled on her heart.

Rusha hesitated. "He's out working. He'll be home tonight. They're going to make the final rescue in Greece tomorrow."

"He's decided to return to his original plans?" Bianka asked, allowing herself to feel hopeful.

Rusha pinched her mouth to the side. "He has. You should have seen Cenric and Volker when he told them they would be moving forward with the extraction. They were completely insufferable. They chopped up half the woods in anticipation."

Bianka giggled. "I am glad that Ammond remembered what the gold was meant for. I only hope this is the end of his endeavors to get me home."

Rusha grew somber again.

"What is wrong?" Bianka asked warily. "Has Ammond *not* found himself?"

"That man is far more confusing that I can account for. He wants an entire troupe of men to escort you home and vowed that Lilia will never harm you again. Once they return, it's your turn, dear."

Bianka wilted back onto the pillow, feeling weak and shaky.

Ammond was willing to pull these men from a life of fighting and survival and throw them at a woman determined to kill her? Had he lost sight of everything he stood for in the beginning?

"Oh, you're probably starving dear," Rusha said. "I can boil some vegetables for a calming broth for you if you'd like."

"Yes, that would be wonderful, thank you Rusha." Bianka closed her eyes. For an instant, she imagined things could go back to the way they belonged. But Lilia seemed determined to cut short any happy moment Bianka found. Her childhood in the castle, her life here with Ammond's troupe. Where could she possibly go next, now that neither place was safe?

"Duplication is a process that may occur after an agent repeats a timeline. If the original agent fails to duplicate the initial jump that caused the split agent, two versions of the same person will exist in the same timeline. When duplication occurs, the unstable agent must be eliminated and the primary agent restrained from ever returning to their past."

-ITTA guidebook

CHAPTER
TWENTY-EIGHT

Zapasnoy Junkyard, Yekaterinburg, Russia
Pause

L ilia held the soldering gun with nimble fingers. Twenty years of living in the castle made the mechanical device feel foreign. Surprisingly, she still had a stable hand. That was more than she could say for her other half; her kidnapper. The woman twitched with age.

"It must be smooth. It must be subtle," the old woman said, running her fingers along the scrappy metal sheet in front of her.

"Who cares about subtlety? Nothing about killing is subtle." Lilia sent a flash of sparks up past her mask. Subtlety wouldn't *stop Bianka*.

"I brought you here to build, not to critique," the old woman snapped. She returned to obsessing over the metal frame before her, inspecting every nook and cranny with shaking fingers. "There can be no broken seams if we want to *stop her*. There can be no weaknesses if we want to *end her*. It must be *subtle*," she whispered to herself.

Lilia turned back to her soldering. She worked on a motherboard panel and tried to figure out the old woman's program as she built. As far as Lilia could tell, she was to place the motherboard in a panel behind a salvaged mirror frame.

The mirror didn't work any longer, not since Lilia shattered it. That was for the best. Lilia didn't trust any machine that could be run by The Mirror.

LILIA POLISHED the glass screen with the hem of her sleeve. Her younger, careless self continually mucked it up with fingerprints. *Subtlety.* No fingerprints meant invisibility. And they couldn't afford to be seen, now could they? This hodgepodge medley of scrapped parts made her proud. It didn't look as natural as The Mirror's creations, but Lilia was a scrap mechanic, not a craftsman.

"Isn't it beautiful?" she asked, stepping back. "This creation of our enemy is perfected under our hands, Lilia. This will *end Bianka.*"

"I'd hardly call it beautiful," her younger self said. "You warped the large panels when you melted them together."

"Beauty lies in function, dearest," Lilia said.

"Well, *your* shaky hand would never have enabled this motherboard to function."

"That's what you're here for, darling," Lilia said to her younger self.

LILIA PAUSED over the finished circuitry. She didn't know what the old woman planned to do with this machine, but she surmised bits and pieces as she worked on the mainframe. And as long as it *stopped Bianka*, did anything else matter? Her best guess was that this machine froze time. Not the most original idea, since The Mirror already invented that.

Put together, the machine formed a long casket with the frame of the mirror as a lid. Lilia didn't know what was inside the metal container. The glass that covered the top was so dark and tarnished, she couldn't see through. She finished the last bit of soldering on the motherboard and stood up to attach it to the box.

HER YOUNGER SELF worked with efficiency, as Lilia had hoped. Her precious invention was finished. Now was the moment to see if it worked.

"Wait just a second, love," Lilia said, stooping over the mirror. She lifted the lid from the box, revealing a hollow casket inside. She plugged the new motherboard into the side panel and activated the mechanism. She closed the mirror lid and it hissed as it sealed itself shut.

"Help me stand it upright," she whispered. Together the two lifted the mirror into position. The glass blinked to life. They came to the front and admired their handiwork.

"What does it do?" her younger self asked.

How foolish of her not to recognize after all this time. "It's a time capsule," Lilia said.

"But you've sealed it with nothing inside."

"Not yet," Lilia said, imagining Bianka's frozen body filling the chamber.

"Sometimes I wonder what my life would have been like without mirrors. Would I feel as lost as I do now? Surely not. I would have been home. Home is where children are meant to find themselves."

-Journal entry of Bianka Cirksena

CHAPTER
TWENTY-NINE

A mmond stood beside Bianka's bedside, dressed in traveling clothes. "We'll only be gone a few moments my dear," he said. "When we return from Greece, we'll have even more arms to defend you."

"I don't wish to pull those tired men directly into another battle, Ammond," Bianka said, not bothering to rise. She still felt weak from the poison and only managed to stand for short spurts of time.

Ammond scowled. "You may not care for your own safety, but I do. You deser—"

"I know," she interrupted him. "You keep saying that. But think about what others deserve as well. Not just me."

Ammond narrowed his eyes. Though he obsessed over her safety, he didn't care much about her opinions these days. She hated the magic that stole his true self away.

"I won't argue with you. We will be back soon," he said, then strode out the front door. Bianka saw most of the troupe waiting anxiously outside, dressed in an array of togas and sandals.

Cenric and Volker snuck down from the loft above her, sending her solemn glances. They had equipped themselves with their old armor, looking more comfortable than they had in months. Their bare arms showcased a myriad of scars that Bianka had forgotten about.

Cenric approached the foot of her bed. "Thank you for your words, Bianka. While we are eager to rescue other unfortunates like ourselves, we don't like Ammond's desire to use them."

"Are these new men soldiers like you?" Bianka asked, nodding at the gladiators.

"No, but they were slaves like us. Their masters underfed them, hoping to shorten their stature even more to fetch a higher price for their novelty."

"How could anyone—"

"Don't upset the girl," Ammond said abruptly from the door. "She's frail enough as it is. No need to disturb her. Soon they'll be strong enough to bear arms like you."

Bianka pursed her lips together in frustration. "Did you sacrifice all the good, kind, gentle parts of yourself to save me? Because I hardly think that was worth it."

Ammond looked hurt and she immediately regretted her words. She never snapped like that at anyone. For a moment, he softened, looking vulnerable. When he spoke, his voice wasn't filled with the authority it usually carried. "Come, men."

A tear of worry sprung up in Bianka's eye as the men left the cottage. What if that was the last thing she said to him? She tried to calm herself by remembering that The Mirror could reverse their errors until they emerged victorious. But even though his magic saved her life more than once, she also saw the cost. It worried her.

Silence filled the cottage as the troupe made their way up the path to the mirror. She snuggled deeper into her bed and listened to a bird chirping quietly in the distance. The breeze rustled the leaves outside the open front door. Then there was no sound at all.

A dark sense of foreboding gripped Bianka while she waited. Hadn't Ammond explained how bringing their new comrades back would only take a few moments? Bianka pushed herself upright. Perhaps she should wait in the chair for a more proper introduction. She slid her legs out from under the covers and moved to the chair near the front door.

Bianka felt light-headed and breathless as she sat. But here she had a better view of the trail.

She waited.

As the minutes passed, her throat dried out and the sounds of the forest grew too lonely.

Bianka stood unsteadily and walked to the front door.

"Rusha?" she called. No one answered her weak voice back through the woods.

Terror pulsed through her. She stepped forward, shivering. They should be back by now. Bianka stumbled forward, grasped the edge of the garden fence, and looked up the empty trail. Her legs trembled beneath her. She didn't have the strength to go after them.

Then, from behind her, came a strange rushing sound. She turned and saw a mirror, appearing by magic in the center of the clearing. Surprised relief coursed through her body. But as the mirror came into focus, she wrinkled her nose in confusion. The scrappy frame looked like mismatched armor hammered together. Cracks ran through the glass, forming shards that jutted out in wide angles, reflecting darkness.

"Mirror?" she asked, painstakingly pushing herself from the fence. The mask didn't appear inside. She caught hold of the frame to help her balance.

Why was this here? Did The Mirror send it to her because he needed her to warn the others of their failed mission? The glass flickered with faint light. But instead of the mask, an apple appeared, resting on a fine wooden table.

Everything around the fruit slowly grew brighter. The image focused even more, revealing a large hall with a fireplace and green velvet seats. She gasped. It was the dining room! *Her* dining room. Seeing her childhood home after so many years brought back all the painful yearning she felt when she first arrived at the cottage.

A man walked into view.

Father.

He looked as young as she remembered him in her very first memories. A young girl followed him into the picture. Her breath caught in her throat.

It was her. Bianka.

The image shattered and faded into darkness.

"What is this?" Bianka whispered.

The Mirror's mask appeared, though his face flickered in and out of sight like flashes of lightning. His voice sounded panicked and unnatural.

"I'm unable to maintain... You must remain hidden... mirror in the forest..." His face disappeared.

"Mirror? What is going on?" Bianka asked, gripping the sides of the frame. The mask faded into darkness and a new face appeared in the glass. Though it was distorted and his skin glowed unnaturally, Bianka recognized the handsome boy.

Charul.

"Margaretha von Waldeck, I am coming to arrest... for violating the... Time Travel Summit of... You will be taken... headquarters to..."

His face disappeared just as The Mirror's had. Bianka shuddered with the strain of fear. Charul was coming here? For her? The reflection flickered again, revealing the apple again. This time, a soft, compelling voice spoke through the mirror though no face accompanied the image. The voice reminded her of Rusha.

"Child, you have been through so much. So many forces pull you in different directions. The Mirror wants you to stay hidden in the forest. The Huntsman wants to take you away. Ammond wants to restore you to your broken home. I grant you the choice to choose your own path. Too long the powers of time have sat out of your reach. Powers that The Mirror, Lilia, Charul, and Ammond all manipulate.

"But I must warn you of the costs. As you know, it is easy to lose your way inside this magic. The Mirror is in peril of being captured. Lilia is no longer the woman you once knew. Charul heartlessly follows orders. And most devastating of all, Ammond and his comrades lie dead in the ancient past."

Bianka clutched the front of her dress, trying to hold back a sob for her friends.

"On the other side of this mirror lies the fate of your choosing. Even, a life without mirrors."

The thought made Bianka's mind whirl. She felt excitement for the possibility, yet fear for what she might lose.

"You may return to your childhood, leave the magic behind you, and live your life as it was meant to be. Without Lilia. Without The Mirror. Without the Huntsman. And without forcing Ammond to split to save you.

"He will be able to complete his missions as he originally wished, return to the cottage with his full troupe of comrades who will never be trapped in the past."

Bianka's heart tightened. She was the root of everyone's misfortune. They often acted desperately to save her, fragmenting their own lives in the process. If she removed the magic from her life, would everyone be healed?

In the mirror's reflection, Bianka saw Father lift his young daughter and gently hand her the apple. The child took a ferocious bite from it and he laughed heartily.

Could she really return? To live again with Father? A chance without Lilia?

"But wouldn't I split? Just like Lilia? Just like Ammond?" she asked.

"This magic is offered to you as a gift. You won't split like the others. Instead, the cost lies in your memories. You won't remember any of this. Life will be as it should have been—everything restored to its proper place, without magic."

Whether she stayed or left, she had already lost the companionship of the wonderful people who had loved her. Ammond and Lilia were broken because of it. Rusha, Cenric, Volker, Urig, Gunther, and Mathilda were gone, lost in the past.

She watched her younger self eat the apple, handing Father a bite every so often.

A life without magic? A life surrounded by the love of her family that she missed so terribly. The love she longed to return to. A life with no deception. Surely there would be heartaches, but it would be a life guided by her own conscience. And most importantly, a life where her friends could succeed. Without her.

Bianka moved before she realized her decision. She reached her hand forward and pushed it gently into the surface of the glass. Her skin prickled from the cold on the other side of the mirror. Bianka felt fear ripple through her arm, remembering the terrifying time she spent inside the eternal forest. She soothed herself by remembering that this time would be different.

Holding the rim, Bianka pulled her foot over the threshold of the frame. She pressed her face into the glass, letting the soothing chill rush over her skin. But, before she passed completely through, Bianka turned, staring longingly back at the life she was leaving behind.

"I am satisfied that there is probable cause to believe that:
[x] Suspect #1: Grammar, Keltson DOB: 3/7/2047, black hair, brown
eyes, 5'8", 190 lbs.
[x] on the premises of 92 Gallowgate Rd. A single standing structure
with grey brick and white trim with the numbers "92" on the front post.
In the city of Carntyne, County of Edinburgh, Scotland, there is now
possessed or concealed certain illegal property described as:
Photon acceleration technology
Stolen confidential database files
Firearms

-Search warrant issued to ITTA special operatives

CHAPTER
THIRTY

"I still can't believe this. You... you are The Mirror?" Baigh asked, leaning over the desk.

Keltson plugged in his external hard drive and began downloading all the information from his computer onto the device.

"I mean, you're one of the biggest myths in the world right now! I thought I was all 'bad-A' getting locked up for chump change when my little brother was breaking international laws!" Baigh threw his arms around Keltson's shoulders and squeezed him like a vice. "I'm not sure if I should be jealous or proud."

Keltson pinched Baigh's arm and he yelped, releasing Keltson. "Look, as long as you're down here, you help out. If ITTA is already watching my house, that means they could arrive with a warrant any second. If I can put this drive into..."

Keltson stopped as his door alarm went off. He looked toward his monitor and saw an entire team assembled on his front porch. They rang the doorbell. Two guys in the back shifted anxiously, looking like they wanted to kick in the door.

Baigh scratched his beard. "So, since you can time travel, can you... You know... make them disappear?"

"It doesn't work that way, Baigh," Keltson said, grabbing a tarp from off a shelf. He spread it on the ground then grabbed an extension cord that would enable the tarp to connect to his vest. That way, anything he laid atop the tarp would transport along with him.

"I'd help, but I don't imagine you have time to train me or anything," Baigh said, shoving his hands in his pockets.

"Just pretend like you're looting the place."

Baigh straightened up and smiled. "Now that, I definitely can do." He jumped on top of the desk and rummaged through the top shelf of equipment, tossing it over his shoulder toward the tarp.

"Careful! That stuff is expensive!" Keltson said.

Baigh nodded from his perch near the ceiling, then picked up a six-inch strand of wire with two fingers and delicately laid it out on the counter at his feet. He even took the time to smooth it out.

"Seriously? We're about to be arrested!" Keltson strapped on his utility belt and set his toolbox on top of the tarp.

Baigh looked over at him and smiled. Just then, the men on the porch kicked in the front door. Baigh looked up at the ceiling and pointed, his face suddenly concerned.

"Just be quiet," Keltson whispered.

Baigh switched gears. Now that the threat was right above them and he heard their footsteps, he ransacked the cellar alongside Keltson with efficiency and precision. They moved everything onto the tarp quietly. The trap door under the water heater might hide them for a while, but it wasn't foolproof.

Keltson still couldn't believe this. He thought he had at least a few days before Lilia gave ITTA enough information to peg him. As much as he hated that Baigh was mixed up in this, he also felt grateful he wasn't down here alone, panicking as he tried to pack up his life's work.

"How exactly did you get in this mess?" Baigh whispered.

"A Russian mechanic named Lilia," Keltson said, pulling a number of electronic records off his bookshelf and scattering them across the tarp.

"Sounds attractive," Baigh said, raising an eyebrow.

"I'll introduce you to the hag sometime," Keltson struggled to conceal the loathing in his voice. "Time changes people. Turns them. In this work, I've learned not to trust anyone but myself—I knew this would happen. I knew it. Why did I expect anything less? Even Ammond..." Keltson trailed off, realizing that none of this made any sense to Baigh.

Baigh shrugged. "That's the trouble when you start breaking the rules. You think you know which rules are worth breaking. But then the people around you start thinking if you can break one rule, why not another? And another," Baigh trailed off.

Maybe Baigh understood better than Keltson thought. "I can't afford to fall through on them. Even if they're all insane. I'll finish what I promised."

There was another heavy *thump* from upstairs followed by the sound of marbles scattering across the floor. Apparently, they already decided to tear apart the house for incriminating evidence. He heard them pull down his media shelf. If they wanted secrets, they'd be rewarded. He knew the media shelf looked suspicious so he had cut a crawlspace into the wall behind it that led under the stairs. Keltson had filled the space with childhood mementos. Hopefully, their discovery would buy him a few extra minutes.

He checked on the external hard drive. It still needed two more minutes to finish the program transfer. Hopefully they had enough time. Keltson joined Baigh throwing things onto the tarp: tools, detectors, battery packs, etc. He wouldn't leave anything incriminating behind.

"Where exactly are we taking all this?" Baigh asked.

"To a safehouse we should be able to crash at."

If he could get all of this equipment to Ammond's, it could potentially save all of his twenty-seven previous clients from being found by ITTA. Once Keltson got to Ammond's, he would do everything in his power to stop Lilia from ever becoming a client in the first place.

He paused.

Stopping Lilia meant restoring Bianka's timeline to its original poisonous fate. If he went to Ammond's, could he honestly stand in front of her and condemn her to return to her old life? Keltson shook his head. He couldn't do this to himself. Lilia was sent back to save her, sure, but instead, she tried killing Bianka. Bianka didn't need Lilia. Keltson could always find another, more qualified client to complete her rescue. He went back to his computer to continue checking on the software wipe.

"Great job, Keltson. Really great stepmother you gave her," Keltson whispered to himself.

"What was that?" Baigh asked.

"Sorry, I'm used to talking to myself down here," Keltson said. A buzz sounded from the computer. The hard drive was completely empty.

Keltson unplugged the cord, and just like that the cellar was retired. He looked around longingly at the empty screens. Band posters and guitars still covered the walls. It killed him to leave this all behind. Keltson couldn't resist. He picked up his acoustic guitar and placed it on the tarp.

"What next?" Baigh asked.

Keltson walked over to the soundboard and looked at the last song he played—it was the Coroners condemnation of ITTA.

He turned it on.

"What are you doing?" Baigh asked. "They're going to hear..." He pointed to the ceiling.

The song began quietly, then grew.

Let them find his cellar. Once he left, the only things they would find down here were a line of monitors and a blank hard drive. He left no other trace of time travel down here. ITTA needed a sign that they were right about him. That way it would hurt more when they knew they couldn't do anything about it. The music would be thundering by the time the agents finally made it down into the cellar. He imagined their faces as the lyrics blasted their crimes into their faces. He picked up his mask from the pile and put it on just as the Coroners' voices came in, singing about the injustice of time travel laws. The footsteps upstairs went silent as the investigators listened for the direction of the music.

Baigh watched Keltson in disbelief. "You know you're not a super-hero, right?" he asked.

"What are you talking about?" Keltson avoided Baigh's gaze by pretending to fix something on his utility belt.

"A mask, theme song, and we're about to jump through time? Maybe dial it back a notch."

Keltson scowled. "I knew you were jealous," he said, lifting his vest over his shoulders. He plugged it into the tarp's extension cord. With half a smile, he pressed his thumb against the ignition on the vest. The entire tarp glowed with the fiber-optic lining that enabled it to correspond with the photon acceleration technology inside his vest. Everything else around them faded into the Pause and formed into the clearing outside Ammond's cottage.

Odd shadows flickered through the warped trees surrounding him. A cluster of trees exploded to his right as Baigh focused on them.

"Holy—" Baigh said, leaping back and wrapping his arms around himself.

"I forgot to warn you. It's cold here. And things explode," Keltson said.

"What's wrong with this place?" Baigh asked, looking around with wild eyes.

"We're in the Pause," Keltson said. He looked around the empty clearing. Perhaps Ammond's troupe still waited near their mirror, helping the newly rescued Grecians process what just happened to them. He turned back to Baigh, just in time to see him step off the tarp.

"Baigh!" Keltson yelled, but Baigh's body fizzled as time pulled him into the stream of the real world. Keltson sighed. It probably wasn't the worst thing, but Keltson wanted to scope things out before he jumped into the clearing.

He unhooked the tarp's extension cord and the entire pile of equipment faded into the clearing along with the now frozen Baigh. Keltson did his best not to focus on his brother. He didn't want to see all the things he could have been. So, instead, he turned his back on him, glancing around the clearing. Things seemed fine.

Keltson jumped out of the Pause and felt the characteristic tingling that came along with re-entering time.

"Gyah!" Baigh shouted as they both materialized into the clearing.

"Don't worry, Baigh. The feeling will wear off," Keltson said. He shivered, trying to dispel the tingling from his skin. The leaves rustled around them, and Keltson took a deep breath of the fresh air. The air never smelled like this in Carntyne. It was a scent with no exhaust, no pollution. Just the forest.

Exactly the way Keltson liked it.

-Sketchbook of Dorothea Wild

CHAPTER
THIRTY-ONE

Bianka found herself inside an icy room as large as the cottage. The frozen air bit through her thin frock. Memories of the eternal forest flashed before her eyes, but she pressed down her panic. Fortunately, nothing here shattered. The stagnant air around her felt as if she were the only disturbance it had ever experienced.

Frosted mirrors lined the walls. Each of them sat lifeless and dark, except for one. On the other side of the room, a mirror reflected the happy scene of her father with the apple. Bianka made her way toward it, her bare feet hating every step on the icy floor. She reached the glass and placed a hopeful hand on the pane. It held solid. Bianka blinked in confusion and pushed on it harder. The glass crackled under her hand and the vision of her childhood disappeared. Instead, a familiar, terrible face appeared.

Lilia laughed at her.

"Did you really think you could relive your life as a child? You know what happens when you repeat your timeline. You've seen it in me and in your pathetic friend. Yet you took the risk." Her eyes narrowed and she shook her head. "Do you believe the rules don't apply to you? You should know better by now. You trusted the bodice. You trusted the comb. And now you trusted in the worst invention yet."

"No," Bianka whispered, stepping back from the mirror. This couldn't be happening.

Lilia caressed her wrinkled hands and leaned forward in the mirror. "You'll relive the past alright... But not your own. Please, observe all the helpless moments when others tried their best to save you and failed. The times they sacrificed everything for you. You'll watch, knowing where all their efforts led... To this frozen time capsule. Frozen forever, never aging, never living."

Tears sprung from Bianka's eyes. She couldn't stay here. She couldn't!

"So, sleep well, fair Bianka. Enjoy your vision of the past one last time."

Lilia's cackle was the last thing she heard as the mirror went dark. Bianka looked around desperately, panic rising inside of her. The mirrors remained blank. How could Lilia have done this? Bianka couldn't save her friends. She couldn't go home.

One of the mirrors on the wall to her left lit up. She took a shaky breath and wrapped her trembling arms around herself. Cracks divided the mirror into three pieces. A little girl appeared on the other side, peering through the frosted glass as if through a window.

"Hello?" Bianka asked.

"There's a girl here," the little girl called over her shoulder to an invisible friend. The girl held a red, lush apple in her hand. Bianka gasped. It was her—the childhood image that tempted her into the mirror. The girl took a bite of the apple and tilted her head as she studied Bianka. In another piece of the glass, a blurred form appeared over the girl's shoulder. Father? But the figure was too short and slight. It came near and her face cleared through the fog.

It was Bianka again, yet this one was older and wore a fine dress as if she were going to a feast.

"She wanted my apple," the little girl said, looking up at the older Bianka.

"Why is she asleep?" the elder asked. The two talked as if admiring a portrait.

"I'm here! Help me," Bianka said, leaning forward. She thumped her hand on the glass. Neither of the girls responded.

"What is she wearing?" another voice asked in confusion. A third form appeared in the final shattered piece of glass. This time, it was an older woman, though Bianka immediately recognized it as herself at an age she had not yet reached. This one wore a thick cloak and removed her hood as she came closer. Bianka shivered, jealously imagining the warmth the cloak offered.

"Her dress is so plain," the older woman said. The other two nodded.

"I think it makes her look pretty, in a simple sort of way," the middle Bianka said.

"She looks nothing like what Lilia would have wanted," the eldest said in a scolding sort of way.

"Or Father," the youngest said, holding the apple in front of her with both hands. The glass mirror began to frost over.

"You must help me! It's so cold!" Bianka fingered the frosty patterns. It was climbing inward quickly.

"Perhaps when she wakes, we can help her find something suitable to wear," the eldest said, taking a step back into the fog.

"Yes," the second said. "I don't want to miss the next dance." She lilted away. But the youngest sat, staring at the mirror, curiously eating her apple as the frost closed in and Bianka could no longer see out of the frame.

"I'm not sure how long Lilia plotted inside the Pause. She used an endless stream of years to create a whole slew of contraptions. Enough time to grow old. Baigh and I can't find any clues about what caused the demise of the safehouse, but I have a suspicion that Lilia may be behind it."

-Logbook of Keltson Grammar

CHAPTER
THIRTY-TWO

L ilia set the dials and moved the casket effortlessly across the clearing. Yes. This spot gave Ammond's troupe the best view of the terrible surprise she had in store for them. The little troupe stood, frozen before her in the Pause.

For the first time in years, the pulsing voices in her head disappeared. All except one.

Subtlety.

"You promised you'd return me after we trapped Bianka," her younger self said, holding up the chain that bound her ankle to the casket.

What was she whining about? Her skin was free of the wrinkles of time that Lilia carried. Her only flaw was the dark circles under her eyes that had grown darker after long weeks of work in the back corners of the Zapasnoy Junkyard. Lilia stood just outside the perimeter of the tether's reach. She might love her younger self, but she didn't trust her.

Still and calm.

"This is the last piece, darling. You will be home soon enough." Lilia tossed a pair of iron-soled shoes to the younger Lilia.

"No. I'm done making things for you. You have your casket with Bianka trapped inside. Now return me to Philip like you promised."

Lilia ignored her plea. "I thought you might recognize these slippers," she said.

Her younger self picked them up and turned the shoes over in her hands. "What have you done to them?"

You must be subtle.

"They are your ticket home, love. You only need to attach the bit of filigree to the adapter. My hands aren't steady enough to manage it."

"And these will get me back to Philip?" her younger self asked, hope flickering in her desperate gaze.

Lilia nodded. "Just complete the circuitry."

The younger woman paused, her forehead wrinkling in concern. She inspected the task Lilia handed her. Those slippers were from her wedding—the prime of her youth, the best years of her life. Lilia smiled. What she wouldn't give to fill those shoes again.

But Philip would never take her back like this.

Only a few more quiet steps.

Her younger self tensed in the middle of her inspection and glared up at Lilia. "I can't see the interface. I'm not working on anything else that I don't understand. Tell me, what will these really do?"

Lilia clasped her hands delicately in front of her, trying to remember the posture she so often assumed in her days in Philip's castle. "It uses the same technology that ITTA shields their Mother Document with. With these, you will never be corrupted. You will live in a circle of eternal youth. A present for your hard work. And for quieting the thrumming in my head."

"Are these for you or for me?" her younger self asked warily.

Lilia laughed, wiping at her watery eyes. "You think I want to stay like this forever? No. Your present is my past. Whatever happens to you will change my life, darling."

Subtly.

"You really figured out how to do this?" the young woman asked, breathlessly.

"Please. Darling. Do you doubt me?" She pulled out a pair of needle-nose pliers and scalar wire. The woman didn't flinch. Lilia sighed and shook her head. "Come. Finish the job. My bones ache constantly now and I can't stop the tremors in my hands."

The young woman relaxed, exhaled, and reached carefully toward the supplies. "Just—don't rush me."

Lilia smiled. Yes, this technology would be a miracle. And it would work. She knew it. With this contraption, she would return to the prime of her youth whenever she felt she was growing too old. Her reign would last into the eternities. Lilia watched the younger woman work with ease, picking up her tools with fluid movements.

The woman snickered as she twisted the wire into the CPU socket. "You know, it's ironic that you intend to remove Bianka from time and give me the ability to endure it."

Lilia smiled. No, it wasn't ironic. It was perfectly planned, calculated over the decades.

Subtle.

The last voice still remained in her head. The motivation meant for herself.

Lilia spent too much time revisiting her stolen years, trying to reclaim them. But after this, there would be no more lost youth, glass ceilings, or forbidden love. Her life would go on happily, *forever* after.

"I struggle to understand how Lilia managed to shatter my mirrors. The devices are unique because they exist in two separate planes. They can be moved in the normal flow of time, or in The Pause with no special equipment. Everything else must be pulled into the Pause with the photovoltaic transmitter to be moved. The Pause causes the mirror's molecules to move so slowly that they are nearly indestructible in real time. And yet, the tool Lilia held in her hand still managed to shatter the glass..."

-Logbook of Keltson Grammar

CHAPTER
THIRTY-THREE

K eltson awoke to the smell of burnt bacon. He stretched and covered his face with the scratchy woolen blanket.

"Are you ever going to wake up?" Baigh asked, banging two pots together on purpose.

"No," Keltson growled. After cramming twelve years' worth of time-line into the last two days without sleep, he deserved to wake up whatever time of day he wanted.

"Well, I'm obviously no expert on camp ware cooking, but this didn't turn out half bad," Baigh said through a mouthful of overly crunchy meat.

Keltson groaned and yawned.

Baigh scraped the cast-iron pot with a fork. "I don't know how you can sleep so soundly when your friends just up and disappeared."

"Whatever happened to them is already done. I can fix it. But it doesn't matter if I work now or later." Keltson pulled the blanket over his head.

"But you blew me off because you had 'work,'" Baigh said, scowling.

"Just because I deal with people in the past doesn't mean I didn't have a schedule. Time still mattered in the present," Keltson said, rolling around, trying to find a comfortable position on the stiff hay mattress.

"You sound like you don't even care."

Keltson threw the blanket off his head and sat up to glower at Baigh who inspected a charred piece of salt pork. He looked over at Keltson and held out the briquette. "Breakfast?" he asked.

"No, thanks." Keltson climbed out of the beds he spent the night in. He went out to the yard and washed his face, feeling unnerved about how quiet the woods felt.

Once back inside, he grabbed a heel of stale bread from a basket. "I'm going to find them today. I want you to stay here and set up a workspace for me." He nodded toward the table littered with equipment.

"You're not taking me on your adventure?" Baigh asked, dropping the pan on the table.

"Only have one vest," Keltson said, lifting it from the table.

"What about that tarpy thingy?" Baigh waved his hand in the direction of the device.

"I'm not taking you, Baigh."

Baigh scowled.

"Don't worry," Keltson said, picking up his mask. "It will feel like one second to you. Unless something goes wrong."

"Then what?"

"Then you should find a nice girl in the local village and settle down."

"Don't you even—"

But Keltson merely grabbed his mask from the table and stepped outside. He set the coordinates to the Pause for the moment Ammond jumped to Greece, put on the mask, then pressed the ignition and appeared in a clearing. Ammond and the troupe stood frozen around the mirror, but he found something odd there. On the opposite side of the clearing, two women looked up at him in fear.

It was Lilia.

Twice.

Keltson didn't even think. He barreled toward them. The younger of the two scrambled away like a scavenging rodent. She stumbled and fell to the ground only a few meters away. A long chain attached at her ankle trailed from a strange metal box, preventing her from running.

The elder one stood with wide eyes, watching as he ran to tackle her.

That's the one he'd take down first. Keltson couldn't afford to lose another single piece of equipment. He didn't care if she was old. He really wanted her to feel this.

Keltson crashed into her, pinning her at an awkward angle to the ground. She squealed and wriggled beneath him. He pinned her hands down to the sides as he looked up into the face of the other.

"What have you done? Why are there two of you? What are you doing here?" His mask muffled his voice.

The chained Lilia looked at him curiously and the woman pinned beneath him laughed, a light witchy sound. Keltson struggled not to pull his hands away from her wrists with disgust.

"Mirror?" she asked, staring blankly up at him.

The younger Lilia smirked. "Even wearing a mask here, too."

Keltson was glad he had thought to put it on *before* coming to the Pause. The old hag chuckled again, her laugh mingled with a hacking cough. "All these years, I imagined you tall and handsome. And here you are a squatty little brute. Not above pinning an old lady to the ground either, I see."

"You aren't anything like a lady." Keltson's voice rumbled with anger. Both women laughed, the sound echoing strangely from both sides of him.

"What are you doing here?" Keltson asked.

"You don't care for us. So, we fend for ourselves now," the eldest Lilia said.

"You were supposed to protect a little girl." Keltson frowned.

"She's a wretched thing."

"Where is she?" he asked.

"How strangely protective of her, you are. A bit like that dwarf." Lilia sneered and her gaze turned cold. "You never cared about us as much as you cared about that girl. *'Save Bianka. Support Bianka. Teach her to be a real countess.'* Well, why should I teach her to be a countess when they already had a perfectly suitable one like me?" She smirked, obviously enjoying the look of frustration on Keltson's face. "Oh, your precious Bianka. Well, you needn't worry about her anymore."

"What did you do?" Terror coursed through his veins.

"That wench cast her net around everyone. That dwarf would do anything to save her. Even become crazy to save her. Crazy, like us," the elder Lilia cackled. The younger Lilia glowered. She apparently didn't like being called crazy.

"No matter how many times you multiply, you'll never be worth even half of Bianka," Keltson said. Both the Lilia's fell silent and he saw the fire flashing in their eyes. Even though the elder one's body was brittle, he feared the wrath coiled within her.

"At first, I only wanted to stop her. When I succeeded, it was the sweetest bliss I've ever known. But when she returned, the voices came too, telling me to *stop her.* I knew that to truly silence the voices, I needed to kill her. But I was too desperate, like this one here," she said, motioning to the younger Lilia. "I forgot one sacred element to murder. Subtlety. A trait that I once believed in and had long forgotten. So now I plot and I plan calmly while others scramble over themselves to save the poor withering peasant." She coughed with a sudden attack.

"So much for subtlety, darling, you gave away your entire plot," the second Lilia scoffed, rubbing her ankle where the chain rubbed her raw skin.

"Well, I've succeeded, haven't I? Am I not allowed to gloat in the brilliance of my plan?"

"Our plan," younger Lilia demanded. "It wouldn't have worked without me."

"Where is she?" Keltson yelled, putting pressure on Lilia's wrists to make her feel uncomfortable. She didn't seem to mind at all.

"My hands are old. I can't hold a wire steady as I once did. Not like she can," older Lilia said, nodding her head toward the younger Lilia. "So, I went back and got her. Isn't she lovely, Mirror?" She nodded toward her younger self, her eyes glistening with adoration. "You don't care, do you? Oh, well. I'm tired of being held in this horribly uncomfortable position." Lilia shifted her weight and her cloak crackled strangely. Blood seeped along the ground beneath her, pooling in the thin wisps of her hair. Keltson pulled back her cloak and saw that bits of shattered glass wove through the fabric like jewels. Keltson's eyes widened as Lilia blinked out from beneath his hands.

"Ugh." The younger Lilia rolled her eyes. "She thinks her contraptions are so amusing. But I can see its benefit right about now." The remaining Lilia backed away from Keltson as much as her chain would allow.

"That shouldn't be possible," he muttered.

"She can jump wherever she wants, whenever she wants. Every time I see her, she's older. It's nice to finally meet you, by the way. I'm far happier to be with you than her. Lilia brought me to the in-between. She promised I could go home if I finished these," she said, lifting her hem, revealing a pair of ironclad shoes.

"What do they do?"

"She said they'd take me home, but so far I'm still stuck here, only able to walk in circles."

Keltson's eyes followed the chain that led from her ankle to the metal box on the edge of the clearing.

"And what is this?" he asked, taking a step closer. But just then, the elder Lilia reappeared directly behind the younger Lilia.

"Watch out!" Keltson shouted as the old woman slapped a magnetic tether to the iron shoes and pressed a button. The younger Lilia shook as electricity pulsed through her. Two seconds later, the elder Lilia fell to the ground and the younger Lilia stopped shaking.

"Are you alright?" Keltson asked. Lilia checked her hands and arms, then touched her face, and nodded quickly. Keltson turned toward the old woman, who lay deathly still next to her. The younger Lilia blinked at Keltson for a second, then knelt next to the older woman. A smile crept along the corner of her mouth, and with a quick motion, she whirled the hem of the cloak around her and pressed the ignition on Lilia's cloak.

"No!" Keltson said, reaching out as the two women disappeared. He lost them! Unbelievable. He turned around, looking at the metal box in the clearing. The chain that once attached Lilia's ankle to the device lay tangled on the ground. The glass face was dark without any kind of projection. The longer he looked at it, the lower his stomach sank.

"You've got to be kidding me," he whispered, recognizing bits and pieces of his hijacked mirror. He groaned and hit the outside of the box with his fist. The Pause made a perfect lair for Lilia to build devices without consequence.

Worry clawed at his stomach. He'd located Ammond and the troupe but found no hint of Bianka.

Maybe Ammond knew. Keltson set the coordinates on his vest for sixty seconds before Ammond arrived in Greece, then made the jump. The clearing immediately emptied of everything except the mirror and he felt relief at leaving the Pause. If he explained their failed mission, perhaps they could help him find Bianka.

Ammond stepped through the mirror first. Confusion set in as he saw Keltson's mask. The others in the troupe followed him through the glass and also paused when they saw Keltson.

"Hello, Ammond," Keltson said.

"What are you doing here?" Ammond asked.

"I've been compromised. And Bianka is missing. This mission…" But before Keltson could say anything else, there was a loud pop. They turned and saw Lilia's metal box fizzle into the clearing. Foreboding settled over Keltson.

Everyone rushed toward the contraption and a few gasps sounded. Rusha covered her mouth with her hand. The glass had cleared with the flow of time and Keltson could see inside.

Bianka lay in the middle of the casket, frozen in the Pause. Her torso twisted as she attempted to look back through the closed mirror behind her. Her hair lay splayed around her face, a thin strand curled against her icy cheek. Keltson leaned against the frame.

He'd seen Bianka so many times through the mirror surveillance. He'd even seen her from the Pause where the light was faded and dark. But he had never seen her while he was in the flow of time.

She was even more beautiful here.

"We have to open it!" Volker shouted, hefting his ax above his head. Before Keltson could stop him, the ax ricocheted off the glass and threw Volker's balance backwards. Not even a scratch hinted the surface.

"Is there a latch?" Urig asked, inspecting the casket.

Keltson scanned Lilia's creation. What did this device even do?

"Can it be lifted?" Ammond asked. The crew strained together, unable to lift the box more than a few centimeters from the ground.

"I've never seen anything like this," Keltson said.

"What do we do?" Rusha asked. A tear trickled down her cheek. The casket grew colder with every passing moment and ice began to form on the inside of the glass. Frosted crystals scattered across the edges of the mirror, slowly threatening to close in around Bianka.

Keltson knelt down and ran his fingers over the welded metal seams in the side of the casket. "We need to get it back home to the clearing. We can figure out what to do from there."

Before they could move, a clattering noise sounded on the road below them. A group of five bearded priests in long white togas with red trim stared up at the group in awe.

"By the gods!" one of the priests whispered in Latin.

Keltson bristled. Not only did he wear straight cut jeans and a t-shirt with a guitar on the front, but an entire troupe of little people surrounded him, standing next to a glass coffin with a frozen girl inside.

He might as well call ITTA personally.

The priests hunched their shoulders and raised their arms in front of them as they stepped closer. Volker and Cenric lifted their spears in warning and the priests flinched. Keltson checked to make sure his mask still sat securely in place. The troupe around him took courage, shouting down at the group to scare them off. The priests didn't back away quickly enough. Their gaze wandered toward the metal coffin. Volker and Cenric didn't wait. They rushed down the hill and the priests scattered just in time to reveal a group of centurions on the road behind them.

"Help us!" the priests cried, pointing at Keltson and his group. "These pygmies attacked us on our way to make an offering to Poseidon."

The centurions drew their short swords and Cenric and Volker stumbled to a halt.

"What did you call me?" Cenric raged, his face turning red. Volker held him back.

"They stole something," another priest said, motioning up to the casket holding Bianka. Keltson's stomach tightened.

"Drop your weapons!" the lead centurion said, raising his sword. "You dare anger Poseidon by threatening his priests?"

No one moved.

"I said drop your weapons," he said again.

"We have done nothing wrong," Ammond said, puffing up his chest.

The centurion smirked.

"You have no rights here, pygmy."

Ammond's cheeks flared red with anger. The insult proved too much for Cenric. He yelled and raised his ax. The centurions moved quickly, darting behind each of the dwarves to cut off any form of retreat. They scooped Urig and Rusha up from behind, lifting their feet into the air and pinning their arms to their sides. Cenric and Volker lifted their weapons, darting around the centurions and deflecting their strikes easily. The soldiers didn't expect a fight and the pair of gladiators were ruthless in their tactics. A life in the arena taught them to fight like it really mattered.

Keltson stepped back as he realized the futility of it all. He still wore the travel vest and could easily escape if he needed to. But he needed to know exactly what happened to these people so he could know what to prevent.

Keltson surrendered and Ammond shot him a hateful glance. He felt stupid giving up so easily while those around him struggled, but sometimes strategy was the only way to win.

Ammond's fist connected with the side plate of a centurion's helmet. He yelled out in pain and a soldier nicked the side of his arm with a sword before tackling Ammond to the ground. Some of the centurions stood back, chuckling at the scrambling troupe. There were at least two trained soldiers for every one in Ammond's group. Keltson glanced at the casket where Bianka slept peacefully.

The fight ended quickly.

"This is what you were sending us into?" Ammond yelled. "A group of centurions and priests? We never stood a chance!"

Keltson had to calm the pit of anxiety in his stomach. No one was at the controls. The group—including himself—were at the mercy of history. If something went wrong, there might not be any going back.

He wouldn't let that happen.

The priests carefully stepped toward Bianka's casket.

"Chione!" one of the priests cried, looking into the frost-bitten mirror. Even from here, Keltson saw the priest admiring the glistening crystals forming on the inside of the casket. The other priests rushed forward and gasped as they saw Bianka frozen inside. A few of them fell and offered worship to the girl in the box. Keltson looked at Volker and Cenric for help. Volker went pale.

"Who is Chione?" Keltson whispered in German, receiving a decent shove from the guard holding him back.

"She is the goddess of snow. Poseidon's lover," Volker said. Keltson closed his eyes and groaned. This could not be happening. Without another word, the priests stood, scattering around the casket and lifting it like pallbearers.

"Whoa! Whoa!" Ammond shouted, struggling again. "Where are you going with that?" he asked the priests. Apparently, he knew Latin from his days at ITTA.

"This is Poseidon's love. We must return her to the temple. How dare you take her!" one of the priests shouted. The rest of Ammond's troupe struggled against the soldiers' grips, complaining loudly in German, a language the Grecians didn't understand. The soldiers laughed and tossed their victims to the ground.

"Bring the prisoners to Poseidon's temple. He will decide their punishment for kidnapping his love and causing this deep sleep."

Ammond struggled against the centurion behind him and earned a sharp knock in the back of his head for his efforts. The soldiers tied their prisoners to a long line and pulled them along as they followed the priests. Mathilda cried. Ammond cast infuriated glances back at Keltson.

After an hour, a clifftop temple appeared. Its marble columns overlooked the coastline. Above the portico was a sculpted depiction of a muscular hero grappling with a centaur. Blackened stones surrounded a pyre built atop an altar. The priests brought the casket bearing Bianka forward and laid it atop the wooden pyre.

"You can't do this! She's still alive in there!" Rusha cried.

"She belongs on Mount Olympus. We shall provide her the quickest route to the gods," a priest said. Both gladiators turned a shade paler than normal. Ammond's jaw muscles clenched and unclenched as he stared at the priests as they mixed water and wine together as a preliminary libation.

Keltson watched in horror as the priests lit the pyre on fire. He fingered the escape button on his vest, realizing that this timeline held no happy ending. Ammond's troupe shouted and struggled. Gunther managed to quietly undo his bonds and ran along the line, pulling his comrades free. Cenric and Volker ran toward the flames. The rest scattered. Mathilda ran for the market. Rusha ran toward a well, shouting for water.

Ammond yelled over at Keltson. "Do something!"

"I *will* fix this," Keltson shouted as Ammond barreled into the legs of a priest.

"You'd better," Ammond growled, pummeling the priest with his fists.

Keltson pressed the emergency escape button and blinked out of the tumult.

"The mirror's glass is embedded with data-storing photo pixels. I can project images on its surface, such as my avatar or my client's future location. However, I took the technology a step further, giving the pixels memory. The glass stores data recordings of everything it sees. I invented it hoping to retain variance recordings, but unfortunately, once the timeline changes, the data adapts to the new history instantaneously."

-Logbook of Keltson Grammar

CHAPTER THIRTY-FOUR

B ianka felt the chill in her bones sink deeper as she looked at her frosted reflection in the mirror. The girls had seen her, but acted like strangers inspecting a dead body in a coffin.

There had to be a way out of this foreboding place. A dozen mirrors still lined the room, dark and blank. She tried to push down her anxiety. Memories of the frozen eternal forest pressed in around her, but being trapped in this metal box felt infinitely worse. Before, she ran through forests, with the hope of a beacon guiding her way. Here, mirrors tempted her with possibilities for escape, and yet, she doubted any one of them would ever let her through. Moving toward a mirror, she tried to pry it off the wall. It didn't budge.

A hesitant glow emanated behind her as another mirror lit with a new scene. She hobbled toward it, her muscles tense from the chill. The mirror flickered as if it yearned to show her something, but didn't have the strength.

"Please," she whispered.

The mirror slowly revealed a stone room with no windows. Glowing pictures lined a long metal desk on one side. On the other side of the room, green starlight flickered on a shelf filled with thin books. Strange lyres hung on the walls and in the distant corner a blacksmith with a rounded knight's helmet held a fiery tool, melting two metal plates together. The glass on the front of his faceplate flickered with the intense light he held. She blinked and had to look away.

At last, the light in his hands died down and the man removed his helmet.

The young man had a square jawline and his dark hair cast upward in odd angles from his helmet. He wasn't tall like Father, but he seemed strong. He picked up the sheets of metal and moved toward Bianka's mirror.

"Hello?" she shouted and pounded on the surface. Walking up to the glass, he held the metal plate up to the base and began fastening it. He ignored her completely. It was worse than when she saw herself on the other side of the mirror. This man seemed completely oblivious to her presence inside the glass. But why was the mirror showing her this? She cast her eyes around, looking for any clue that might help her.

Bianka stopped breathing.

On the desk behind him lay a single white mask. Was this the face behind the mirror all these years? Someone her own age?

She knelt down to the level of his face so she could study him as he worked on the base of the mirror. He had such a kind face, full of so much expression as he worked. Not at all like the emotionally dead mask he hid behind. She leaned her hand against the mirror for balance. The cold from the glass sank into her palm.

His eyes were dark, like hers.

"It's you," she muttered, pressing even closer to the glass. The corners already began to frost over, just as the first mirror had done.

He reached behind him and pulled a tool from his craftsman belt. She never realized The Mirror might be a craftsman. Was this really magic then? He used human tools to create the mirror. There was no conjuring going on. But how could she explain the starlight on the shelves? Or the glowing pictures on the desk? Or the way the mirror transported people from one place to another?

Could it be these were nothing more than contraptions of science? She shook her head and pulled her arms in to warm herself. Her chin quivered. The frost on the mirror continued to grow.

The man on the other side of the glass hesitated. He stared at the corner of the glass. Then, pulling out a cloth, wiped at a spot. Bianka's palm had left a handprint in the quickly forming ice. He leaned in closer, examining the fingerprints of her hand.

Bianka's heart leaped. Could he truly see?

He muttered a few words in a language Bianka couldn't understand. She pounded against the glass again. The mirror would be completely frozen over any second.

"Help! You must help me!"

The man compared her handprint to his own hands.

"You must find me!" she shouted, banging on the glass until it froze into solid ice.

"Keltson,

The mission fails. Abort current directives. Replace with the following:
Leave Bianka in the clearing. Get the troupe home immediately through
the mirror. (Don't hang around or you'll split.)
Coordinates: Depart- Greece 7:35, Arrive- Cottage 9:10
Duplicate this note and place it in the clearing to complete the loop.
Depart- Cottage 9:15, Arrive- Greece 7:25 (the night before)
Jump to the clearing after troupe has left.
Depart- Greece 7:33, Arrive- Greece 7:45
Follow Bianka to the temple of Poseidon and observe events at the pyre.
See if variances occur. However, if her fiery fate still remains the same,
good luck."

-Note found in the clearing

CHAPTER
THIRTY-FIVE

K eltson appeared in front of the cottage and grabbed his head as a new memory rippled through his brain. He remembered inspecting a foreign handprint inside his mirror in the cellar. It remained an unsolved mystery that he struggled to reconcile.

Baigh stepped out of the front door. "I really don't think you should be going out there alone, Kelts. Anything could happen."

"I'm already back." Keltson groaned, pressing against his forehead.

Baigh's eyes widened and he rushed forward in concern. "What happened to you?"

Keltson pushed past him. "I'm fine, it's just—a memory."

He needed to get back and stop the tragedy in Greece. Inside the cottage, Keltson rummaged through the pile of tools. He needed to send himself a message, but none of his communication equipment ran without electricity.

"What do you mean you're already back? Where'd you go?" Baigh asked.

"Greece," Keltson said, plowing through the disorganized piles on the table. "I can't work like this!"

"Did you find who you were looking for?"

"Yes. And I have to leave them a message or they'll be captured. I need to send myself a message, but for that I have to set up a monitor, get my generator going, upload my masked avatar interface. Then I can isolate the coordinates and make the broadcast."

"Or," Baigh said, reaching into his back pocket and pulling out a pen. He held it toward Keltson, who stared at it blankly. Keltson hadn't thought of using a pen. He'd spent so many years relaying messages through the mirror that it felt like the only way.

"Yeah. That works." Keltson grabbed the pen and rummaged around for a piece of paper.

He scribbled on a half-used notepad, giving departure and arrival times. He might not know how to save Bianka yet, but at least he could get the troupe back home. It required a lot of jumping back and forth, but he would manage. It felt odd writing directives for himself the same way he did for clients.

He thought about bringing the tarp to lay beneath Bianka's casket after it fell.

No, while the troupe had managed to lift the casket a few centimeters, it was only for a moment. He couldn't risk ripping the device as they tried to slide it beneath the jagged metal. Blast. He would have to watch to see if the priests still took the casket along with them without the troupe there.

"All this makes sense to you?" Baigh asked, peering at the directives over Keltson's shoulder.

"Perfect sense." Keltson scribbled out a departure time, realizing it was too small of a window and rewrote the directions. "It'll get me as far as I need to go. I'll bring a few friends back in a minute. I want you to wait outside and welcome them. They only speak German. Do you still remember how to speak it?"

Baigh massaged the back of his neck. "I haven't spoken a word since Oma died."

"Well, do your best. I'll warn them you're here."

This would work. Keltson picked up the note and set the coordinates for Greece then jumped back into the clearing early in the evening, a day before anyone else arrived. He wanted to give himself plenty of time in case he needed to come back again and change directions. The sun lay low beneath the tree line. Keltson found a long, straight branch and hammered it into the ground with a rock. Then, he speared the note on top and took a step back. Hopefully this worked.

Because he was changing the course of his own past, there was a loop to complete. He needed to follow the directions on the note so he ended up exactly where his new memories would put him. Otherwise he'd run the risk of duplicating. While having two of himself floating around sounded tempting—and helpful—it also put him at greater risk for splitting. So, he glanced down the list to step three, set his coordinates and skipped forward, hoping against hope that the troupe actually left.

The sun instantaneously changed position in the sky and Bianka's casket appeared in front of him. A nerve in the back of his head snapped as a new memory popped into his brain. Finding the note had offered him hope. He liked knowing that someone watched over him. Ammond's group hadn't gone easily. They fussed over the coffin, but ultimately trusted him when he said it was the only way. Relief rushed through his body as he realized they had made it back through the mirror and to the safehouse. At least that part of the directive came easily.

Yet even as the new memory settled, he felt the old knowledge remaining inside him. While completing a loop couldn't heal a split, it did allow you to retain both memories, the old and the new.

The priests would arrive any minute. He did his best to cover Bianka's casket with fallen boughs so it wouldn't draw their attention. But the sound of their footfalls arrived all too soon up the road. Keltson slipped into the trees to hide.

Just like before, the priests and centurions found the coffin, calling her Chione. They carried the casket toward the temple of Poseidon. Keltson followed at a distance, watching as the soldiers escorted the priests to the temple of Poseidon. Just like before, the priests lit the pyre.

Keltson closed his eyes and pressed his fingers against his temples. He didn't know what to do beyond this. What would he have told his clients to do?

Don't do anything stupid. Report and I'll guide you.

He pressed the ignition and jumped back to the cottage clearing. He found Baigh waiting nervously by the door and Keltson heard Ammond and the others make their way from the mirror in the forest toward the cottage.

Baigh rubbed his temples and squeezed his eyes shut. "I'm not going to get used to this, Kelts. I'm just not. You popping back and forth like this... How are you staying sane?"

Keltson chuckled. "I'm not, Baigh. I haven't felt sane for a long time." He turned to face Ammond and realized too late that he wasn't wearing his mask. The troupe paused at the base of the hill and froze. The wall he'd carefully built around himself was gone. He was completely exposed and vulnerable

"I knew you were a kid!" Ammond shouted, pointing his finger at Keltson.

"We don't have time for this. I need your professional advice."

Ammond walked forward. "I don't like leaving Bianka behind."

"I'm going back to get her, but I need a plan. I need your help." Keltson explained how Bianka's coffin would burn at Poseidon's temple. He gave Ammond the time frame restrictions and coordinates.

"Now, how do I save her?" Keltson asked.

"You're usually the one with all the answers." Ammond folded his arms and frowned.

"Yes, well, I had to leave my research library and surveillance behind."

Ammond still stood in his defensive stance, his eyes darkening every second. Keltson opened his fists and held his palms toward Ammond. "This is all I have. You are my new library. Teach me."

Ammond only watched Keltson. His eyes searched him, looking for something. Keltson swallowed and waited, hoping that his sincerity showed through.

Ammond sighed. "What kind of equipment do you have?"

"My newest mirror is malfunctioning. I can't explain it. The surface sometimes fogs, lighting up when I haven't activated it. The other day, I found a handprint. Smaller than mine. Sometimes I feel like something inside it is breathing."

-Logbook of Keltson Grammar

CHAPTER
THIRTY-SIX

Another mirror lit in Bianka's room. She struggled to convince her feet to move across the cold floor. Inside, the un-masked man sat at his desk, looking into one of the illuminated frames. Images flashed like pages turning in a book. He shook his head and leaned back, muttering something at the ceiling. Bianka wished she understood him.

A new picture lit up the entire surface. It was a portrait of her—one that she never saw commissioned, perhaps from a different life. She wore a white dress and looked about eighteen. He drummed his fingers on the desk, but before anything useful happened, the mirror began to frost over. Bianka desperately clawed at the glass. Perhaps if she could leave him a message through the mirror.

*Don't trust...*were the only words she was able to scrape into the frost before it became too thick. Her shoulders tensed and she yelled in frustration.

"Lilia! Don't trust Lilia!"

Another mirror began to light up. She scrambled toward it as quickly as her tired limbs allowed her. This time he spoke in German. Finally, something she understood. She saw the face in the frame.

It was her.

She remembered the day her suspicions about Rusha and Ammond led her to confront The Mirror. Again, she heard him speak the harsh words that drove her to dig deeper within herself. But instead of disinterested or critical, the man seemed genuinely intent on their conversation. She watched as the girl in his frame backed away from the mirror, defeated.

But instead of looking pleased with himself, the man seemed concerned. He scribbled notes on a pad, then paused to pull the painting back into the frame. But the picture had changed. Instead of a young teenage girl in a delicate white dress, she was a woman in her twenties. She wore a gossamer crown and simple homespun gown. In the background of the painting was her father's castle. The man leaned back in his chair and exhaled.

Was this a moment in her future? Had he helped shape another path for her? A path that led her back home? The Mirror had never given her permission to return, so she assumed he didn't desire it. But watching him study her, it made her wonder if perhaps she was wrong.

The mirror began to frost over again. She couldn't imagine scratching her numb fingers through the ice again. Instead, she leaned forward, hoping that her warm breath would prevent the ice from forming so quickly. Her breath fogged in front of her and the man looked up. She could barely make him out through the fog, but he stood and crossed toward her.

She tried to wipe a message into the fog, but it had already formed into the thinnest layer of ice. The scene on the other side of the glass dimmed.

Again.

She needed another mirror to light up. If the fog could capture his attention early on, perhaps she could write something in it before the glass froze over.

Two mirrors aside from where she stood, the glass lit with a scene. The man spoke in frustration to Lilia in one of his miniature frames.

"Do you remember why I sent you there, Lilia?" he asked.

Lilia spoke with a flat tone, her spine rigid. "To stop Bianka from being sent away. To save her from being killed."

The words gripped Bianka's heart.

"And do you know what will happen if you get caught by ITTA?" he asked.

"I'll be extracted, arrested, and live the rest of my life in prison."

"Yes. But that's not all. This timeline will be returned to its original state. A place where you never arrived, where Philip marries Katherina, and where *Margaretha* dies. Every mistake you make, you put her life on the line. Are pockets and compacts really worth that?"

This was a moment before everything went wrong- before Charul had tried to arrest her- before it was too late. Bianka's heart raced. She had to warn him. She had to let him know what Lilia was about to do.

Bianka breathed on the mirror again, but the man's focus was so fixated on Lilia that it didn't matter. Perhaps she could leave a message and it would freeze into the ice for later. He had tried to wipe away the handprint. Perhaps he would see this.

Lilia betrays us all

The glass fogged over and she hoped it would be enough.

But, as the seconds ticked on, she remained locked away in this horrible room. It didn't work. Lilia still ran through Bianka's past, trying to kill her. More than half of the mirrors in the room were frosted over now. Her opportunities were running out.

The next mirror lit up with a scene. Though this time, the man wasn't in the windowless room. Instead, he stood in a time-frozen alley-way. The light bent oddly around him. He looked tired and disheveled, like he hadn't slept in far too long. He put on a pair of black gauntlets and stared intently at the mirror, bracing himself for something. His dark eyes studied the mirror and he leaned forward, slowly.

This was her moment. Bianka leaned forward to expose the last bit of warmth her breath possessed onto the mirror when his hands suddenly jutted forward toward the glass. She shrieked and fell back with the unexpected movement. She saw him struggling to pull something through the mirror. Light flared around his gauntleted hands. He growled in frustration.

Suddenly, the mirror shattered and darkened.

What had happened? She wanted to yell in frustration. She didn't understand why the mirrors surrounding her were showing her such things. As she sat with her eyes closed, trying not to let the cold seep deeper into her bones, Lilia's last words to her recounted through her mind.

"Please, observe all the helpless moments when others tried their best to save you and failed. The times they sacrificed everything for you. You'll watch, knowing where all their efforts led... To this frozen time capsule."

Bianka's eyes flew open. How often had this man worked to protect her? For years she saw Ammond and Rusha's efforts. They were held close to her heart. But in her mind, she always believed that The Mirror didn't think once about her.

But piecing all these moments together meant something more.

"Do you remember why I sent you there, Lilia?" he had asked. From the very beginning, he meant for Lilia to save her. Had that been his entire intent this whole time?

To help *her*?

The cold didn't bite her skin so fiercely as she stood in the center of the room. Despite her trembling body, she waited with a focused intensity for the next vision to begin. She must help him. He had worked too hard to fail.

-Sketchbook of Dorothea Wild

CHAPTER
THIRTY-SEVEN

K eltson held his head in his hands waiting for the pain to subside. Ammond stood with his hand on his shoulder as the memories came in a wave, one after another.

Don't trust...

Unexplained fog in the mirror.

Lilia betrays us all.

Bianka was trying to warn him. He wasn't sure how, but she lived and breathed inside the time capsule, doing all she could to help them. Her efforts only set his resolve even more.

Keltson sat up, his headache rushing away as quickly as it had come. In the clearing, Baigh ran back and forth from the river, filling every bucket, basin, and barrel the cottage had with water. The troupe gathered blankets, brooms, shovels and other items they needed to put out the incoming fire.

"We can do this." Keltson closed his fists, then looked at Ammond.

"You're sure you can't rescue her before she is put on the pyre?" Ammond asked.

"Until the priests set her down, the tarp won't work."

"Try to get her here before it burns too much, will you?" Ammond growled.

"I will," Keltson said. It had taken a lot of convincing to get Ammond to stay home, but he agreed once Keltson put him in charge of managing commands and the fire brigade. Together, they had worked out a new set of directives and etched them firmly into Keltson's brain.

"Good luck, kid." Ammond held out a flashlight and Keltson attached it to his utility belt. Ammond watched him, not blinking, his chest rising and falling heavily with concern.

Stepping back, Keltson nodded to everyone in the clearing before jumping back to Poseidon's temple. The cloud-covered night sky prevented the moon from lighting the temple courtyard. Unfortunately, the steps ahead were dimly lit by torches. They lined the perimeter of the sacrificial altar. Keltson crept up the stairs and lay the tarp down in the center of the altar, spreading it out and wincing with each crinkle it made.

Even with the invisibility feature, it stood out like a lumpy rug. In the daylight it would be worse. Perhaps if he built the pyre atop it himself? He folded the corners of the tarp to fit the stone slab, then lined it with split logs that rested along the side of the temple.

Sweat dripped down the sides of his face and his back by the time he finished, but hopefully, no one would recognize the tarp underneath the wood. The extension cord trailed along the edge of the pyre, so he set it in a location that hopefully wouldn't be too guarded by Centurions. He planned to jump directly here, plug it into his vest and transport the entire thing away to the clearing. Keltson only hoped the troupe could douse the fire before it did any damage. He didn't want any harm coming to Bianka inside it and he didn't know how heat transferred through the mirror.

He adjusted the settings on his vest and got ready to jump. He needed to arrive after he left the burning pyre so he didn't accidentally duplicate himself and split. He pressed the ignition.

The world around him brightened instantly with daylight and he squinted. The priests standing closest to him stumbled back, startled by Keltson's sudden appearance. Ahead of him, flames began to climb up the sides of Bianka's coffin.

"Hermes!" a priest yelled, picking up a long staff to defend Bianka.

Keltson rolled his eyes in frustration and bent down to pick up the extension cord. Before he could plug it into the vest, the priest struck him in the chest, knocking him onto his back. The group of priests surrounded the casket protectively, and the centurions rushed toward Keltson, holding out their spears.

Keltson ground his teeth and pressed the emergency jump button that transported him back into the middle of the night. Everyone disappeared. Perhaps he could draw them off of the cord? He pushed himself up from the ground and walked to the other side of the newly built pyre. He braced himself, then hit the return button, appearing back immediately after he disappeared in front of the priests.

He felt the warmth of the flames. The soldiers stared in disbelief at the place where Keltson disappeared mere moments before. Behind them now, he shouted and they whirled toward him in shock. He backed away, hoping to draw them to this side of the pyre, away from the extension cord.

A few men started after him, but to his dismay, a priest with the staff leaned down and picked up the end of the extension cord and ordered the others to make a protective ring around the pyre.

Keltson wouldn't give up. He darted back and forth, jumping strategically around priests as they swung their fists at him. A centurion grabbed him from behind and Keltson pressed the emergency transport button, disappearing from his arms.

Back in the still of the night, Keltson pounded his fist against the stones. He stooped next to the cord and picked it up, looking at it in frustration. It was right here in his hands, so easy to access now when the coffin wasn't available to transport. However, when the moment came, it was impossible. But he wouldn't give up. Not yet. If he moved its location, perhaps it would be unguarded. He pulled it to the other side of the coffin and dropped it on the ground there. But as he jumped forward into the daylight, he found the priests still huddled around the wire. A new memory arose—he struggled to remember which thought held the true location of the cord.

Each time Keltson jumped back and forth, the fire grew larger, turning the metal box with Bianka inside a deeper black. Again and again and again he tried. About fifty people surrounded the coffin, determined to keep him away. Some pointed spears in his direction. Others swung swords if he came too near. This wasn't the way. Keltson jumped back to the clearing, breathing heavily, the idea of Bianka burning in the timeless coffin ate at him. He couldn't allow that to happen. He needed to save her.

He jumped back to Ammond's clearing panting and sweaty. The entire troupe looked at him in concern.

"I can't do it. There's too many of them. I couldn't get through."

A solemn silence fell over the clearing. Rusha started to cry.

"I'm not giving up, I just... I need to find another way."

He looked at Ammond, whose eyes were focused and fiery. "I have another idea. But it's drastic," Ammond said.

"I think we have to be drastic at this point," Keltson said.

"YOU'RE ASKING me to bury you under a burning pyre?" Keltson asked in disbelief.

Everyone gathered around the equipment on the newly cleared table.

Ammond leaned forward on his elbows. "You said you can't get to the extension cord because the others are guarding it. If I hide inside the pyre with the vest hooked directly to the tarp, then all I have to do is wait for Bianka and transport her back here. There's no fighting, there's no chance for failure."

"If I were to bury you in the pyre at night, you'd split again in the morning when the whole troupe shows up."

"It's a sacrifice I've made before," Ammond said. Though his shoulders remained square and his chin lifted in confidence, Keltson saw a glint of fear in the back of his eyes. If Ammond recognized the risk, that meant there was enough sanity within the man to save him. But splitting again might be enough to break him entirely. The others glanced nervously at each other.

"No, I'm not letting you split," Keltson said firmly. Ammond looked ready to argue, but Keltson held up his hand. "You've already split twice. If you were to do it again, you may not survive the mental strain."

"We don't have any other options!" Ammond shouted. "We have to save her!"

Keltson looked across the table at Ammond. The man was split enough to think of something crazy like this. He closed his eyes and shook his head.

For years, he sent others back, coaching them to fight through impossible situations. But now he couldn't even solve his own vigilante mission. He looked down at his arms, covered in a multitude of cuts and scrapes from the swords as he threw himself desperately toward the cord. The determination to succeed fueled his desperation.

"I'll do it myself," Keltson said.

"Keltson," Baigh said, looking worried.

"Bianka is stuck in that infernal machine because of me. I have to save her. No matter what. I can't let Lilia win at this."

"But splitting?" Baigh said. "Even I know how dangerous that is."

Keltson pursed his lips together. "It's the right thing to do."

"Chione, named after the goddess of snow, boasted she was more beautiful than the goddess Artemis and was killed by her arrow. Her father, Daedalion, overcome with grief, tried to jump into the funeral pyre with his daughter and was stopped by the priests."

-Greek myth of Chione

CHAPTER
THIRTY-EIGHT

LILIA'S TIME CAPSULE
PAUSE

The mirrors stopped showing images of the man. In fact, the ice had begun to melt and the room felt warmer, though despite the humid air Bianka's teeth wouldn't stop chattering.

The mirrors around her flickered with the faintest of warm red lights. It made her wish even more earnestly for home; for the hearth near the table, or for Rusha's stove. Bianka felt herself slipping in and out of feverish memories. She was still so weak from the poison and now the cold wore her down even further.

The floor was finally warm enough to lie on. Bianka closed her eyes and wondered, for the first time, why she felt warm inside the mirror.

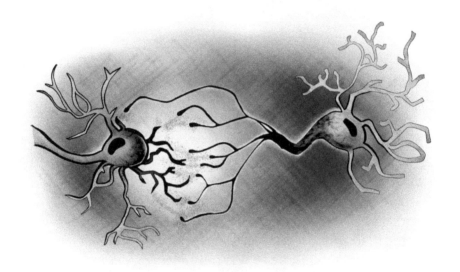

-Sketchbook of Dorothea Wild

CHAPTER
THIRTY-NINE

K eltson lay under the wooden pyre, breathing hard. Could he really do this? He'd spent all night rebuilding the pyre in the dark. He created a hollow tunnel in the center of the logs then crawled beneath it, using short pieces of wood to close up the end. Then Keltson lay on top of the tarp's plug and connected it to his jacket.

Any minute now, the sun would rise and the priests arrive. If they discovered him, everything would be lost. He hoped they weren't suspicious enough to investigate the pyre closely.

Footsteps approached and he heard them muttering around the mysteriously constructed pyre.

They didn't stay long. With the first obstacle averted, Keltson waited for the more painful part of the morning. His split.

The sun grew warmer and Keltson welcomed the heat. Before long, he hoped to be in the frozen chill of the Pause. Thinking of Bianka frozen in that box made him feel more determined to succeed.

Any minute now, he would be arriving to meet Ammond. He had left an addendum to the note in the clearing. Instead of telling himself to follow along and watch the pyre's fate, he detailed exactly what he must do to reach this moment. Instead of hundreds of splits as Keltson jumped around trying to get to the extension cord, Keltson told himself to go straight to the pyre. Only one split. Only one sacrifice.

He looked at his watch. One minute. He chanted his motivation. The idea that would become all-consuming after this. He couldn't afford to accidentally think about something else.

Do the right thing.

Do the right thing.

Do the right thing.

Then it hit. His head felt like it exploded. It was all he could do not to scream out and alert the priests in the temple. He splintered like firewood into hundreds of pieces. His burning skin felt hot enough to light the pyre surrounding him as he writhed against the rough wood.

As the pain subsided, the only thought in his head was of Bianka. He must save her. *It was the right thing.* His fear and frustration bubbled to the surface.

He heard the clang of swords as the centurions walked and the grunts of the priests as they hoisted Bianka's coffin onto the pyre. The wood settled around him, Keltson suddenly felt petrified. *Was* he doing the *right thing?* Would this work? What if the tarp malfunctioned? What if Ammond and the others couldn't put out the fire in time? Would he burn along with Bianka?

Do the right thing.

The flames began. They ate through the wood at his feet and he waited to see if he had obeyed his own instructions. There were no gasps and shouts of men as Keltson appeared, desperately trying to get to the extension cord. He still remembered fighting hard, receiving nicks and cuts from the soldiers, but the memory seemed to fade into a mist, like it was a dream instead of something real.

Do the right thing.

Now.

Keltson pressed the emergency return as the heat penetrated through the bottom of his shoes. The air changed. For a moment, Keltson wondered if it worked. The smoke and flames were so thick around him that he couldn't see anything. Then he heard a familiar voice.

"Over here!"

The flames quickly grew thicker and hotter, crawling up his sides as they ate up the oil-covered logs. The heat pressed in on Keltson and the smoke began to smother him. He coughed, but he doubted anyone could hear. There was far too much shouting and grunting going on around him.

Wood creaked as the flame-weakened logs crumbled. The coffin pressed down on his chest. It was impossibly heavy but chilled his skin. At first, he welcomed the relief, but then it crushed the air out of him. Keltson tried to push it away and failed. He couldn't even cry out for help.

"He's still down there!" another voice cried. Keltson heard the sizzle of water as it was thrown atop the fire. His panic grew. He could feel his pant leg catch on fire and the flames burning his skin.

"More water! Tear the pyre apart!" the voice shouted.

It was the right thing.

Only the pain from the intense heat was keeping him alert.

He heard the sound of axes and scattering wood. The coffin pressed down even harder, then slid off the top of him. He took a desperate gasp of air, and his lungs filled with smoke. Water drenched his hair, covering him in muddy soot. The ash and heat sizzled all around him. Keltson reached out with dizzying desperation and felt a hand grab his. It pulled again and more hands wrapped around his wrists and arms. Hands and blankets smothered the flames on his legs. He lay on the ground, coughing and wheezing as the smoke refused to clear from his lungs. He saw Mathilda first and felt a damp handkerchief rubbing the soot from his face. From the side, he saw Ammond looking frantically over the coffin, searching it for damage.

It was safe.

He closed his eyes and let the blackness take him.

KELTSON AWOKE to the horrible sensation of fire and ice at the same time. He turned his head and saw a haze of smoke rising into the air. The memory returned. The fear of being burned alive. He felt feverish and frozen. Water ran across his legs. Rusha stood in the stream beside him cutting off the remainder of his pant leg to look at his blistered shins.

She seemed serious as she turned to a blurred form beside her. "It's bad. He may have trouble walking for a while."

"He needs a doctor."

"Hide the casket, then go into the village."

"I will."

"Thank you, Gunther. You know the way?"

Keltson heard someone splashing through the water. Keltson lifted his hand shakily.

"Shh." Rusha tenderly took it and laid it back down into the water. More hands felt along his chest.

"The damage seems to be the worst on his hands and legs. The rest of him was spared by the coolness of the coffin." Rusha tossed the scraps of fabric behind her into the river as she cut them from his body.

"I split," Keltson mumbled.

Rusha nodded solemnly.

"It was the *right thing*," Keltson trailed off. His lungs felt tight. Ammond came into view next to him with a fatherly kind of protection glinting in his eyes. Keltson coughed again.

"Smoking isn't as relaxing as they say," Keltson said.

Ammond smiled. "You need rest." He patted Keltson on the chest.

Rusha laid cold rags on Keltson's limbs, trying to sooth the red skin. He laid his head back in agony.

THE DOCTOR'S POULTICE HELPED. Rusha's orders to place Keltson in the stream had saved his skin from getting any worse. The first few days after that were full of fitful sleep and feverish nightmares about the wall of fire closing in on him. Rusha was a faithful nurse, though he suspected everyone was only being so kind to him because they wanted him to continue his quest to get Bianka back. He didn't mind. He wouldn't fail them.

It still took Keltson nearly a whole week before he could hobble around the house. Bending any joints in his legs was excruciating, so he hobbled around stiff-legged, which was hard in the miniature cottage. He felt like a broken marionette.

Rusha refused to let Ammond talk to Keltson about Bianka's casket until he'd recovered enough to walk. When Keltson finally hobbled into the clearing, he found his equipment neatly gathered up and organized into a pile.

"I may not be ready for action yet, but I want to start planning. I'll need my vest fully charged with the generator…" Keltson trailed off as he saw the look on Ammond's face. He wandered over to the pile of equipment and picked up the vest. Keltson's heart sank.

The vest had melted.

It was still largely intact, but the wires and main power component was warped and metal dripped down the sides. Keltson set his jaw.

"We still have the mirror though," Ammond said.

"That won't work," Keltson whispered. "I need to get into the Pause. The mirror is programmed to transport to Greece and the only way to change those commands is from the Pause."

Ammond wrung his hands and stared at the ground. Every second that passed showed defeat growing in his gaze.

Keltson tossed the vest angrily to the ground. "Lilia made a blasted mess of everything. If that casket is anything like the mirrors, the only way to disarm it is from the Pause. Otherwise, it's indestructible."

Keltson couldn't believe it. All that sacrifice just to hit a dead end because he didn't have the equipment he needed.

Ammond stared at the casket laid next to the cottage door. "It's killing me to have her back but have no way to get her out."

Mathilda sang a French lullaby while she scattered wildflowers around the casket. Gunther held a rag, trying in vain to polish the blackened metal. The glass remained the only clean part of the capsule, still frosted by the cold interior. Ice formed on Bianka's lashes and hair.

Could he bear looking at the coffin of failure every day? He stood and leaned over the casket, staring down at the beautiful girl. He'd do anything to save her.

He wouldn't give up.

It was the right thing.

"Hand me that vest," Keltson said. Ammond obliged.

As Keltson looked over the damage, he sighed. It was totally destroyed.

He couldn't think like that. If Lilia could make an eternal coffin and vest from scraps of glass and metal, he could do this. He opened the motherboard and found the programming and hard drive untouched. Perhaps he could substitute the power supply with something from his equipment pile?

Ammond's organizational skills put Keltson's to shame. The tools had been organized by category. But as he glanced over them, not a single one could help him. Lilia had stolen and destroyed everything substantial. He imagined himself stranded here for the rest of his life, and ITTA stumbling upon this rotting pile of equipment...

He paused, then looked up sharply at Ammond.

"I know what we have to do," Keltson said.

"What?" Ammond asked.

"I need a pen," Keltson said.

-Sketchbook of Dorothea Wild

CHAPTER
FORTY

LILIA'S TIME CAPSULE
PAUSE

The heat and warmth subsided and the cold bit into Bianka's skin with even more fury than before. The dripping water quickly formed into icicles that framed the mirrors with jagged crystalline teeth. One reflection on the far wall lit with the image of the man in his windowless room again. He seemed agitated, fumbling with tools she didn't recognize.

The mirror closest to Bianka lit up at the same time.

It showed Lilia.

Bianka flinched and pulled away from the glass. Lilia was inside the eternal forest, meddling with the back of a mirror, pulling threads from their places and attaching them in different spots.

Both mirrors faded. But before the man's mirror went completely dark, it brightened again and showed him stooped before the mirror, inspecting the mess Lilia had made of his invention.

A mirror on the other side lit up. This time, it showed Bianka as a young girl running through the eternal forest. The man heard her and stood to investigate. And then the two images in the mirror stopped in their tracks. They stared at each other. Bianka watched the two, captivated at the realization that she had stood before this man, face to face and never realized how well he knew her.

The young girl screamed and ran away.

Ran away from the only man who could truly help her. She watched as The Mirror desperately searched through the forest for her. How different would things have turned out had she allowed him to find her?

The images faded and the cold wrapped her up in its arms, cradling Bianka to sleep. She curled into a ball, trying to keep herself warm for just a few moments more.

"When I first entered the Pause and saw things shatter, I thought I broke the world. Now, I know shattering is the universe's way of showing me what could have been. At first, it was enchanting. But as I lingered in the Pause of my childhood, I saw myself split in front of my very eyes. I saw the possibilities I could have had and I realized that none of them were happy."

-Journal entry of Keltson Grammar

CHAPTER
FORTY-ONE

K eltson sat at the table, writing careful details on a piece of parchment. His fingers were finally healed enough for him to hold the quill steady. Even though he had healed significantly over the last few weeks, the skin on his legs still felt tight and was covered in scars. But it was enough, he was finally ready. He folded the note and sealed it with wax. Cenric had whittled a seal press into the form of Keltson's mask. On the front, he addressed the letter to:

ITTA agent Charul, deliver in 2069.

Keltson handed the letter to Gunther. "Deliver this to the village priest and instruct him to place it in the archives."

Gunther nodded and ran through the front door. Volker followed him to guard him as he passed through the woods.

The letter gave Charul the coordinates for the cottage. It was a risk, but a necessary one. Keltson hadn't received any new memories since his rescue in Greece. He didn't tell Ammond, but it made him fear the worst. What if Bianka hadn't survived the flames? No. He wouldn't think like that. Keltson stood up and walked to the center of the clearing.

"The rest of you, scatter. You can watch, but don't allow yourselves to be seen. I need you safe if this goes wrong."

They nodded and ran into the trees.

Keltson waited. If Charul didn't appear at 10:00 am, it meant the letter didn't survive through history and they'd have to try again. Keltson wore his mask to prove he was the man in the mirror. He also wore short trousers, leaving his burns visible. That, paired with his hobble, would hopefully convince Charul that Keltson wasn't a threat.

Only minutes before ten, a tall, tan-skinned teenager with perfectly styled hair stepped out of the woods. He looked at Keltson and let out a breathy laugh.

"I expected more than this. A trap maybe?"

Charul held up the letter Keltson had just sent with Gunther. The edges were brittle and torn and the wax seal was smeared and faded. Keltson couldn't believe it worked.

"I'm confused. Are you actually turning yourself in?" the boy asked.

Keltson stood straighter and threw his melted vest to Charul, who caught it and glanced down at the device, his eyebrows raised in surprise.

"You have no idea what it's like to be stuck here."

"So, you called me to take you back to jail?" Charul asked, skeptically.

Keltson took a step backwards, motioning to the casket behind him. Charul crept forward with cautious interest. Peering over the edge of the glass case, he caught his breath. "Bianka? What happened to her?"

"One of my clients, Lilia, split and gained an unsavory hatred for the girl. Bianka hid here for a few years, but Lilia found her and did this."

"What is this contraption?" Charul ran his fingers along the melted metal seams.

Keltson swallowed the knot in his throat. Exposing Lilia's invention felt like the worst possible thing he could do. After this, ITTA would know about the Pause. But he had to do it, for Bianka.

"It's a time capsule. She's frozen in a separate dimension where time doesn't exist."

Charul looked up in amazement. "Is that possible?"

"Lilia repurposed some of my equipment."

"But we have Lilia in custody, how could she…"

Keltson interrupted, holding his hand out in front of him. "Like I said, she split and duplicated. As soon as you arrested one version of her, the second one took over here."

Charul's eyes widened. "You made quite a mess, didn't you?"

Keltson set his jaw. He was fully aware of the jumbled timeline he had created. It hurt knowing he needed to rely on this teenager and ITTA to set things straight.

Charul turned his attention back to Bianka. "She's even more beautiful now. She's much older."

Keltson's gut tightened as he saw the admiration in Charul's eyes. He had never considered that Charul and Bianka developed some kind of relationship during the weeks they knew each other. Keltson pushed back the wave of anxiety. He needed Charul. There was nothing he could do for Bianka without him.

"Why is it frozen inside and burnt on the outside?" Charul asked, fingering the blackened trails climbing up the sides of the capsule.

"We had trouble saving her from a Roman temple," Keltson admitted.

"Is that how…" Charul trailed off as he eyed Keltson's burnt calves.

Keltson pursed his lips and nodded slowly. "I just want to do *what's right*."

Charul pushed himself up from the casket. "I thought you were all about screwing things up?"

"I don't have to justify myself to you," Keltson said, trying to hide the venom in his voice.

"That's true. It's the judge you'll have to answer to." Charul pulled out a pair of handcuffs.

"I'm willing to accept responsibility on one condition," Keltson said. "That you do everything in your power to remove Bianka from this time capsule and return her home. But not the life she knew before. Her original future was not a good one. If you care for her at all, you won't let her be poisoned. I've worked too hard to save her from being murdered at twenty-one to have her put directly back into that timeline."

"So, you're asking for me to arrest you, but not to revert all the damage you've done to the timeline?" Charul asked incredulously.

Keltson nodded.

Charul sighed. "You're being arrested for tampering with the integrity of the Standard Timeline as recorded by the International Summit of 2042. Under this violation, I am responsible for taking you in without further notice, where your case will be investigated and a fair trial will be held."

Keltson clenched his teeth. These were the words he had dreaded for years. His own personal game-over. He sighed and held out his right hand. Charul looked surprised at his willingness to submit but took his wrist anyway. As he fastened the cuff, Keltson pulled his left hand forward for Charul, but at the last second, twisted Charul's arm and covered his emergency escape button exactly where Ammond said it would be.

"Now!" Keltson yelled. Ammond jumped from his hiding place beneath a leather oilskin and ran at Charul with a pair of wire cutters. Meanwhile, Baigh ran from the front door and helped Keltson hold Charul down, keeping his hand away from the ignition. Luckily, a spindly teenager was no match for three men. Ammond knew exactly where the wire was in Charul's sleeve and snipped it, disabling the vest.

"No!" Charul yelled just as the vest short-circuited. A wave of electricity rippled down Charul's body.

"It feels good to take down prince charming," Keltson said, breathing heavily.

Charul regained his composure quickly and grabbed Ammond by the shirt collar. "You traitor!" he shouted. He raised his hand as if to strike Ammond, but without a word, Rusha appeared behind him and smacked Charul on the top of the head with a cast-iron frying pan, knocking him out cold. Ammond and Keltson looked at her in shock.

She straightened up and smoothed down the front of her skirt. "I didn't like the way he looked at Bianka."

Keltson smirked at Charul's once perfectly smooth hair now smudged with dirt. He bent down and pulled the severed device off the boy, then took a box from his shirt pocket and opened it to reveal the motherboard from his own vest. He opened a slot in Charul's vest, detached the ITTA board, and inserted his specialized programming.

"It fits?" Ammond asked,

"Yeah, but I won't know if it really works unless I try it," Keltson said.

"What do we do with this guy?" Baigh asked, nudging the unconscious Charul with his foot.

"Well, we can't keep him here, can we?" Urig nudged the boy with his foot.

"I don't want him," Rusha said flatly.

Keltson rubbed his forehead with his hand. A few weeks ago, he wouldn't have felt any remorse for what he planned to do with the boy. But after the split, morality had become starkly black and white again. Growing up, Baigh had always given him a hard time for his moral compass. Over the last five years, he learned to see the grey between the lines for the greater good. But now, he felt a knot in his stomach.

"We can't afford to have him going back to ITTA now. He knows too much and would put Bianka at risk," Ammond said.

Do the right thing.

"I visited France once and hated it. Why not drop him there?" Urig said. Mathilda let out a stream of French expletives at him.

"You hate everything, Urig," Cenric said.

"Perhaps *he* would hate it more," Urig said, prodding Charul with his toe.

"France in the twelfth-century doesn't have any ITTA ports for him to get back through," Ammond agreed.

"What's an ITTA port?" Keltson asked.

"They're secure bases for stranded agents. Kind of like your stationary mirrors. Only they lead to ITTA headquarters. It'd be a good thing to abandon him somewhere that would be too difficult to get back to the future and rat us out."

Do the right thing.

Was abandoning a teenager in the past the right thing to do?

"Perhaps you should go after Bianka first. Then we can take care of this guy," Ammond suggested.

"Ammond," Keltson said, "I, of all people, understand the overwhelming urge to follow the instinct of our split, but my voice constantly pushes me to *do the right thing.* And right now, it's definitely telling me to get *him* out of here."

Ammond sent him a short nod, then stepped back, opening the way to Charul. "We should at least make the man a survival pack."

That felt like a good idea.

"I'll drop him, then head immediately for Bianka." As Ammond stepped forward and set the dials of his new vest to twelfth-century France, Baigh brought Keltson a pack from Rusha and gave him a reassuring pat on the back.

"Be careful, Kelts. And good luck."

Keltson felt a tinge of jealousy. If he successfully saved Bianka, Baigh and the others would get their happy ending in a matter of seconds. But he still had a long, treacherous road ahead of him. One that was likely filled with plenty of trials and errors before reaching a resolution.

He waved goodbye, wrapped Charul in the tarp, then pressed the ignition and transported them both into a beautiful forest.

"Welcome to your new home," Keltson said, grabbing the still unconscious Charul under the arms and dragging him toward a tree. "This isn't so bad. I don't know what Urig was so fired up about. There shouldn't be anything remotely close to you here, so I prepared you a survival pack. It's mainly boy scout equipment from the 1500's, but hopefully, you know how to find food on your own. If I remember right, you didn't mind bragging about your hunting skills."

Charul's eyes fluttered.

Keltson patted his head, purposefully mussing his hair out of its perfect wave. "Now remember, it would be REALLY nice if you could just hang out here forever instead of going back to the agency and bringing all of Hades down on us. We already had a run in with Poseidon and that was a terrible experience."

Keltson straightened and looked down at the awakening Charul. "Seriously though, dude, don't come back," he said. He gave him a casual salute then jumped into the Pause near Ammond's cottage to look for a way to free Bianka.

The space felt smoky and the trees were so dense that when they shattered, there was hardly room for them. Ammond gazed at the spot where Keltson disappeared. Keltson searched around the coffin, hoping to find the best way to open the device. But as he looked at it, he realized the top was completely dark.

His heart clenched in his chest. He moved forward to inspect the casket and as soon as he touched it, his surroundings melted into the floor. An immense stone ballroom rose around him. Cracked mirrors lined the walls. He startled and jumped back as they each cast beams of light onto the floor across the room. The light grew into shadowy silhouettes of Bianka. The faded woman filled the room on every side of him. Some were young, merely children. Others had grown gracefully old. All of them dressed like the countess she should have been.

Some danced, others spoke to invisible companions. It was as if he saw a hundred different moments in the lives Bianka might have lived. Had he really tampered with her life this much?

"Are you lost?" a young voice asked from his side. Keltson startled and looked down at the girl. She seemed about eight years old. She blinked up at him sweetly.

Before he could respond to the child, a teenage version of Bianka whirled by, spinning with an invisible partner. She bumped into him and apologized with a giggle as she was whisked away in a silent waltz.

Keltson stood on the edge of the immense crowd of variances, his head whirling at all the changes he had made.

The young girl spoke again. "Are you lost?" she asked.

He looked into her deep brown eyes. "Um, yes. I am," he said.

"Who are you looking for?" she asked.

"You, actually," he said.

"No one has ever come to see me here before." Her eyelashes fluttered as she spun gently from side to side. "But at home, Father is called on quite often."

"I believe that," Keltson said.

"I love having guests. Are you a guest?" she asked.

"Actually, I'm here looking for someone like you, but, older."

The young Bianka's smile faded. "One of them? Not me?" she asked, motioning to the crowd of Bianka's standing in the center of the room.

"Yes, could you help me?" he asked.

"I wish you well. But I should see my other guests. There are so many who wish to call on me," she said, whirling back with a swish of skirts.

Keltson watched her curls bounce behind her as she walked into the never-ending crowd. Everyone around him was dressed in finery. His Bianka would be dressed in simple linen. At least, that's what she wore in the casket. Keltson stood a perhaps ten centimeters taller than Bianka so he could see over the heads of the entire crowd. But everyone looked identical, making it impossible to pick her out.

"Excuse me!" Keltson shouted, hoping to gain their attention. No one responded. His shoulders slumped. He was about to set out around the perimeter of the large room when someone else spoke.

"They don't listen very well," another young voice said behind him.

He turned, surprised, and found a *very* young Bianka, sitting on the side of the room behind him, eating an apple. She couldn't have been more than four years old. Behind her stood a frosted mirror laid into the wall. As he stepped closer, he could barely make out a hazy shape in the center. He peered through the glass and gasped when he saw that Bianka lay inside, frozen and white as a ghost.

The little girl recognized his gaze and looked behind her.

"The pretty lady wanted a bite of my apple," the young girl said.

"She did?" he asked, taking a step forward.

"Yes, her face appeared in the glass, watching Father and me. He got me this apple, you see. They're my favorite. She wanted it, but when she tried to reach for it, she froze. Now I wish I could give her some, but she might choke."

Behind Keltson, the dancing Bianka whirled by again, her skirts brushing his boots.

"You are a very smart little girl," Keltson said, examining the frame around the mirror. She smiled, then hesitated.

"Father says others must call me 'milady', or just 'lady'. But, you may choose."

"My apologies, your majesty." Keltson gave her a dramatic bow. The girl giggled.

"Why do you think she wanted your apple?" Keltson asked.

She ignored him and turned back to admiring her apple. "Father must have sent the servants to search the deepest parts of the cellar for it. They must be very brave to go down there in the dark. He knows that I love apples." She smiled, her dimples carved into her round cheeks.

Do the right thing.

This girl was so young, younger than he had ever seen her before. Was this Bianka's original life? He turned and looked at the girl frozen behind glass and began to doubt. Which life would she have chosen for herself?

"The pretty lady wanted a bite of my apple," the young girl said, holding up the apple again. He looked down at her, confused.

"Yes, her face appeared in the glass, watching Father and me..." He listened as she repeated every word, exactly as before, as if stuck in a loop.

A skirt brushed against his boot as the dancing Bianka whirled past him. Again. Keltson looked through the mirror at the sleeping countess. Her hair curled over her cheek as she slept and her body was slightly twisted as if she looked back through the mirror as she passed through. Had Bianka regretted the decision she made?

Of course she had regrets. She must have just realized it was a trap.

Do the right thing.

Why had Bianka wanted to step into this time capsule in the first place? Was she attempting to leave the life she knew? Was she that unhappy? He looked at her, looking back, now frozen in time, in a place where she didn't exist at all.

Around him danced all the tragic lives that Keltson wanted to change. The women who flitted around the room might seem contented, but...

He turned back around to look at the face in the glass. This most recent Bianka was different.

Through every timeline, Bianka remained kind, but often kind to all the wrong people. She was quiet and non-confrontational, but at the most crucial times when speaking up was necessary, she maintained her silence. She was confident, but only in her beauty.

This girl in the casket was different.

Bianka was happy despite all the horrible things that happened to her. She was kind, yet stood up for herself. She was quiet when others needed her to listen. She was confident in her compassion toward others.

Dressed in simple linen with frost forming in her tangled hair... This Bianka was the most beautiful in the room. She looked back longingly at a life of hardship, near death, and betrayal. But also of friendship, bravery, and honor. In this room, where he could choose from a multitude of women to take back with him, Keltson wondered which life would Bianka have chosen?

The right choice.

He looked back down at the young girl, who continued to loop through her story about her father. "Enjoy your apple, your majesty. Make sure you thank your father for it," Keltson said to the young girl.

She smiled brightly and Keltson leaned over, touched the frosted glass of the mirror, and felt the room melt around him.

-Sketchbook of Dorothea Wild

CHAPTER
FORTY-TWO

Bianka's eyes flew open and she let out a startled gasp. The man knelt over her, his eyes wide in surprise. Everything was icy, dark and frigid. Crystals covered the walls and glittered on the floor. The ice underneath him crackled as he shifted his weight.

"Mirror?" she asked. Her lips barely formed the words. The sound came out as a breathless whisper, no more than a puff of moisture that drifted up into the air. The man immediately stooped to pull her from the floor. As he moved her, her thin linen dress crackled. He wrapped a long, stiff blanket around her and pulled her onto his lap. She shivered into his chest, her breath creating a thin cloud around his face.

He rubbed her arms. "I'm here. I'm so sorry. I'm here."

Bianka couldn't speak. She only shook violently.

"Ammond and the others want you home. I came to find you," he said.

Bianka blinked, but no tears came. It was too cold for tears. She recognized the hints of a beard she had seen in all her visions of him. In the back of her mind, Bianka knew it was improper to study him so closely, but she also deserved to inspect the corners of his jaw, the shape of his brow.

You have seen my face a hundred times, she thought. *But this is the first moment we are no longer strangers.*

"I need to get you out of this cold," he said, shifting his weight against the floor. She stared at him as he lay on the floor beside her, keeping her wrapped in his arms. Bianka burrowed her head into his chest and he blew out a quick foggy breath as he pressed a button on his vest. The cold ate through her skin. Her eyelids fluttered, then closed.

~

GLASS SHATTERED AROUND THEM.

Keltson barely had time to close his eyes before he felt the scratches digging into his skin. Bianka burrowed even deeper into his chest, the tarp protecting her. Warm air rushed over them, thawing the ice that sank into his bones. He opened his eyes, looking around through the glittering glass.

Bianka's head poked out from beneath the tarp. The frost finally began to melt from her face. In the sparkling remains of Lilia's invention, this was the most beautiful version of Bianka Keltson had ever seen.

A face peered over the edge of the casket.

"Bianka!" Ammond cried out.

The girl shook uncontrollably but tried to turn toward his voice. Her breath broke into little sobs as his hand reached over the side of the casket, brushing her cheek.

"You're like ice! Rusha! Blankets, hot water!"

Keltson lifted Bianka up. Baigh helped him remain steady as he stepped from the casket while he cradled her in his arms. She blinked, still studying his face. He sent her half a smile and carried her through the door of the cottage, ducking low through the frame. He lay her gently on her bed and Rusha rushed forward, kissing Bianka's forehead as she threw piles of quilts on top of her and pulled them up to Bianka's quivering chin.

"Out of the way. Hot stones coming through," Urig shouted, holding a pan with five large river stones heated inside. Rusha quickly arranged the quilts around them so they would warm Bianka's feet without burning her.

Bianka glanced at Keltson with wonder in her eyes as often as she could through all the happy reunions going on around her. Keltson couldn't help but send her a smile whenever she caught his eye until Ammond sent him a warning glare. Keltson tried to remain somber after that. The girl was freezing after all and likely in shock.

Rusha attacked Keltson's hands with kisses each time she passed him. Cenric and Volker tried to hide the tears in their eyes. Mathilda brought in a single wildflower for Bianka, laying it by her bedside.

"With her temperature regulated, she should sleep. Who knows how long she was in there," he whispered.

Everyone left for the yard. Cenric and Volker began hacking up the remnants of the coffin and tossing the metal and glass into a fire they had built. The noise didn't seem to bother Bianka, who slept heavily. Keltson's limbs ached, still weak from their wounds. The day's ordeal carried plenty of adrenalin and worry. Now, with Bianka resting safely in the cottage, Keltson sat quietly in the corner with his eyes closed in sleep.

BIANKA AWOKE IN THE COTTAGE. The large main room where she rested was empty except for the man, sleeping in a chair across the room. His arms and legs were covered in burns and scars. His face was dark and he looked utterly exhausted.

She didn't move for fear of waking the poor man. She remembered his warm arms closing around her, stealing her from that wretched frozen room. The man's fingers twitched and her gaze was drawn to the small table to his right. Set on top, very carefully, was something that a few days ago would have made her heart nearly stop in her chest.

His mask.

This man was The Mirror. This man had caused every calamity in her life. He'd sent Lilia back in time to be her stepmother. He'd allowed Ammond to split after Lilia killed her with the bodice. Bianka had stepped through *his* mirror and into that horrible frozen waste. And yet, he was also the man who rescued her time and time again.

The man's eyes opened, suddenly, as if he felt her studying him. He didn't move. They stared at each other for a moment. He looked ashamed and she wondered what crimes he accused himself of inside his head.

"You're The Mirror," she said, simply.

He straightened, hesitating before he answered. "Yes," he said, in his strange accent.

"Why do you wear a mask?" she asked, studying every feature of his face. Did he feel uncomfortable being exposed before her?

"I wear the mask to protect myself from people like Charul and those he works for. Pretty much everyone else too."

"So, you're done hiding now?" she asked, nodding toward the abandoned mask beside him.

"No," he said, looking down at his hands. "I don't think I'll ever be done hiding."

"I am," Bianka said, adjusting herself against the pillows. He looked up at her from beneath his dark eyebrows. "I've realized that there is nowhere I can hide. So, my only option is to confront those that threaten me."

"That's not..."

Bianka raised her hand, cutting him off.

"I know you prefer me to be a peasant over a lady. But I need to go back."

"I don't prefer you any different. But I won't let you fall victim to feelings of revenge."

"It's not about revenge," Bianka said. "I want to return because I think I can do good there. I'm capable of making a change. Whether or not you believe in me."

The man pushed himself from his chair and knelt near her bed. "Bianka, I absolutely believe in you. Years ago, when you asked me what kind of person you were, I didn't know you well enough then to tell you. But now I've seen you in circumstances ranging from countess, to rebel leader, to simple peasant. But, no matter what position you hold, you are always kind. It was the core of who you are. Always. I thought your compassion came from your life of privilege. Life was soft on you, so being sympathetic was easy. But, then…" he paused, looking like he didn't want to mention the things she had been through. "Whatever happened to you only made your kindness run deeper."

"Thank you," she whispered.

She realized exactly how close he was, leaning against the side of the bed as he spoke and she pulled the blankets closer to her chin.

He smiled self-consciously and backed away. The Mirror had never said anything complimentary before. His mask had only looked at her with flat, expressionless features and offered her sharp, biting words. But now, this face—these warm, human eyes—looked at her with admiration and care.

Just then, Ammond walked through the front door. He glared at the man who stood so near her bed. The Mirror cleared his throat and stepped backward.

"Wait," Bianka said, reaching out. She swallowed, the words weighing heavy in her throat. "When I first came to Ammond's clearing, I was angry at you. I thought I lost everything because of you. But I saw you in the mirrors of that horrible room. I saw you struggle to help me. I saw your anger over Lilia's betrayal.

"Those years ago, when you first spoke to me, your words hurt. But then I saw that you meant them. Life wasn't about focusing on myself. It was about helping others. So, I stopped caring about revenge and all the things that were eating at me inside. And now I realize I need to go back home, not because it is a position of comfort. But because, like you, I could make a difference. I need to go back now. Not for the ease. But for the change."

The man looked down on her with warmth in his eyes. He stepped forward, lifting her hand in his and gave it a gentle kiss. She felt warmth rush up her arm, melting away all the remaining ice inside.

"I will do whatever it takes for you to get your desire, my lady," he said, looking at her directly.

"Does this mean I'm your… *client?*" she asked.

Keltson laughed. "Pro bono."

Bianka smiled, understanding his Latin.

"Might I ask a liberty then, that no other client has ever been bestowed?" she asked.

"Perhaps," he said, warily.

"Might I know your true name?" she asked.

He pinched his mouth up in a crooked smile. It was a rather charming smile.

"Keltson Grammar, at your service," he said.

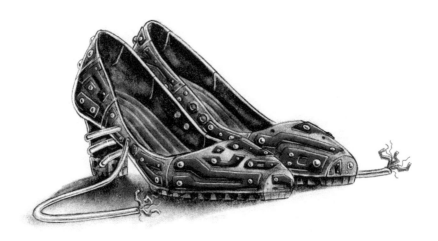

-Sketchbook of Dorothea Wild

CHAPTER
FORTY-THREE

B ianka rode through the silent stone gates on a brown mare the citizens had loaned to her. Morning dew dripped down the sides of the gate and a low mist radiated the morning light in the familiar courtyard. Dirt covered large patches of the cobblestones and scaffolding encased the southern face of her old home. Yellow plaster covered parts of the walls while others remained the old medieval stone from her childhood. It felt like half of her life had been erased from the kingdom's memory.

On either side of her stood guards and peasants, whispering, staring, and pointing as she passed. Bianka twisted the reins in her hands, forcing herself to remember how to breathe. Despite her preparation, her entire body felt tense. A million emotions flooded her heart, like a river cutting a new path through a mountain.

Lilia's prophesy flashed through her memory; the story she related as she sold Bianka the deadly bodice. Lilia claimed an arrow pierced Bianka's ribs. She ran her fingers along her un-armored stomach. She fit Lilia's vision exactly.

Bianka wore the filigree crown and a linen robe made by her sweet Rusha. Ammond rode at her left with Cenric and Volker, who had steeds that suited them. The villagers shied away from them, intimidated by their Roman armor flashing in the sunlight.

And then, on her right, rode Keltson. She knew how uncomfortable he felt on a horse, but at this moment, he hid it well. The only hint of his emotions was his white-knuckled grip on the saddle's pommel. He wore peasants' clothes, there were no fine tailors in the villages, but his strong arms and straight posture gave him the aura of a nobleman.

His dark hair had grown longer over the weeks since she met him, though she couldn't remember most of the beginning days. She'd drifted in and out of a constant fever. Rusha whispered that Keltson spent most of his time by her bedside, tending to her needs. The cold had reached her very soul and had nearly taken her despite Keltson's rescue. She still felt weak, but the others reassured her she wouldn't have to do any fighting, even though she had trained with the best.

The guards looked up in awe as she rode through the courtyard.

"Welcome, beautiful Countess," one man said, kneeling as she passed. The way Keltson glanced at her as the man said it made Bianka blush.

"Thank you," she said, struggling to smile.

Keltson stared at her curiously. After they passed far enough, he pulled his horse closer to hers. "What's wrong?" he asked.

"Do they see nothing more than my appearance?" she asked, thinking about her portrait over the fireplace. She didn't come back just to be beautiful.

"Give them time. They'll love you for other reasons soon enough," he said, smiling.

She blushed again.

Keltson leaned forward to pat his horse's shoulder. "Face it. You won't have trouble topping their last countess. She doesn't have many admirers."

Bianka wrinkled up her nose then shushed him playfully.

They stopped in the center of the courtyard where soldiers and citizens pressed in through the gates. Keltson jumped from his horse and reached up to help Bianka dismount. She slid off the saddle and into his arms. He held her steady for a moment before stepping away; her legs still weren't as stable as she needed. Bianka glanced around the courtyard, hungrily searching for a familiar face. It had been so long.

And then, she saw Father, rushing out from the main door at the top of the stairs. He paused as he looked down on her. He was older now. She tried not to let herself tremble as he struggled to recognize her.

She had changed more than he.

Mere seconds later, he wrapped her up in his arms.

After everything she had been through, she was finally here. Her father's warm embrace overwhelmed her. The crowd lowered in reverence.

"Where have you been?" Father asked, his eyes welling with disbelieving tears. "Why did you run away?"

"Lilia..." she began, but her voice cut short as something clattered against the cobblestones, coming to rest at her feet.

An arrow.

The entire crowd looked to a darkened window in one of the stairway towers. A familiar face, full of venomous hatred, looked down on her from inside.

"Lilia," Bianka whispered. She had tried to kill her. Again. A feeble effort, but another attempt all the same.

"Guards, to the tower!" Father shouted and his men darted toward the stairwell. He wrapped his arm protectively around Bianka's shoulder and escorted her toward the main door. Bianka looked over her father's shoulder to ensure that Keltson followed her. The entire troupe moved after Bianka, not willing to let her out of their sight. Father hesitated for a moment, eyeing her troupe of friends, but seemed to accept their presence and moved on. Once the crowds could no longer see, her knees buckled.

"Bianka?" Father asked, grasping her hands as she sank to the floor. Keltson stooped and picked her up in his arms.

"What is wrong?" Father asked.

"She has been deathly ill," Keltson said. "She's still recovering."

"We should get her closer to a fire." Father motioned to the main gathering hall. Keltson carried Bianka up the winding stairs and through the corridors. As they stepped into the formal room, memories overwhelmed Bianka. It was like stepping back in time. She clung tighter to Keltson.

Just then, a group of soldiers burst through the doors. "The countess... she, disappeared through a mirror, Sir!"

Bianka looked toward Keltson in concern.

"We have to let this happen," Keltson whispered. "Otherwise everything will change and there will be new fights to be won."

Her father argued with the soldiers about Lilia's escape. Bianka leaned her head closer to Keltson and whispered. "But is this fight over? She's still out there."

As if in answer, the doors around the great hall slammed shut and the lanterns were doused as if by a ghost. The guards crouched, gripping their weapons.

Bianka slid from Keltson's arms to face whatever was in store for her on her own two feet. The world held still as a figure materialized in the center of the room. It was Lilia. She was young again, but not tall and straight as Bianka remembered her. Her shoulders twisted at an odd angle as she looked across the room hungrily at Bianka.

"*Stop Bianka,*" she hissed.

Father stared in confusion at the young version of his wife. Lilia's mouth moved behind closed lips. Her clouded eyes focused intensely, and Bianka felt a wave of sadness at what her stepmother had become.

Lilia disappeared from the room and appeared only a few steps in front of Bianka. She reached a jagged hand toward her.

"*End Bianka,*" Lilia said.

Keltson jumped forward to tackle Lilia, but the woman disappeared again. Bianka's entire body trembled and she felt as if she would fall without Keltson to hold her steady.

"Witch," Father whispered.

Lilia appeared again, this time next to one of the guards near Father.

"*Subtlety.*" Lilia grunted as she shoved a knife into the guard's ribs. His voice caught in his throat and he fell. Father looked at the woman in horror as she let go of the knife and the guard. Lilia straightened and lifted a hand to caress Father's cheek. He caught her wrist and stared harshly into her eyes.

"Witch," he said again, this time more resolutely. Her gaze hardened and she pulled her hand from his grip and disappeared. Father ran to the wounded guard who had slumped to the floor.

"Get Bianka out of here!" Father shouted to Keltson. Bianka knew that wouldn't do any good. Lilia would follow her wherever she went.

Lilia appeared again, along with a network of cords that sizzled as they ran toward Bianka, encircling the ground around her. Keltson stood outside the perimeter of their reach.

"*Stop Bianka. End Bianka... Be Bianka,*" Lilia said, smiling her most devilish of smiles. Bianka's heart twisted inside her.

Keltson disappeared into thin air and reappeared beside Bianka. He threw the tarp around her and pressed the ignition. She closed her eyes as the familiar cold surrounded her. She tried not to let the anxiety overwhelm her.

They were no longer in the great room at Bianka's home, but instead outside the empty cottage they left a few days ago. But, in the Pause, it didn't look like the welcoming place Bianka remembered. Keltson kept his arms wrapped firmly around her, pressing the tarp close to her skin so as not to let her slip back into the flow of time.

"What did you do? Why are we here?" Bianka asked, pushing back to look up at him.

"I had to get you away from there. I've seen that invention before." Keltson looked around the clearing warily. Did he expect someone to come here? Was that possible?

"What does it do?" she asked. Keltson ignored her, holding her close as he turned to inspect the frozen world around them. Bianka reached up and turned Keltson's face toward hers. "What does it do?" she repeated.

"When Lilia was older, she kidnapped herself—a young and less corrupted self—and hooked her up to the machine. It put the old mind into the younger body."

Bianka looked in horror at Keltson. "She was trying to steal my skin?"

Keltson's fingers gripped the tarp more firmly.

"Will I never be safe at home?" she asked, tears threatening to jump from her eyes.

"I won't let Lilia win. She must be stopped."

"But how can we stop someone who can jump through time? We're constantly driven backwards by her. Ammond split multiple times. You split. But no matter what you did, I have always been tortured by her inventions..." Bianka trailed off.

For a moment, she imagined herself sparring with Volker in this very clearing. She remembered him circling her, constantly driving her back, but her never taking the offense. Bianka gained small victories over him, like putting her back to the sun, but there was always another strike coming.

She wanted to be kind by never attacking, but was it truly kind to wait for others to take the offensive for her?

Bianka swallowed and stood taller. "You're right. We need to stop her."

"I don't know how," Keltson said, shaking his head.

"We can't merely react. We have to come up with our own offensive strike," she said.

"What do you mean?" Keltson relaxed his grip on Bianka's waist.

"When Volker taught me to fight with a long sword, he told me of a tactic called a feint. I never used it, because it required an attack afterwards. It revealed a 'weak spot' to your opponent, leading them to attack. While in reality, you used their motion to set up a strike yourself. When you know exactly what they are going to do, you can know where they will be weakest themselves."

Keltson's brow furrowed as he thought. "What kind of a feint do you have in mind?"

"There's only one thing Lilia wants... Only one thing she will go after," Bianka said, pulling the tarp closer around her for warmth. "Me."

Keltson shook his head again. "I'm not leaving you in the middle of that contraption of hers. That's far too dangerous."

Bianka shook her fists, rustling the tarp with the movement. "But don't you see, that's exactly what she wants! It's the only move she will make that we can rely on."

"If we don't instantly kill her and you're stuck in the middle of all those wires, she will take your body. Bianka. She will live inside of you." Keltson's brown eyes looked desperate. His grip on her waist tightened. It gave Bianka the courage she needed.

BIANKA STOOD in the tangle of wires, exactly as before, still wrapped in Keltson's tarp. "This will work," he said.

She nodded nervously and looked into his dark eyes. This man who continually found reasons to hold her close, to pull her from danger's path, had done so much for her. Bianka trusted him. But now she needed him to trust her enough to jump back into the treacherous situation Lilia built.

He set his jaw and took a step backwards, pulling the tarp from her shoulders and she gasped at the warm tide that rushed over her.

Keltson disappeared, revealing Lilia on the other side of the room. Fury flashed on her face, still reacting to Keltson's attempt to save Bianka. But, seeing that the girl still stood in the middle of her contraption, Lilia's eyes changed from anger to pleasure in the matter of a second.

Lilia shook her head. "Mirror, Mirror," she clicked her tongue disappointedly.

Aiming her hand at Bianka, Lilia revealed a metal button resting inside her palm. Lilia pressed it, and a loud crack sounded. Lilia's shoes lit up with fiery light and light traveled down the wires that surrounded Bianka.

But before it reached her, the light shot backwards, redirected by Keltson's guiding hand in the Pause. Lilia wouldn't have noticed the tangled wires at her feet. She was too focused on Bianka across the room.

The light on Lilia's iron shoes grew brighter and brighter. Bianka flinched and raised her hands to guard her face. Lilia flickered for a moment, shuddering as if light only illuminated every other movement.

Her jerky motions seemed desperate, though she made no noise that they could hear.

Keltson appeared at Bianka's side, watching as Lilia's shoes grew red hot with the light of the disabled device. Her face grew older, more wrinkled, and sagged with pain as each second passed. Philip and the guards cringed away from her. Lilia moved, flickering in a desperate dance around the room. Bianka's eyes struggled to predict where the woman would appear next. The light trailed like lightning around the dining hall. Then in a bright flash, the device flickered out.

Lilia crumpled to a heap on the floor. It seemed there was no life left in the woman. Keltson stepped forward and turned her over, placing his hand on her neck to feel for a pulse.

A tear rippled down Bianka's cheek.

Keltson turned and solemnly looked up at Bianka. "She's dead."

"Lilia Vaschenko was a miraculous inventor. She could deconstruct a foreign device and not only understand how it worked, but how to transform its function into something new. She knew how to bend laws of time, consciousness, and sadly became one of the greatest villains I have ever known."

-Journal of Keltson Grammar

CHAPTER
FORTY-FOUR

On the dining room balcony, Bianka and Ammond looked over the castle courtyard. Peasants had come to town from the very outskirts of the county and danced in the square below to celebrate Bianka's return. Fiery torches flickered on the walls surrounding the castle, and stars blinked down at her as if in congratulations. Bianka knew, though there was time for celebration tonight, tomorrow would bring a long list of revelations that needed to be made in the presence of her father. The thought weighed heavily on her heart. She knew it wouldn't be easy to speak to him of such things. Father had retired to his rooms after Lilia's death.

Someone cleared their throat behind her and Bianka turned to see Keltson, dressed in the clothing of her era. He had worn the new clothing for the first time today. Around the cottage, he still preferred to wear the stiff blue leggings and the stretchy shirt with the strange lyre on front. This version was quite handsome.

The time travel vest peeked out from beneath his jerkin.

"You could be down there dancing, your majesty. I know how much you enjoyed that," Keltson said.

Bianka smiled. "Is that an invitation?"

Keltson blanched and quickly shook his head. "No, no, I don't dance."

"I haven't the strength anyway," Bianka said, smiling as she motioned to the balcony rail she held on to for support.

~

KELTSON CLEARED HIS THROAT AGAIN. Bianka's face was illuminated by the celebratory bonfires below, giving her skin a gentle warmth the Pause had never afforded her.

"I came to offer you congratulations on your return," Keltson said, trying not to clench his fists. Bianka's smile disappeared.

"There is a hint of goodbye in those words," she said, drawing back. He wanted to reach forward and take her hand, but instead he kept his face as stark and sullen as the mask.

"I have a list of clients that I left behind. I need to ensure that ITTA doesn't erase their resolutions and yours."

"I see." Bianka ducked her head politely. She bit her bottom lip, then looked up. "How long do you think your task will take?"

A hint of hope flashed in Keltson's chest. "You'd like me to return?"

Ammond cleared his throat and stepped between the two. "What do you think is going to happen to you after you return to the present?" He folded his arms and narrowed his eyes at Keltson.

Keltson's face fell. "Last thing I knew, the agency was looting through my house. I don't exactly have a lot to go back to. It'll be dangerous, but it's the right thing to do."

Ammond snorted. "You wouldn't last ten minutes back there. They have technology you don't even know about, kid. If you're flagged, that's it. Going back would be suicide. Not to mention mess up everything we've worked for here."

Keltson felt a rush of adrenaline pulse through his veins at those last words. He looked up at Bianka. "I promise you, I will never let that happen. I'm not letting your fate return to its original course."

Ammond grunted and shook his head.

"As hard as you try, son, you'll never be able to afford Bianka that."

~

"You don't believe Keltson can keep his word?" Bianka asked.

Ammond sighed. "I wasn't going to say anything today, Bianka. You've been through so much and you deserve at least one day to enjoy your success, but... by staying here, Bianka, your life will create another red flag and ITTA is going to come back to set your life straight."

Bianka's eye widened. "Is that true?" She looked at Keltson, who pressed his lips together in solemn confirmation.

"As hard as you've both worked for it, Bianka can't stay here." Ammond said. He grabbed Keltson's hand and led him back to Bianka, placing their hands together. "You're the only other person I know who cares about Bianka as much as I do, kid. I might be a crazier than you for it, so I'm not necessarily the best person for the job. I think you've got just the right amount of crazy in you for her."

Bianka blushed and looked Keltson in the eyes. He still wore the undaunted expression of the mask, though his dark brown eyes couldn't hide the amount of emotion pulsing behind his gaze.

"What are you suggesting?" Keltson asked.

"Give me the vest. You can't function in the future as the Mirror anymore without getting tagged. So, send me instead. I'm a million times better with this junk than you are anyway."

Ammond swatted Kelton's stomach.

"What does that mean for us?" Bianka asked.

"I've got connections with the agency and I can establish a place for you. You'll see." Ammond turned back to Bianka, his penetrating gaze convincing her that what he said was true. "I can watch your timeline and make sure things go the way they should."

Keltson's forehead wrinkled in concern. "But my other clients?"

"I'll do it all," Ammond said. "Besides, I've still got some little people to save."

Bianka stooped down to hug Ammond. "You were like my father all these years. And now you're just going to leave?"

"I'll keep on protecting you, darling," Ammond said, running his hand over her hair. "And you," he said, pointing to Keltson, "keep her safe."

～

AMMOND WAVED HIS HAND, motioning for Keltson to hand over the vest. It felt wrong to give up his last link to the future, but his instincts did their best to calm him, telling him it was *right*. Keltson hesitantly unbuttoned his shirt and handed the vest to Ammond, who grabbed Bianka's hand and gave it a gentle kiss before he blinked out of the room.

Bianka turned to Keltson and was about to speak when a rustle sounded in the corner behind them. Together, they looked over and saw a new mirror forming from thin air beside the wall. Bianka smiled and grabbed Keltson's hand, pulling him along to the other side of the room.

The mask formed inside, the same one he had hid for years. Although for the first time ever, Keltson was the client. For years he had hidden behind a desk and coordinated orders. Only recently had he taken action into his own hands. Despite the danger, Keltson liked the feeling.

"There you are, my dear. Keltson," Ammond said, nodding toward each of them respectively. "I'm busy getting things set up out here, but I thought I'd let you know I'm alright and can speak to you whenever you need. Most of all, I wanted to give you these. Keltson, I found you and your brother, Baigh, a decent place in history. As for Bianka, I managed to rewrite the Master Doc to hide you so you can stay with your family in the castle. It's not perfect, but I think…"

"Wait, wait, wait," Keltson said, shaking his head. "You rewrote the Master Doc? How did you know where it was? I searched for years and never found the location of the vault inside ITTA!"

"That's because it wasn't inside ITTA." Ammond said, shaking his head. "How do you think they kept the document from corruption every time history changed? They placed the database in prehistoric times before anything ever changed. Its location is highly surveyed and guarded, but with your Pause trick, lots of things are possible." The mask gave the flicker of a mischievous smile.

Keltson stepped back, stunned. Then he laughed.

"In fact, I have a business proposition I'd like to propose to you, Keltson," Ammond said. "I have a house built for you and your brother in Westphalia in 1810. You would assume the identities of two brothers who died in a carriage accident."

A folder slid out of the glass and drifted to the floor.

"Do you have a mission for us there?" Keltson asked, picking up the manila envelope with his and Baigh's names on the front.

The mask smiled. "Better than that. I have big plans. And I need someone to cover up for me. Bianka's life created such a large variance that I couldn't directly rewrite all the changes in the Master Doc. So, I had to find a way to reinterpret it so that if other details were discovered, they could easily be explained away. There were so many radical details that I couldn't let any of it become historical fact, so instead I made it something else entirely—a fairy tale. I need someone to compile the stories in the past. That will be you and Baigh," Ammond said. "The brothers were historians with access to the royal library. Their names were Jakob and Wilhelm Grimm."

"BIANKA, I have rewritten your story so that you can live the rest of your life here in this castle with your family. You deserve a happily ever after, darling," Ammond said.

Something else slid out of the mirror. A piece of paper. But Bianka didn't pick it up.

"Do you honestly expect me to just stay here while the rest of you are off adventuring?" Bianka asked. The mask's eyes widened. "Ammond, I want to go too. Whatever you're doing, I want to be a part of it all," Bianka said. A steady warmth built inside her, a confirmation that this decision was absolutely right. She felt it chasing away all the memories of the cold. The frozen capsule, the eternal forest... They left fragments of ice inside her. But this? This choice would chase them away.

"But my dear, you just returned home." Ammond wasn't questioning her, he was reminding her.

"Yes, but I need to do more than focus on myself." She looked at Keltson and smiled.

Ammond tilted his head, studying her. The image inside the mirror went dark momentarily. Bianka worried that he would refuse, his over-protective split demanding that she accept his gift of an easy life without arguing. But seconds later, he returned and two new papers fell through the mirror.

"Bianka, I only ever wanted you to have what you deserved. If you want a life of adventure, then I'll help you have it. But you better know that I won't let you do anything too stupid," he said sternly.

Bianka nodded, an uncontrollable smile breaking through.

"Then here's your new identity and the revised Master Document. I'll leave you two to read it. I'll be checking in with you later. Got to get to work. Read your new directives and I'll be back in a week to transport you," Ammond said, his face flickering out.

Bianka settled onto the floor with her skirts billowing around her and glanced up at Keltson. The paper with her name trembled in her hand.

"Read yours first," she said.

KELTSON CAREFULLY SLID OPEN the manila envelope and pulled out the top page.

> Keltson,
>
> Bianka's story went down through history, creating an incredible number of variances in the world; affecting companies, culture, and household names. However, after some manipulation I managed to alter the Master Document. You and Baigh will assume the identities of the brothers Jakob and Wilhelm Grimm. As historians, Jakob and Wilhelm will be able to gather facts for upcoming clients and record them in a very unique way. Rather than historical legends, you will publish your findings as 'fairy tales', compiling them into a book of stories for children.

The following pages were filled with biographical information, settings, and other facts for Keltson to assume. He would have to help Baigh brush up on his German before they departed, but all in all, the Grimm brothers seemed to fit them perfectly. Their struggles, their dedication. He knew Baigh wouldn't argue. Keltson marveled at the amazing details Ammond worked out for the two of them. He was sure to be a better Mirror than Keltson ever was.

Keltson looked up at Bianka and leaned toward her, resting his arm behind her back. "Let's see what Ammond has for you," Keltson said.

"It looks like a story," she said, brushing a few black curls away from her face.

"Will you read it out loud?" Keltson asked.

Bianka nodded. She held up the page and read a beautiful retelling of her life, told in terms that anyone in her kingdom would understand. The bits and pieces of the past years came together, leaving her sleeping in a beautiful glass coffin. Bianka smiled as it told of the handsome prince that came to save her and the bit of apple flying from her mouth.

"They got a few parts wrong," she said.

"You mean the handsome part?" Keltson pointed to the mention of him.

"No, that part is accurate," she said, smiling.

Keltson nudged her with his shoulder and she continued to read.

"Where am I?" Snow White asked.
"You are with me," the prince said joyfully. "I love you more than anything else in the world..."
Snow White loved him and she went with him.

BIANKA HESITATED. "What do you think of this part? Another inaccuracy?" she asked, carefully.

Keltson thought about it, turning the words over in his head. "I think, that often when we hear stories, they are told after the end when the 'happily ever after' is determined. But right now, you and I are at the very beginning of a story. There are many things that will yet be discovered."

He stared into Bianka's eyes and she smiled. He leaned in and kissed her gently and knew that this was the happiest path he could ask for.

"My son, Charul, has been missing for two weeks now. He left no documented trail, but his vest is missing. If he betrayed the agency, his head shall stand for an example."

-ITTA Director Banu Shazad

EPILOGUE

Charul sat up, feeling stiff like he'd been in a car accident. What had happened? He tenderly patted his chest and his heart sank. His vest was gone. Looking at the forest around him, there were no signs of it anywhere. A ragged pack lay on the ground hear him. He rummaged through it, finding basic necessities. What was going on?

He rose to his feet, wincing as his knees buckled under the pressure of his weight. Thick trees and blackberry briars surrounded him. The branches above him chirruped with the songs of delicate birds. If he hadn't been so terrified for his life, he would have found the location lovely. Usually, there were safe transport locations for agents who were stranded. He had to figure out when he was and make his way to a portal. What if there was no civilization near him? How was he going to get back?

Don't think worst-case scenario.

He could figure this out.

He found a sturdy tree that extended higher than the others and climbed. His best chance to find civilization was to look for smoke. He only needed to get high enough to see the sky. He climbed further and further into the greenery, scratching his hands and arms on the sharp twigs that protruded from the unmanaged forest. With each step, he cursed the man called The Mirror.

Charul would arrest him. He would see it done.

Reaching the top of the trees, Charul shaded his eyes from the sudden blast of sunshine. It was an absolutely perfect day with a light breeze billowing against the leaves, casting an almost musical ambiance that should have been soothing. Instead, he only felt the loneliness of such natural noise. There was no other soul besides him to disturb it. He glanced around and saw no telltale smoke rising into the sky. His fear sank deeper.

He turned to look in the other direction. Still nothing. But then, his eyes fell on a large mound of greenery. It was taller than the trees surrounding it and he suspected there was something hidden beneath it. It reminded him of many of the covered ruins in modern-day South America. After the invention of time travel, they no longer needed to unbury civilizations in order to study them. If he could go to the mound, perhaps he could use the archeological hints to determine his location and calculate the time and nearest civilizations.

The mound looked to be only two or three kilometers away. He should be able to be there in an hour, depending on how rough the terrain was. He climbed down and set off in its direction.

It was difficult to keep his path straight. The sun wasn't always visible through the thick forest, constantly redirecting him through an unsurpassable clump of trees. Rabbits and squirrels scurried away as he stepped through the thick briars. He tried to guess what region he was in from the foliage and animals. It seemed like either eastern North America or Central Europe.

He finally stumbled into a clearing overgrown with plants and ivy. This was unmistakably a road at one time.

A deer trail meandered around the infant pines. As he followed the path, it darted into the woods, sometimes ending entirely before picking back up again. The day grew warmer and Charul felt eager to get back home. If only he hadn't been so brazen and had documented things as well as he should have. He still held the letter in his pocket that The Mirror had used to lure him to the past. Deep inside, he worried The Mirror was smart enough to know when and where would be the hardest place to get out of. The location where he'd found The Mirror wasn't a historically relevant site. In fact, it was obscure enough that there weren't any ports established within a hundred years of the location. Perhaps that's why The Mirror chose it.

Charul marched forward, determined to find a sign of life somewhere.

His heart nearly stopped when he heard a rustling in the trees beside him. He crouched low. The noise was large enough to be caused by a bear. A donkey laden with baskets walked out of the trees and the thudding in his chest calmed. Behind the donkey followed a peasant, wearing a linen top and rough brown trousers.

Unfortunately, that exact peasant wardrobe spanned a timespan of about 500 years, so there was no way of narrowing down the time he had been dropped into. He stood and carefully stepped among the plants, raising his hand in friendship.

He hoped the gesture would encourage the man to reveal which language he spoke. The man hesitated, staring through the clearing with wide eyes. Charul put on his most charming smile, so as not to frighten the man.

"Good day," he said, finally, taking a wild guess. The man continued to stare. He tried another salutation in German. The man's gaze widened but remained incomprehensive.

"*Parlez-vous...*" Charul tried again, the man jumped.

"*Oui, monsieur,*" he said, reaching out with both hands to acknowledge his recognition of the tongue. Charul's shoulders relaxed. France. He was in France.

"What is wrong with you, *monsieur?*" the man asked, tapping his forehead. Charul reached up and felt the spot where the man had motioned and felt thick crusted blood in his hair.

The Mirror would pay for this.

"My caravan was attacked," Charul said, motioning far down the overgrown street, hoping there was something in that direction for the man to assume he had been traveling on. "I fell from my horse and when I awoke, I was lying on the ground and my company was gone."

The man studied Charul's clothing. He again cursed himself for being so brazen and coming back in regular garb. It was likely that if he ever made it home, his mother would kill him for disregarding the rules. He thought this would just be a quick jump back and a hero's welcome when he returned.

"You are a prince, *monsieur*?" the man asked. Charul hesitated. What had drawn that conclusion out of this man?

He laughed. "No, sir. I'm just lost. Is there a town nearby?"

"Come, come with me," the man said, waving his hand for Charul to draw near. "My home is not far. I will answer your questions."

Charul nodded and followed the man into the clearing. As they rounded a bend in the overgrown road, the hill Charul saw from the treetops loomed before them. Spires of kudzu and walls of ivy were surrounded by a thicket of ferocious looking briars.

"What is this place?" Charul asked.

"Only the departed forefathers know the truth," the old man said. "But my favorite story is that a princess lies inside the chateau, waiting for a handsome prince to awaken her from her hundred-year slumber."

Charul stopped mid step. "A hundred years?"

"*Oui, monsieur*," the man said, chuckling and continuing on down the path.

Charul smiled as he followed the man. A hundred years. This had time travel written all over it. The legend, the strange concoction of Japanese and other alien plants covering the whole of the castle. Someone was trying to cover something up here. And if that was the case, he just might be able to find a way home and stop The Mirror once and for all.

ABOUT THE AUTHOR

Rachel Huffmire grew up in the middle of a Utah wheat field where she found plenty of time to read and dream in the simple pace of the country. Her mom paid her a dollar per classic novel she read so, in a quest to amass a small fortune, Rachel read over 200 classic novels by the time she reached junior high. She performed in over 16 musicals through high school, learning about character development, directing, and storytelling. After dabbling with writing novels and stage plays, she ran to the BYU bookstore for her first job. She sat behind the register, voraciously reading Shannon Hale novels while Brandon Sanderson and other internationally selling authors held book signings in front of her. It was then that she began dreaming up plots of her own.

She found time to write each day during her baby's nap times and on long road trips. While attending her first writers conference, Rachel met the wonderful girls at Writing Through Brambles and became a part of the supportive mommy-writer group. She found a home for her debut manuscript, "Shattered Snow" with Immortal Works and a few months later joined their team as an acquisitions editor.

Rachel currently lives in Southern California where she enjoys sand at its finest: the beach and the desert. She home schools her two little boys, writes about time travel, virtual reality, and djinn, and reads bedtime stories to her husband every night.

ACKПOШLEDGEMEПT8

One of the significant blessings in my life is a wealth of people who cheer me on, make me better, and trust me when I want to take a crazy leap-- like become a writer. God absolutely listened to my prayers over the last few years as I pursued this dream of mine, and I genuinely have to thank him for all the incredible people he put in my path to help me along.

I am deeply grateful for the family at Immortal Works. Thank you, Holli Anderson, for listening to my pitch and being one of the first people to celebrate "Shattered Snow". James Wymore, thanks for teaching me how to self-edit on a whole new level. Melissa Cox Meibos' masterful touch as an editor and countless personal affirmations made the experience of editing an absolute joy. I'm particularly grateful for Jason King, who supported my vision for illustrations and coordinated production details with an ideal sense of humor. To Amanda Wintch for her stunning fact-checking skills and her masterful ability to keep an entire array of dates, times, and locations straight, thank you! To everyone else at Immortal Works, you all are my champions.

I'm exceptionally appreciative for the array of friends who helped me through the exciting and daunting new territory of becoming a debut author. Bree Moore, Dacia Arnold, and Sarah Dunster, thank you for your sage wisdom. To the incredible girls at Writing Through Brambles who have been a part of every step of my writing journey, I love you all and couldn't have done this without you! To my beta readers, Rachel

White, Amanda Hakes, Ruth, Bryce, Michelle and Bethanie Twede- your critiques refined this novel to be the wonderful form it is today.

To my Mom, who paid me a dollar for each classic novel I read when I was ten. Without that, I don't think I would have discovered a love for old literature. To my dad, who recorded "The Wonderful World of Brother's Grimm" on VHS for me to watch over and over again, making the Grimm brothers seem like real people to me. To my kids who constantly encourage me to see through young eyes, even though they are the wisest people I know. And most of all, to my remarkable husband for supporting my passion and celebrating every little milestone with me. You claim to not know anything about storytelling, but you never fail to get me out of a jam when I hit a storytelling wall. I love you and wouldn't be here without you.

This has been an
Immortal Production

CPSIA information can be obtained
at www.ICGtesting.com
Printed in the USA
LVHW110726210319
611369LV00001BA/166/P